BINDINGS
KATE ROTH

Bindings
Written by Kate Roth
Copyright ©2015 by Kate Roth
Edited by Erin Roth, Wise Owl Editing
Additional Editing by All Good Things Editing
www.allgoodthingsediting.weebly.com

All rights reserved. No part of this book may be reproduced or transmitted in any form or by any means, electronic or mechanical, including photocopying, recording, or by any information storage and retrieval system, without permission in writing.

This is a work of fiction. Names, characters, places and incidents are the product of the author's imagination or are used fictitiously, and any resemblance to any actual persons, living or dead, events, or locales is entirely coincidental.

The author acknowledges the trademarked status and trademark owners of various products referenced in this work of fiction, which have been used without permission. The publication/use of these trademarks is not authorized, associated with, or sponsored by the trademark owner.

All rights reserved.

Recommended for ages 18+, contains strong sexual content, graphic scenes, explicit language and a consensual, intense BDSM relationship.

You can discover more about a person in an hour of play than in a year of conversation.
-Plato

PROLOGUE

WATCHING THE WOMAN scribble something on her yellow legal pad, I sat up a little straighter, attempting to see what she'd written. I cleared my throat and she met my eyes with a soft smile. She had her hair pulled back in a bun and an average but surely expensive pair of black heels capped off her outfit of a cream silk blouse and charcoal gray slacks. Dr. Keith tugged her reading glasses off of her nose and titled her head to one side. I resisted the urge to roll my eyes. Silence hung in the stuffy office, as it had for the last few minutes. Was she trying to force me to be introspective? I was paying her to do that for me.

"So…yeah. That's it. That's the whole story," I said with a nod.

"What is it you want me to tell you, Sloane?" I scoffed. "I want your thoughts on it. Your professional opinion. Am I crazy?"

Dr. Keith slid her glasses back on and my stomach pitched. "Have any of the...*encounters* been against your will?"

Blinking a few times before I lowered my eyes to the ground, I replied, "No."

Her pencil made its way to her lips. "Have you enjoyed them?"

I gulped and whispered, "Yes."

"Would you consider yourself happy right now? With your life, everything that's gone on, and all these recent changes...him included?"

A deep breath filled my lungs, and as I blew it out my gaze lifted to my new doctor. I'd searched for her on a whim—in a frenzy, really. After my last night with him, I hadn't been able to stop obsessing over the *how* of it. How had I become this person who felt a little like a stranger but more like the truest version of myself I'd ever known? How would I survive if I ever lost him? How had I allowed him to stitch himself into the fibers of my soul?

"I've never been happier."

A smile spread her mouth and her arched brows came together in the center. "So what's the problem? Why do you think you need my thoughts? Would you like to explore the reasons why these sorts of experiences appeal to you? I don't really think that's what you came here for..."

The back of my neck flushed with heat and a bead of sweat tickled as it slid from beneath my breast to my navel. I huffed and threw my hands up, feeling more lost than when I'd walked through her door.

"Do you think it's healthy?" I barked.

Dr. Keith's head reared back as though I'd swung at her. I bit my lip and recoiled, embarrassed by my outburst. She grabbed her yellow pad of paper again and put her pencil to the page just before she glanced at me.

"Do you?"

ONE

"NO... NO! WAIT!" The muffled sound of my voice pulled me from sleep and I sat up with a heavy groan. Sucking a sharp breath through my teeth, I winced and clutched the back of my neck. A twinge in the muscle shot lava-like pain down my shoulder. I squeezed the throbbing spot, kneading my thumb into the rigid flesh until I felt a little relief. As I exhaled the tension from my lungs, I cursed internally.

This was becoming a horribly unwanted habit. It didn't matter, day or night; I always woke up like this. First, I'd wake up from a stress nightmare, usually about unfinished high school classes, the loss or destruction of my family photos, or—the kind I'd just awoken from—the vague *left behind* dream. The dream varied and took on different scenery and tones from night to night, but the concept was always the same. I was being left behind. I was being forgotten. I was suddenly but seemingly forevermore, alone.

Next came the blinding pain, forcing me to pinch and rub the kinks out of my neck, back, or shoulder. It'd been going on for weeks, ever since I saw the news…

Rolling out of bed and clearing my mind, I slipped into the robe I'd thrown on the floor this afternoon when I pathetically crawled into bed for a midday nap. I made the effort to shower, shave, even throw on some perfume before my clothes only because I had dinner plans with my sister and I figured I wouldn't make it back to my apartment before I had to meet her.

I grabbed a cardigan and walked the few blocks from my place to Calloway Books—the little old book shop that'd become my home away from home. It was unlike any other bookstore I'd ever set foot in and from the moment I found it, it'd become my favorite place. I shopped there, read there, wrote there—sometimes I just went in to look around and breathe in the heady mixture of freshly brewed coffee and books, new and old. Stress didn't leave my body too often these days, but something about the atmosphere there brought me momentary relief.

I'd been foolishly trying to write a novel for the last six months and shortly after I wrote the first sentence, I stumbled upon the store. By now, the owner, Oliver, and I were more than acquaintances. I suppose we we're friends. If I arrived early in the morning, I helped him open the store, starting the ever-flowing pot of coffee for the day and raising the blinds. If I stayed until close, I helped him clean and lock up. I'd even hopped behind the counter once or twice to ring up a customer when he'd been short staffed. Oliver never seemed to mind me setting up shop with either my laptop or my notebook, drinking the free coffee and enjoying the quiet of the reading nooks tucked in the back or the little room on the second floor where he kept most of the leather bound antique classics only collectors looked for and some overstock inventory. I'd claimed that room as my own at some point. Oliver was even kind enough to put a table and chairs inside for me.

The words of my novel had never poured out of me as easily as I wished they had, but throwing myself into the project was my way of trying to get over the past. To get over Warren and what I'd left behind. But over the past few weeks, the words stopped altogether. I kept going, I kept trying. I needed to. At this point, the bookstore and my non-existent novel were all I had. I knew one day I'd break through the wall blocking my mind—something would release me—and I'd be able to tell the story or at least let go.

The bell above the door rang when I walked in and I headed straight to my spot. I didn't see Oliver, but that wasn't uncommon. He was always on the move through the store. The sound of hushed voices around the stacks didn't stop me as I grabbed a coffee and climbed the rusted metal stairs for the second floor.

With my laptop on and a paper cup of coffee steaming on the old oak table, I drew in a breath. I smelled the familiar scent of musty books, leather, and coffee grounds. Staring at the screen, I tried to think of Warren and the story. Our story. It hurt every time I pulled it to the surface, heavy and covered in splinters of shame and regret. My heart ached as I attempted to fling myself back in time to relive it all over again.

While the book I was writing was fiction, the truth marbled its way through the words. Moments we shared wove into the storyline and the emotions that consumed me—from the butterflies of the beginning to the agony of the bitter end—drove the plot. I hadn't decided if I could give it a happy ending yet or not. I was still trying to keep from killing him off in chapter two.

"Screw this," I mumbled, pushing back from the table. I scanned the shelf behind me for something to flip through to quiet my mind. A dark laugh crept from my lungs when my eyes fell on a fitting tale—the kind of story to really stir up my self-loathing. I sat down once more with the classic in hand and sighed, set on escaping into someone else's ill-fated story instead of my own.

"Wait—" My voice jolted me out of the captivity of a dream and as I sat up, my arm flailed in front of me, colliding with something as it moved through the air.

"Shit!"

Warm liquid trickled onto my lap and my eyes flew open to see my paper cup once full of black coffee spilling over not only my favorite pair of jeans but also the leather bound edition of *The Scarlet Letter* I'd read three chapters of before dozing. Keeping my eyes open lately was a challenge. All I wanted to do was sleep—depression gripping me twenty-four hours a day.

Thanking God I hadn't doused my laptop in dark roast, I snatched my cardigan off the chair next to me and tried to sop up the coffee before it seeped into the pages of the book. I tossed the drenched sweater to the side and glanced at my phone.

"Fuck! Motherfucking fuck fuck!" I snarled at the ceiling.

It was nine forty. I had sixteen text messages from my sister, Ellie, and nine phone calls. It was the second time I'd stood her up in three weeks. The heels of my palms knocked into my forehead as I growled again. My stomach pitched wildly as everything sunk in. It was like a snapshot of the current state of my life right now—messy, infuriating, out of control, and completely my fault. The book was the most urgent situation, though, and I decided to take care of it first before I called and begged for Ellie's forgiveness.

Grabbing the book, I held it open as I hustled down the staircase to the sales counter. They'd be closing in twenty minutes and as far as I could see, I was the only person there who didn't get a paycheck. Expecting to find Oliver, my feet froze when I saw a man I didn't recognize crouched down beside the checkout desk, rifling through a cart full of books.

He rose and turned to me, his eyes narrowing. "Yes?"

Blue, nearly deep violet, eyes drilled through me—unsettling me for reasons unknown. His face was familiar, but I knew I'd never met him. I shook my head, knowing the book was more important than introductions, and jutted it out toward him.

"I spilled my coffee. I didn't know what to do. I'll pay for it, I just…"

He frowned and took the book from me carefully, tearing his gaze away from my face. I felt my skin chill at the loss of his eyes on me. He examined the pages quickly then ducked under the counter. The slight movement wafted a tempting scent my way and I breathed it in shamelessly. Was that cologne or the lingering trace of clove cigarettes? He popped up with a stack of paper towels and placed one gently in between each coffee soaked page. Watching his fingers care so delicately for the book mesmerized me. With each damaged page padded by a paper towel, he slammed the book shut and stared at it for a moment before eyeing me.

He pushed a hand through his espresso hair and raised his brows. "You must be Sloane."

I squinted, still studying him, filing his image away in my mind for some reason. "How do you know my name?"

"Oliver had to leave early. He told me you'd be upstairs. I'm Leo."

Staring at him blankly, I tried to think of anything other than the shape of his lips when he'd spoken my name.

"Calloway," he clipped. "Oliver's brother."

"Oh!" I felt like an asshole. "Right." Oliver had been talking about his brother for days. He was thrilled to have him back in town and even happier to have his help at the shop.

"You just moved here," I said foolishly. I couldn't remember the details of where he'd been or why he was home—something about a girl maybe.

One corner of his mouth ticked up in a subtle smile for an instant before he nodded slowly. "Just moved back, actually."

His smoky voice made me gulp a breath, but his penetrative stare riveted me. He held my gaze firmly, a mixture of awkwardness and fascination melding within me. I nodded, pulling my lips tight, then turned on my heels, ready to gather my things from upstairs. After an apologetic call to my sister, I'd need to crawl back into my bed for more stress-induced nightmares.

Spinning back to him, I let a pained smile touch my mouth as I tapped two fingers beside the book on the desk between us. "Seriously, I feel awful. So whatever the price, Oliver knows I'm good for it."

Leo's expression remained rigid, but his eyes lit up with some unknown emotion when his deep voice crept out, "I'm sure there's a suitable punishment for you, Sloane."

My heart seized in my chest as his lips twitched, never forming the smile they fought. His words sent a shiver down my spine. My ears pulsed with heat and the rich sound of my blood pumping to my brain, helping me form thoughts—visions of punishment. My mind propelled me to a foreign plane where I pictured this stranger darkening my world with the most forbidden of fantasies.

"Good night," he added before stooping down to the book cart once more.
I swallowed hard and took a step toward the staircase, noticing only how my legs trembled as the sound of his voice echoed in my mind.

Though I hadn't thought about it in ages, my sudden salacious desires brought on by Leo's choice of words weren't new. During my freshman year of college, a guy I'd been casually fooling around with wanted to watch porn with me. I think I surprised him when I said yes and I think he might've proposed marriage when I suggested we smoke a little pot first. We got high and he showed me some of his go-to video clips on his laptop as we lay barely dressed in his dorm room twin-sized bed.

"Wanna watch some kinky shit?" he'd asked, peering down to where I rested against his side. I remember mumbling a yes, not caring what he put on the screen because porn had never really thrilled me.

But then he pulled up a video of a naked woman with her hands tied behind her back, bent over a leather bench, blindfolded, and the sight of her made me sit up a little straighter and open my heavy eyelids a little wider. A man wearing a leather mask over his eyes walked out and without a word, he picked up some kind of whip. It looked like a long-handled black cheerleading pom-pom only with thicker strips of material. She squeaked each time he lashed her with it and I felt my pulse begin to race. When the camera closed in on her creamy white skin, every flick of his wrist turning her flesh redder from the soft-looking weapon he wielded, my core throbbed.

He clicked the mouse suddenly, advancing the video to the end. I would've smacked him had my eyes not been glued to the sight of her bare ass turned deep maroon from the lashing. I licked my lips and squirmed a little in the bed beside him.

"Well that one wasn't good," he said. "I thought he was gonna fuck her."

I pulled in a ragged breath, told him I was tired, and started shrugging into my clothes. I had never been so thankful that my roommate was out late as I spent the rest of the night watching every video like that I could find. At first, I just watched, wide-eyed and curious, fidgeting in my bed with my laptop on my thighs. But eventually I set the computer to my side so my fingers could find their way to my clit.

I'd never told anyone about that night and I only occasionally sought out those kinds of videos again. But the moment Leo had said the word punishment, with his brooding eyes staring me down after I'd doused myself and *The Scarlet Letter* in coffee, flashes of those videos lit up in my mind. I'd wanted to be disciplined in that way for a long time but I'd never had the guts to admit it.

After an excruciatingly guilt-laden hour-long conversation with Ellie where she made sure to tell me how worried she was about me and remind me that she just didn't understand why I'd felt the need to move two towns away, I slipped into bed, knowing my addled mind needed rest. I tried to doze—I hadn't needed to *try* to sleep in weeks—but my racing thoughts made me resort to the one thing I knew would help. The scent of him, that word on his tongue, the unspoken proposal…everything about Leo and our quick interaction had made me wet. With my head still swimming with thoughts of him, it didn't take much to work myself into a frenzy then sigh as I fell into darkness.

The next evening, when I pushed through the front door of the bookstore, a little flutter filled my abdomen remembering the private dreams I'd conjured.

"Hey," Oliver's voice pulled me into the present and caused me to turn. I smiled when I saw him. "I missed you yesterday."

"Hey. Yeah, I uh…" I gulped, cataloguing the similarities of the brothers' appearances and remembering just how filthy my fantasies of Leo had been alone in my bed. "I met your brother."

Oliver's face fell. "Was he a dick? He can be kind of a dick."

"What? No. Not at all. But about the book—"

His brow knit together. "Which book?"

I opened my mouth to speak as a young brunette touched Oliver's elbow. "Excuse me, do you have any German cookbooks?"

"I'll come find you later, okay?" he whispered and shot me a quick apologetic smile as he turned to lead the young woman to the cooking section.

I nodded and headed up to my quiet room and wondered why he'd seemed confused about the ruined copy of *The Scarlet Letter*, but didn't let it keep me from putting pen to paper to outline the book. I forced the words down on the page, struggling to keep my concentration on the story while thoughts of Leo's voice swam through my mind.

An hour passed and when I'd drained my cup of coffee—with a lid tightly secured on the top—I decided it was time for a break. I stood and stretched the kinks from my neck and took my hair out of its ponytail for a minute to relieve the tension at my scalp. I was just about to head down to refuel and have a quick glance at the new releases when I heard the doorknob turn.

I wet my lips at the sight of him, but he didn't meet my eyes at first. Leo pulled his gaze slowly up my body from my flat gray boots and black leggings to the heather gray sweater that hugged the curves of my breasts and waist before finally finding my face, a faint smile on his mouth. His brow rose in a silent greeting and I watched as he carried in a stack of leather bound books. I studied him as he searched for the places they belonged on the shelf. He wore dark jeans and a gray tweed blazer over a crisp white button up shirt. One side of my mouth kicked up in an amused grin, surprised by such an impeccable fashion sense from a young man.

"Hello again," he said, still facing the shelves.

"Hi." My voice was a pitiful scratch and I pressed my lips together the moment the syllable emerged.

Staring at his hands gently maneuvering the soft leather bindings, I couldn't help but imagine him gently maneuvering parts of my body. It was only once I watched him inhale that I noticed he'd finished shelving the books while my thoughts had strayed. He was simply standing, not facing me, just breathing the same air. I found it oddly comforting.

"You didn't tell Oliver about the book I ruined, did you?" I blurted.

I saw him stiffen before he slowly turned to face me. The same ghost of a smile touched his full lips before he spoke. "You looked like you were having a rough night; figured you could use a little mercy."

My lips parted and I expelled a gentle sigh. "Thanks." I took a seat again, turning the chair to see him. A light, shattered breath escaped me unexpectedly before words tumbled out. "Mercy's good. I thought maybe you'd come to dole out my punishment."

In a split second, with my idiotic jest hanging in the air, my chest tightened and my stomach plummeted. Leo blinked once then tilted his head a bit. "Would you like that?"

The trembling in my gut raged with new strength and my mind blanked out. His voice, his eyes, his posture—he was completely serious. Last night, I'd tried like hell to convince myself he was joking, but I knew he wasn't. I was glad. The response running around my head was *yes*. I would like him to punish me. He must've seen it in my face or read my thoughts because he stepped toward me. "Stand up," Leo commanded.

I did without hesitation.

Another quick smile pulled at the corner of his mouth but he willed it away as he reached into the inside pocket of his blazer. He took out a pair of black leather gloves and my eyes widened as he pulled them on. My heart raced, the kind of energy coursing through my veins new but certainly welcomed. I was utterly spellbound. Completely aware and complacent—fuck, I was eager—to allow Leo to do whatever he was about to do to me. Without question.

My last few months and every moment leading to this one, I'd been depressed, hopeless and even catatonic at times, but I'd never been reckless like this. And I'd never felt so alive.

"Turn around and put your forearms flat on the table."

The quiet, peaceful place I'd claimed as my writing domain rarely had visitors but I wondered if today would be the day someone would come looking for something from one of the shelves surrounding us. The idea of getting caught sprung a whole new twist of excitement through my body. The sound of my ragged breathing pulled me from my thoughts as I turned and with surprisingly steady hands, bent over the table, doing exactly as Leo instructed. My sweater rode up to my waist with the move and I felt very aware that my ass was presented to him, my thong leaving my leggings as my only protection. Just one thin layer of cotton.

Was he about to fuck me? Hit me? Maneuver me in random ways, making me his puppet? I didn't know and while I cared, I didn't have a preference. My heart rebounded under my breasts at the realization that I'd placed absolute trust in a man I'd spoken with once and been aroused by twice.

Looking down at the table, I saw the plot notes I'd scribbled earlier, but I didn't recognize my own handwriting. His presence had changed me. I wanted to laugh, thinking about my novel as I was bent over, anxiously awaiting the repercussions of my actions. The fact and the fiction of it suddenly seemed trivial. This…whatever was about to happen…felt critical. Pivotal.

I sucked in a sharp breath, feeling him lean over me. The hard wall of his chest pressed into my back as he put his gloved hands on either side of mine and exhaled against my ear. "You've disappointed me, Sloane," Leo whispered.

Every tiny, fine hair running along my spine flicked up, standing at attention, then bowed down again, surrendering to what was coming. "I'm sorry," I murmured.

Leo straightened and I stared at the wood grain of the table, waiting. The sound of something slicing through the air rang out quickly and then I simultaneously heard and felt a thick crack as his black leather palm spanked my ass.

I gasped at the sting I felt through my leggings. Another strike came and I thrust forward from the force. With his hand gone, I felt my skin burn and buzz, trying to comprehend the damage, but another quick blow came down on my ass and I cried out something between pleasure and pain. With that, he struck me again and again, and each time his hand landed on me, I tried to catch my breath—desperate for air.

And each time he reared back, I missed his touch—desperate for more.

One final slap choked out of me the kind of groan I'd only ever heard myself expel during sex. I snapped my lips closed the moment I heard it. Quiet filled my ears, my skin flushed and stung, then I straightened to turn toward Leo, leaning my weight against the table behind me even though the edge pressed into the tender flesh of my buttocks.

When our eyes met, I shuddered. The silence only served to make it feel all the more surreal. His expression softened into something affectionate as he closed the gap between us. He lifted his hand to my cheek carefully. His palm cupped my face and as his thumb swiped under my eye, I registered the feeling of moisture on my skin. I hadn't even known I'd cried until his gloved fingers wiped my tears away.

He pulled away to reach into another jacket pocket and presented a handkerchief which he blotted across my cheeks, drying my tears and removing the black residue of my mascara. My eyes danced across his face as he tended to me, wondering who he was and why I'd just allowed him to lay his hands on me that way—and why I'd enjoyed it.

His fingers slipped through my hair to the back of my neck and he coaxed me forward, pressing a kiss to my cheekbone. My eyes closed at the sensation of strange lips on me and I finally felt the burning of the salty tears I'd already shed. The silent exchange made my heart ache. A thousand questions bombarded my mind though I didn't have the strength to ask a single one aloud.

Leo let go of me and took one step back, preparing to leave without a word. But my greedy hands reached out to him, gripping his lapels to pull him to my lips, not caring but also not understanding why I needed him so badly. His mouth crushed mine and our tongues tangled without subtle sweetness or build up. I felt the kiss in my tailbone where the muscles below it still hummed. With his hands in my hair, moving me the way he wanted me, attacking my mouth with no romantic fanfare, just pure carnal greed, I felt the kiss tingling between my legs as I grew wetter by the second.

I reached my hands to link behind his neck and those thick leather gloves snagged both of my wrists, our lips never unlocking. He lowered my hands to my sides and easily laced his fingers back into my hair. When the kiss ended, he panted against my mouth for a moment. I feared he'd leave at any moment.

"Leo…I—"

His firm posture returned and he removed the leather gloves, returning them to his breast pocket before he gently touched his bare index finger against my lips.

"Are you okay?" he asked softly.

"Yes," I breathed.

His eyes traced the curve of my face then he smiled sweetly. I didn't know the man at all, but I instantly knew that the smile was genuine and possibly one he didn't often share.

"Thank you," he said, pressing his lips to my forehead before opening the door and disappearing from sight.

TWO

MY EARS RANG as though I could still hear the crack of his palm against me. I stood staring at nothing for seconds that felt like hours and when my mind quit spinning, I knew I should leave. My legs trembled beneath me as I picked up my purse and my notebook, not unlike they had after I'd first met him just twenty-four hours ago. But I was different now. Changed by one moment in time that seemed to have been the culmination of my entire life thus far.

"Hey, Sloane!" A familiar voice called out and I met Wendy, another employee at the store, with a wide-eyed stare. She smiled and tossed her dark blond curls with a quick flick of her hand.

I gulped and tried to play cool. "Hey."

"How's the novel coming?"

I nearly laughed. What novel? Screw that sorry excuse for a book, my life just got a whole hell of a lot more interesting.

"It's...okay, I guess."

Her bubbly grin grew and her rosy cheeks rounded. "You'll get it. Can't wait to read it!"

A staggering breath fell from my lips and I nodded, forcing a smile. "Right," I replied. "Well, goodnight, Wendy."

The hairs on my neck prickled and I turned, compelled to catch the eyes that I was sure had settled on my back. Seeing the blue eyes drilling into me from the office door, I sucked in a sharp breath though my nose.

"Night, Sloane! See you tomorrow?" Wendy said.

A barely perceptible smirk tugged at Leo's lips, reminding me of their taste, and he tilted his head to one side, yet again examining me from a distance.

"Yeah, maybe," I whispered as I forced my feet to lead me out of the store without looking back.

For the first time in as long as I could remember, I slept like a baby. I woke up to the sound of my alarm instead of my panicked voice crying out from the depths of a nightmare. My body felt as pliable as a down comforter. Dreams spun around my mind a few times in the night—all pleasant. It felt so foreign to enjoy a night's rest but even more foreign to wake up and want to relive my dreams.

Of course I wanted to relive them. They all starred Leo.

I didn't know anything about him. One second he was Oliver's brother, the hot new guy at the store, and the next he was commanding me as though he owned me—an enigma who ruled me for no reason. Who was he? I should know something more about him but I didn't. With the chemistry we had, did it really matter? In the dim light, with that palpable lust filling the space around us, we were nameless and faceless. All we were was our mutual desire. Nothing mattered but his gloved hand on my body, the sound of my cries through the air, and the primal drumming of my heartbeat.

I stretched my arms over my head and let out a sigh. When I stood to make my way toward the bathroom for a shower, I winced. Hooking a thumb in my panties, I pulled them down and craned my head around to look at my ass. Though not a hint of redness remained, Leo had marked me. The notion made me bite my lip and grin.

Ellie stared at me cautiously over the brim of her glass. Ever the worried sister, she'd barely taken a breath in between inquiries. She gulped her water then smoothed her fingers along the linen tablecloth after setting the glass down again.

"Are you looking for jobs?" she asked. She'd asked me the same question a handful of times, a hundred different ways over the past three months.

I stabbed at my salad and shook my head. "You know I'm not. I'm working on the book."

Ellie sighed heavily, but I refused to look up from my food as she started in. "Since when are you a writer? I know you've been going through something—something I still don't understand—but it's been almost a year since you moved here and I'm not sure if I should be sending you money or what. How are you affording anything? What the hell happened?"

My eyes slowly rose to meet hers. "If I need money, I'll ask for it. But I don't."

"Are you—" My sister paused then ducked her chin, lowering her voice. "Are you selling drugs?"

My torso quivered and my shoulders bobbed before I registered the noise in my ears as my own laughter. It had been so long since a decent chuckle consumed me. Lips split in a wide smile, I rolled my eyes. "Elle, please. I get that I've thrown you for a loop lately, but come on…do you actually believe I'd deal drugs before asking you for help?"

Her face didn't move. Her entire body looked rigid—paralyzed—as she stared at me from across the table. Firming up her jaw, she swallowed and dropped her gaze to the tablecloth once more.

"Honestly? I don't know what to believe. I don't think I know you at all anymore. I almost asked you if you're whoring yourself out. I wish you'd just explain what happened that made you leave. If you moved somewhere full of opportunities, I might be able to see some benefit for your future, but here in Salem? What are you doing?"

Ellie thought I was whoring myself out *here*? Despite the fact that I'd let a stranger spank me last night, this town wasn't the place I'd become a whore. She wanted to know how I could afford to live for a year, write a book (like I had any clue what all that entailed), and never have to get a job…

How did I begin to explain to my sister than I'd spent the last three years of my life having my bills paid for me? I had nearly three years' worth of my income saved due to Warren's indulgence. His guilt. His conscious hold over me. At first, I was his girl, the one he loved to dote on and spoil. Then I was his secret, the one he paid to hide and wait and slowly lose her mind.

I wasn't ready to tell anyone about Warren, least of all my overbearing sister. I took a long drag off my straw, swallowing down icy water that attempted to cure the intense pain that rolled through my chest when I'd thought his name.

"I'm going to pretend you didn't say that. I'm fine. Financially and otherwise. Can you just trust me and be happy for me?"

Ellie tucked her top lip in her mouth and sucked in a breath through her nose, her brows lifting high at the same time. I kept my gaze pinned firmly on her, my question still hanging between us. Finally, she softened, her face falling, and she nodded.

"Yeah," she said. "I'm sorry. I'm always here though. When you need me."

One corner of my mouth lifted in a pained half-smile. I was thankful I'd gone easy on her. Scolding her for scolding me wasn't what I wanted. She was just doing what she thought she needed to do as my big sister. Ever since our parents died, she'd attempted to be both sister and mother and father to me. It'd never been necessary, but I had a feeling one day I'd need her in one of the three assumed roles. I just wasn't sure what I needed right now. An electric pulse rippled around my heart when the image of Leo slipping his hands into the pair of black leather gloves flashed in my mind.

Need.

That's how I'd gone home feeling after our…encounter. I'd *needed* that. That sweet release. And now, I not only felt as though I needed it again, I also wanted it. I wanted more. I wanted to know all of the endless possibilities of Leo Calloway and that dark, dusty book room on the second floor.

I waited three days to go back to the bookstore. Long enough for me to work up the courage to speak to Leo again. The moment I pushed through the front door, I sighed. I nearly groaned at the delicious coffee aroma hanging in the air. Slipping out of my jacket, I made my way to the back of the store near the office where a few hooks waited. My hands fidgeted, already anxious to see Leo. To talk to him, if my mouth and lungs decided to cooperate. I slid my fingers down the sides of my dress then smoothed over my hair, smearing the few misted raindrops that peppered the top of my head.

"Look," I heard Oliver's hushed voice suddenly creep out from behind the cracked office door. "Wendy, I just…I'm sorry. I don't think we…" He sighed and my brow furrowed. I should've walked away and stopped eavesdropping but Oliver's tone held me there.

"God, Oliver. Grow up," Wendy spat at full volume. "I quit."

The office door swung open fiercely and Wendy stormed through it, barely glancing at me as I turned to the coat rack again. The watery look in her eyes made my stomach pitch and as I turned back to the office door I saw Oliver, his shoulders sagging as he shook his head and breathed in deeply.

"Oliver?" My voice was a mere wisp.

He pulled his chest up, straightening and met my eyes with a forced smile. "Hey there," he said. My lips twisted as I contemplated overstepping my bounds by acknowledging whatever had just happened between him and Wendy.

"Where've you been hiding? Haven't seen you in a few days," he said, running a hand through his chestnut hair, walking toward me after pulling the office door shut.

"Just busy I guess," I replied before softening my gaze on him meaningfully. "You okay?"

Oliver smiled. "Ah, don't worry about it," he said with a shrug. "You don't happen to want a job though, do you?"

I coughed out a laugh and opened my mouth, emitting only silent breaths instead of my polite refusal. Maybe a job wasn't such a bad idea. It would please my sister. Eventually my savings would dry up and I'd need to find something. Why not get paid for being here a few days a week? Oliver wouldn't need to train me…

His smile grew as he watched the wheels turning in my brain at the idea. I huffed and rolled my eyes with barely upturned lips. His brow rose, urging my answer. With a reluctant but surprising yes on the tip of my tongue, I let my mouth part once more just as I saw Oliver's eyes look past me, his chin tilting up.

"Leo, tell Sloane what a good boss I am. Help me convince her she should take the part time position."

My flesh lit up with chills at the sound of his name, a delicious shudder travelling to my tailbone when his smooth baritone voice rang in my ears.

"I didn't realize we were hiring," Leo clipped as he came into view. "But I'm sure Sloane would be great for the job."

His wavy sable hair laid smoothed back perfectly, not a strand out of place, and the straight line of his Roman nose led me to stare at his lips and the soft smirk formed on them. I suddenly couldn't think of anything other than our kiss. Heated and rushed and the kind of erotic spontaneity fantasies were made of. Coming here to write was one thing. I could hide in my corners and closed rooms and choose whether Leo gazed upon me or not, but if I worked here…

"You should know though," Leo added, his eyes twinkling, "I own half of the store, which means I'm the boss…too. I know we just met, but you wouldn't mind taking orders from me, would you?"

Fuck. Staring my sudden sin in the face, I swallowed the rest of my hesitancy and did what I knew had already become a habit when it came to Leo Calloway. I complied—easily, willingly, without a second thought.

"That won't be a problem," I said, pulling my eyes away from him and back to his brother. "When do I start?"

THREE

RAINY DAYS ALWAYS brought the most business to the store, so the monsoon happening outside the large front window made my first day on the job a bit hectic. I'd been in the store on a busy day before but without a name tag, I'd never been asked as many questions. It was a good thing I knew the store so well on my own, otherwise I would've been chasing down Oliver every other second.

I captured a quiet moment and began shelving a few new books that had come in with the most recent delivery. Opening the next box and pulling out the brown packing paper, I gasped when my eyes fell on the two titles on top. *Pain for Pleasure: A Guide to Sadomasochism* and *Different Loving: The World of Sexual Dominance and Submission.*

When I pulled the two books from the box, two more titles on the subject made my ears burn. I could only assume who'd placed the order, as I didn't imagine the Marquis de Sade had strolled into Salem in the last week.

Or maybe he had.

Lifting my head, I stared at Leo's profile where he stood on the other side of the store, helping a father and his young son in the children's section. As he crouched down to the little boy, handing him a copy of *Where the Wild Things Are*, a sweet smile on his lips, I marveled at how unassuming he seemed. But I knew those black leather gloves hadn't been in his breast pocket because of the approaching autumn season. Somehow, I knew they were a permanent part of his ensemble, even tucked away out of sight.

I swatted away rogue thoughts of Leo and our one and only intimate interaction and filled a rolling cart with the new books, heading for the section marked *Human Sexuality*. Each title drew my attention but I kept myself from reading the backs or opening a single page. I needed to do my job. *Google it when you get home*, I scolded myself. When I'd placed the last of the new order on the shelf, I took a step back and shook my head with a smile. A section that once consisted of a few books on how to spice up a marriage and basic gender studies would now surely be cause for teenage giggles and blushing grandmothers. Who in Salem would need fifteen titles on kink?

My curiosity got the better of me and I reached out a hand to the selection once more, placing my index finger on the spine of a book, inching it out of place.

Before I allowed myself to slip it off the shelf and into my eager hands for a glance, I turned my head to see if anyone was around. I gasped and my cheeks flushed as Leo's indigo eyes danced over my mortified face. I jerked my hand away from the book, but it was barely balanced on the edge of the shelf and it clattered to my feet with the sudden move.

"Shit," I whispered, ducking down to pick it up. My hands shook as I reached for it, but the moment another hand covered mine, I stilled. Snapping my head up, I watched as Leo examined me from the same position I was in, crouched down between the book cart and the shelf. His soft gaze kept me immobilized and the feeling of his hand on mine caused a wicked thought to prance across my mind.

I wish he were wearing those gloves.

"Hi," he whispered.

"Hi."

Taking the book from beneath my fingers, Leo rose and I followed. "How's your first day going?" he asked. He returned the book to its place on the shelf and I swear I saw him smirk as he scanned the line of new titles.

"It's okay."

"Just okay?"

I dropped my eyes to study the wood grain of the floor my black flats pressed into. "I haven't worked in a while so I'm just getting used to it again. H-how are you?"

Leo gave a soft smile and stroked his jaw before leaning one shoulder against the bookshelf, folding his arms across his chest. He looked casual, at ease, and yet with his eyes on me I still felt like his captive. Well...his willing captive.

"I'm doing well. I haven't had a chance to tell you how happy I am that you decided to take the job. Oliver can be a bit obsessive about this place so if you get overwhelmed just let me know," he said. "I'm looking forward to spending more time with you."

I was certain Oliver would never have the power to overwhelm me, but Leo was another story. I felt overwhelmed just breathing in front of him. Knowing he was looking forward to spending time with me made me want to squirm. How would I ever be able to look at him without thinking the filthiest of thoughts?

I noticed a shy half-grin form on his lips and his eyes fell to his feet briefly. "So I was thinking maybe I could—well... Okay, look, I—don't want you to feel pressured..."

"Pressured? What, to entertain Oliver's OCD? I don't," I blurted.

His grin grew to a beam as he looked at me through dark lashes, his tongue touching his top and bottom lip alternately before he straightened. He took one step, erasing any comfortable space between us, and I sucked in a sharp breath watching as he reached into the inside pocket of his dark blazer. A ripple of delicious chills scattered over my skin as I waited to see him retrieve the gloves.

"No. Not about that. About this," Leo said, handing me a thick white envelope from his jacket.

My brow furrowed as I took the weighty envelope, turning it in my hands. Glancing up at him, confusion washed over me. In a matter of seconds, his entire demeanor changed. As though I held the confidence and power he usually exuded in the mystery envelope, Leo had lost the supremacy I'd felt radiating off of him from day one.

His hand rose, gliding through one side of his hair before scratching the back of his head. He avoided my eyes. "Maybe it's too forward, but," he said, "I wanted you to have that in case you want to…play. Again."

My throat worked to swallow hard as his words chased through my mind. I hadn't even opened the envelope yet but I knew to what he was referring.

"You call that playing?"

A little smile formed on his face and though my stomach pitched with worry, I bit my lip at the sight of his curling, wicked mouth.

"Don't you?"

I gulped again and shook my head, still clouded by his every word. I tore the envelope open and scanned the first page. Medical records. STD tests dated two days ago from the local clinic. Leonardo E. Calloway was apparently clean as a whistle and he wanted me to know. My head whipped up, pinning him with a wild look.

Leo's face fell and paled as his hands shot up and he took a step back. "Like I said, this isn't to pressure you. With you working here, I know it could be awkward to… I just always try to be transparent. If it was a one-time thing, I'm fine with that," his voice dropped to a whisper, "but I figured however frank it seems, you should know, I haven't been that satisfied with a scene or a sub in a while…maybe ever."

Dizziness swarmed me, darkness crept in on the outskirts of my vision and my palms dampened with sweat. His words were foreign and yet I knew deep down I understood what he was telling me. A thousand questions and retorts flickered in my mind, aimed silently at Leo, but I didn't know where to begin. The scene—our scene—had more than satisfied me as well. It set fire to a whole new inferno of cravings that now raged in me, begging for release. Of course, I wanted to *play* again. And I didn't even know what that truly meant. Couldn't he see it in my eyes?

His word—*sub*—slipped under my skin and slithered its way to my soul the same way his word "punishment" had that first time we spoke. Without ever cracking one of those new books, I knew what *sub* meant and I knew that even if I never did anything like it again, our solitary tryst had christened me as one.

"Oh, God," he whispered before a deep sigh.

I looked up at him and pulled my lips in my mouth to keep quiet. He stepped into my space once more and it wasn't until he hesitantly reached out for me that I differentiated the sound of the rain beating on the roof from my thudding heart. He didn't take my hand, but knowing he'd reached for it was enough. He wanted to comfort me; I could see it on his face. I could feel his protective nature leeching out from his attempt to shroud me. My forehead wrinkled as I watched the waves of emotion crash over his expression.

"I'm so sorry," he started. "The other day you…you seemed like a natural. It just sort of started and I thought you were…" His voice trailed off and his eyes glazed over as he began shaking his head solemnly. I took in a few deep breaths, unable to respond, and then he met my eyes.

"I can't believe I did that. You didn't consent. You didn't even know. You're not—you don't—" Leo paused as horror painted his face. "No wonder you've been so jumpy around me. I assaulted you."

I moved my hand to touch his, linking our fingers for an instant, my voice breathily finding its way out of my body. "No. You didn't," I assured him. Looking deep into his eyes, I saw him accept my words the same way he'd accepted my silent consent to the spanking. I'd never known it was possible to speak such volumes without a single word. No connection had ever felt this pure or strong. We might've been strangers on the surface, but the intimacy we'd already stolen from one another threaded something through us that couldn't be easily undone.

Leo reached for the papers he'd given me, but I held them back and dropped his fingers. He squinted and just as another sinful grin began to lift his mouth, I heard the sharp noise of a throat clearing beside us. We both turned to see an exhausted looking Oliver.

"Could one of you come help me unload the rest of the new inventory please?" Oliver huffed.

Leo pushed a hand through his hair and nodded at his brother, walking with him to the front of the store, leaving me. My shoulders slumped back against the shelf, supporting my weight as a breath heaved from my aching lungs. Shutting my eyes, I let my head roll back. When I straightened a few moments later, ready to get back to work, I let my gaze fall on the alluring titles one last time, secretly deciding which one I'd order online.

Slipping into my jacket, I heard Oliver close the cash drawer after his final count and call out to his brother. My spine tingled and I froze when his smoky voice echoed from the top of the stairs. We hadn't spoken the entire rest of the evening. The store stayed busy until just a half hour before closing and I'd been occupied with either customers or some Oliver-delegated task each time Leo locked eyes on me, begging me to pick up where we left off. Did he know how badly I wanted to move toward him? He was a magnet and I was iron, desperate to bond to him yet weighed down by my own composition.

"So…" Oliver said with a smile, breaking me from paralysis. "Think you might like it here? You kept up like a champ today."

"Thanks. Yeah, I think it's gonna be good. It's kind of nice to be working again."

He pulled the shades down over the front window and craned his neck to glance back at me. "The paycheck may not thrill you, but if you want anything off the shelves just let me know. You're allowed freebies every now and then."

"Oh, that's awesome. I'm sure I'll find something I want to take home before too long."

I let out a steady breath when the sensation of eyes searing into my neck struck me. How could I feel him so clearly? I couldn't turn around for fear the sight of Leo would turn me permanently maroon. Keeping my gaze on Oliver as he picked up the children's area, prattling on about the newest bestseller he'd been reading, I flinched when a hand came down on my shoulder. A ghost of a breath next to my ear had me leaning into the hand for support.

"This one will do," Leo whispered against my skin, pulling the strap of my purse down my arm so he could slip a book inside. I glanced at the spine, not surprised to see one of the new titles that had tempted me earlier. It was the one I'd dropped when he caught me pondering a glance at it. He pulled the leather strap back up to rest on my shoulder easily, keeping the book tucked inside our little secret.

I turned to see his thrilling smirk had returned. "What makes you think I want that book?" I asked, my voice hushed so Oliver wouldn't overhear. Who was I kidding? I wanted the entire new shipment. I wanted to devour them cover to cover—dive in headfirst.

Leo's eyes flicked up and down my body twice before wetting his lips. "Well, it seems for whatever reason, I'm pretty damn good at reading you," he said. "You wanted what I gave you the other day, you kept the envelope, so you want the book. Trust me."

"And if I read it…and like it…what happens next?" I whispered, fear and intrigue lacing the question.

The devilish way his full lips curved, brightening his eyes, made my heartbeat fall out of synch to hear his answer better.

"Oh, Sloane," Leo said. "I can't wait to find out."

FOUR

"I KNOW WHAT I said before," I laughed, "but Oliver needs someone part time and I'm there a lot so it'll work out for both of us."

Ellie continued to blather on the other end of the phone, spewing questions at me. How much was I making? What were my hours? Was I still working on the book? What does Oliver look like?

Another sharp laugh escaped me. "It *really* doesn't matter what Oliver looks like. Believe me. Anyway, I just thought you'd be happy to hear I'm employed again," I held the phone to my ear with my shoulder as I cleared my breakfast dishes into the sink and moved to find my shoes. "But I've gotta go or I'll be late."

As Ellie accepted my nudge to say goodbye, telling me she loved me before hanging up, my eyes fell on the book on my coffee table. I'd spent the past few days reading it, every day finding something new that spoke to me. Each morning I cracked it open and read with my coffee in hand and each night I climbed under my covers to learn even more. The day after Leo slipped the book in my purse, he didn't show up for work. Oliver told me he was taking a personal day and my stomach tied in knots wondering if he had fallen on a sudden change of heart. Maybe he didn't want to hear my book report after all. His day off didn't keep me from flipping through the rest of the pages though, marking the most enticing segments with bright yellow sticky notes. By the time I'd finished reading, the book looked ten years old. Cracked spine, earmarked corners, sticky notes and even a few water spots from when I'd attempted reading in the tub. I smiled sheepishly to myself when I remembered where that attempt had led me.

 Leo's day off was followed by one of mine—a day I'd spent making a bold trip to the local clinic, hands trembling long after I'd driven home with my same-day results. I didn't know what would happen next or what our mutual negative testing documents would mean for us. It had been months since I'd had sex and the idea of Leo putting an end to that dry spell made my insides feel like I'd just unleashed bottled lightning. But sex aside, the most exciting thing about Leo and this swift and shocking revelation of shared desires was that the rest was completely unpredictable. Just like the moment he told me to turn around and bend over, I didn't know what was coming next. It made me want it that much more.

Two and a half of my three years with Warren were the epitome of predictable. Even though I constantly tried to convince myself otherwise, I always knew what was coming next between us. I knew when he was lying and when he'd disappoint me. Almost every day. And I knew where I stood with him—in second place.

He'd say he'd spend the day with me. He wouldn't. He'd say he'd call. He wouldn't. He said he'd leave her. He didn't. He said he loved me. He never did.

I worked to swallow the lump that had formed at the base of my throat. I'd wasted so much time and subjected myself to so much pain and I didn't even have the marks on my rear to prove it.

I shook away the waning thoughts of Warren and picked up the white envelope sitting on top of the worn copy of my new favorite book, readying myself for the thrill of the unexpected.

I stilled with my hand on the coffee pot, hot breath that smelled of cool mint tickling my neck. The day had passed in a blur. The moment I walked through the door, Oliver ushered me into the office, intent on teaching me how to place orders and check inventory. By the time he took off to pick up change from the bank and run a few errands, my eyes burned from the glare of the computer screen and my head ached, overfull of new information. I'd only caught a mere glimpse of Leo through the sliver of the office door. With every passing minute, my bravery had diminished, suddenly apprehensive of Leo's reaction and his next impulse. But feeling him at my back, knowing a little smile had to be on his face while he held me without restraint, catapulted my bravery into pure audacity and I dug for the envelope in my back pocket as I spun to face him.

The smile I accurately envisioned spread across his lips, a sight I could easily drink in as his mouth was directly at eye level. My tongue slipped out to capture my bottom lip, pulling it between my teeth. I didn't want to lose this moment—this courage. The feelings he lit inside of me…I'd never felt so alive. Leo's chest broadened as he inhaled smoothly and my hand flicked out, pressing the envelope to his sternum. His brows dipped together and the smile fell from his face, my hand shrinking away from him once he grasped the paper against his chest.

"What's this?" he asked, slipping a finger under the seal, popping it open.

I scoffed and turned away from him and back to my coffee. "Oh, come on. You know exactly what it is."

"Watch your tone."

The deep rasp of his voice was as powerful as the sight of black leather gloves and I slowly turned my head to look over my shoulder at him and then down obediently, controlled by words alone.

He stared at the results and grinned. "I take it you've done some reading. We should probably talk about what this means," he whispered.

I faced him again, warm coffee cup clasped between my palms, and felt lightning resurge inside of me. "Do we have to?"

Leo threw his head back with a laugh then wagged a finger at me. "That sharp tongue of yours could get you in a lot of trouble."

"I hope so."

My knees buckled at the sound of my own retort and nearly collapsed out from under me when a growl snuck out of his throat. He stepped close, taking my elbow in his grasp. "God, it's taking everything in me not to bend you over my knee right here. I need to know limits. Did you write them down?"

His admission stole the air from my lungs and I brought the piping hot coffee to my lips, knowing words had evaded me the moment he growled at me.

"Sloane," he pressed, his voice a thick blanket of black smoke smothering me magnificently.

"Guys, there's a line," Oliver snapped from behind Leo. "The caffeine break can wait."

Leo's eyes darkened and he took another steady deep breath, the wicked words he wanted to say stagnating in the air between us. Swallowing my coffee, I boldly turned a cheek and smiled breezily at Oliver.

"Coming," I chirped, thankful not a hint of a tremble came through in my voice.

Pulling out of Leo's grip, I felt a spinning cocktail of emotions flow through me as I walked away. The thrill of my bravery, the lust for our impending plans, and the puzzling but liberating feeling of joy—something I hadn't felt course through me in a very long time.

By the time dusk fell on Salem, my insides hadn't settled. A stolen glance from Leo or a pass by the human sexuality section—every second had my body alight with energy, the first glowing ember in the form of his primal and enticing snarl.

Oliver locked the front door behind us and headed toward his car. "Night, Sloane," he said before setting a stare on his brother lingering at my side.

"Where's your car?" Leo asked me.

I glanced up at him and tightened my coat around me as the wind picked up. "I walked. I always walk."

His face contorted. "You walk here every day?"

"Yes."

"And you walk home at night? Alone?"

I didn't answer with words, just a tightening of my lips and lowering of my eyes, knowing he wouldn't like my affirmative. Salem was a sleepy little town and I could take care of myself. The fresh air cleared my head, something I needed now more than ever.

Leo turned to Oliver and sighed. "I'm going to walk her home."

"I could drive you guys…" Oliver offered.

A sudden wave of embarrassment crashed on me and I wished Oliver hadn't driven Leo to the store today. The way he watched us worried me, like he knew something.

"It's three blocks, I'm fine," I whispered up at Leo pleadingly.

Another little grumble rattled inside his chest and he put a hand at the small of my back. "We'll walk," Leo said to Oliver. Definitely not to me.

"And how are you gonna get home?"

Leo huffed, halting before turning to his brother across the parking lot one last time. "I'll call Ben. I'm having drinks with him anyway. He'll pick me up. See you tomorrow."

My eyes swept to Oliver and watched as his eyes narrowed and flickered between us. He noticed Leo's hand at my back and I stiffened under the familiar touch. I forced a smile and willed my feet to move forward, not looking back at Oliver's critical stare. Our first few steps were silent until Oliver's car sped past us and we made it to the damp sidewalk.

"You didn't have to walk me."

I didn't dare look at him. Those mesmerizing indigo pools had a way of catapulting me into a trance. Of course he had to walk me. This was the dynamic, I knew it. Though he was still a stranger—an acquaintance at best—I felt what he aimed at me. It was a mixture of something bordering on possessiveness but softened by what appeared to be genuine concern.

"It's not safe. You could get hurt."

A laugh sprung from me. "Says the man intent on leaving handprints on me."

Leo halted and I cringed. "This is exactly why we need to talk," he clipped.

"I was kidding," I replied, defeated.

Leo went on without acknowledging my tiny voice. "You're new to this, which is dangerous…because I'm not and I've already proven I can't restrain myself around you."

I nearly laughed again. Neither one of us could actually say it. He'd given me a spanking but had never mentioned it by name even when he spoke of it. He slipped me a book called *Pain for Pleasure*, but continued to veil what we were embarking on—a sadomasochistic relationship, most likely sexual since we'd both gone and gotten tested as though the next step was not only sex but unprotected sex. How insane was I? Clearly, I'd unearthed my masochistic, submissive side, but this was nearly negligent. Nearly. Not completely. He'd been right when he said he could read me. I didn't know how because I'd never allowed anyone to read me before and I wasn't sure what internal lever I pulled to drop the walls specifically for him. It was as though he willed it of me and I merely consented…

Pulling in a deep breath, I continued walking toward my apartment and blew it out in relief when he followed. "You're right. This is new for me. But I wouldn't consider it dangerous."

"*Sloane*," Leo barked, raising his voice and cutting me off.

I stopped and turned to him, firming my shoulders and refusing to let him silence me. Right now, we were on equal ground. "Just listen to me. I'm sure I'll have limits—I probably have some now—but my guess is you already know them. Everything about that moment upstairs…that…*scene*," I said with a pause, taking a split-second to fall under the spell of his gaze as he scraped his teeth along his bottom lip hearing me use the language we both knew. "Was perfect. But it was perfect for a very specific reason. I may not have a list of boundaries for you, but I know what I want. Spontaneity."

He sighed and raked a hand though his dark hair. "That's unconventional to say the least. It's not really how it works. Thus, dangerous."

"You say you're not new to this, but you also said you'd never been more satisfied by what you experienced with me. Maybe unconventionality is the key."

His silence didn't worry me as he began walking in the direction I'd pointed us earlier, taking his time as he considered my offer. Turns out, I could read him too. As the idea festered behind his eyes, narrowed and introspective, I waited.

"Elaborate on spontaneity."

A smile began to spread on my mouth and I shut my eyes, remembering. "Not knowing what you'd do or how you'd do it or when it would end gave me this breathtaking feeling inside…unlike anything I've ever felt before. I was floating. Suspended in midair, helpless, levitating in an endless spin."

"Sounds a little terrifying," Leo remarked.

"It was freeing."

He shot me a glance, surprised and pensive, that morphed into a smile briefly before tightening into concern once more.

"Say I agree. We don't discuss it further, we start this and we don't plan…" he huffed. "How will I know where to draw the line?"

"You'll know. You'll see it in my eyes."

My boldness had consumed me. The fresh air, the cool breeze, and the heat of the man beside me whipped my senses into a state of vibration from which I couldn't come down. Who was I? Leo reached for my hand, staring down at it while I reminded myself to breathe.

"I'm not sure I trust myself with the freedom of what you're suggesting," he rasped.

I squeezed my hand around his, butterflies unleashing in my belly with the knowledge that he'd all but agreed. "I trust you with it."

Leo inhaled sharply and squeezed back, though his expression hardened.

"And I'll have a safe word, jeez," I breathed around a quivering laugh.

He lifted his face to look over me and smiled, shaking his head as he let go of my hand. I saw my answer in his eyes.

My steps slowed as we approached my apartment complex, not wanting Leo to leave my side just yet. He matched my pace and the sound of his careful breathing finally made me speak my thoughts.

"I can't imagine going over every little will and won't ahead of time. Where's the fun in that? Not to mention, it's sort of strange. It's weird enough to think about the fact that you and I have essentially agreed you're going to fuck me—"

"Have we?" Leo asked with a laugh, turning my way with a cocked brow.

Rolling my eyes, I shook my head as a little smile pulled at my mouth. Of course we had.

"The wills and the won'ts are important. Communication is important. Trust is important, especially between people who don't know each other yet. It isn't something to go into lightly."

I held him with a glare, feeling my cheeks heat without warning. "Is that what you think I'm doing?" I asked in disbelief.

"No," he retorted. "I'm just saying maybe we should go to—"

My temper flared, leaving no room for the end of his statement. "You're right, we don't know each other, and sure, I've never sorted out the details of sex without at least having a meal first, but I'm not going into this lightly at all. I read your fucking book, I know what could be coming. I'm not naïve and I'm not afraid. Communication is important and I've never been able to speak to someone without words the way I seem to with you. Trust is important and I've never felt, let alone resigned myself to such immediate and unfounded trust in a person the way I did with you. The last few years of my life have been sad and boring. I don't want to be sad or bored anymore and those feelings stopped consuming one hundred percent of my day the minute you slipped on those gloves for me. And as for the wills and won'ts…you *will* fuck me and I *won't* stop you."

A staggering breath blew past my lips and I tongued the back of my teeth, suddenly regretting my bratty tirade. I looked right, staring hopelessly at the entrance to my building, wishing I had the guts to walk away after spewing that last bold line at him. But I couldn't…or rather, I wouldn't. Because my wish for the will to walk away was a lie. What I'd said to him was true; everything prior to my move to Salem had left me depressed and jaded. Even my first few months here hadn't helped despite the distance from the things I was trying to forget. I'd struggled with this feeling as if I already knew the ending to my story…not the one I was writing, the one I was living. I felt like the end already happened and the rest of my days would just be a footnote. Something no one would read. Then came Leo.

He could be my turning point and I, his open book. Leo was the plot twist I'd never intended on and my life could remain unscripted if I allowed it. Thinking about the novel I'd thrown myself into to work through the sins of my past, I suddenly didn't care if I ever finished it. The future of this...with Leo...would be my manuscript of relief and reformation. His hands on me would be pen to paper. The look in his eyes would be my flowery prose. The changes his welcomed savage passion had already prompted showed me the freedom of blank pages—thousands of them.

I inhaled deeply and felt my heart pulsate in my chest. What if he backed out now? What if my sharp tongue had ruined this opportunity? My eyes rose to look at Leo and I stilled, taking in the way his head nodded absently, longing to know what it meant. He dragged two fingers over his lips, his thumb anchored on his jaw. With one step, he invaded my space, looming over me and triggering my obedience as I lowered my gaze.

His hand gripped my chin and lifted my face close to his, a whimper cracking at the back of my throat when I melted into his touch. "Let's get one thing straight, you *won't* ever tell me what I *will* do again," he said darkly just before dipping his mouth to brush my earlobe. "And if you do, you'll pay for it. Understand?"

My muscles twitched and I ached at the sound of his commands. "Yes," I breathed.

His grip loosened and a smart grin took over his face. I gulped and let one side of my mouth flicker in amusement. When his brow rose in unspoken challenge, my face fell and I nodded, passing the test.

"Good girl," he whispered.

My eyes fluttered shut, gratified by the praise, and I felt him step away. Leo turned his back to me, preparing to leave without another word when I called out to him, "What should I call you?"

"What?" he asked, looking over his shoulder before making his way to me once more.

I flushed, the question in my mind making me feel as vulnerable as his stare. "When you…when it happens again—what do I call you?"

His expression never faltered though I knew a smile was begging to form on his perfect mouth. "What do you want to call me?"

"I don't know," I started, tucking my hair behind my ear. "What are my options?"

"Hmm…Master?"

I shook my head barely. It didn't fit.

His eyes sparkled and his smile turned playfully sinful. "Daddy?"

Cocking one brow at him, I shook my head again, chagrin painting me. I hated how titillating I found the potential title, fueling my internal conflict even more all while making me consider a trip to the psychiatrist. But "Daddy" didn't suit Leo either. It was almost as though no name would do.

"Call me whatever feels right in the moment. Call me nothing for all I care, so long as you obey."

My insides lit up the moment I watched the smile break free on Leo's lips as he looked me up and down. Sizing me up. Drinking me in. Perhaps fantasizing about our next moment together. God, I hoped so.

I nodded as his feet led him away from me, his final command the end to our conversation, and I considered leaving him nameless. I'd only know when the time presented itself, but for now, he was simply Leo.

FIVE

"AND TURKEY FOR the lady," Oliver said, handing me the paper-wrapped sandwich as we both sat down to eat. He didn't often close the store for a lunch break, but it had been slow and Leo hadn't yet shown up for the day, so Oliver put out the *Back in Thirty Minutes* sign so we could have lunch peacefully.

"What do I owe you?"

He shook his head with a slanted smile. "Please. You taking this job so quickly completely saved our asses. The least I can do is buy you a sub."

The back of my neck flushed with heat as I took my first bite. He was talking about the sandwich, but it seemed my thoughts turned everything into a roundabout reference to my newfound preferences.

"Thanks," I muttered. "So…um…how come you never mentioned Leo being a part of the business until he came back?

I shouldn't have asked, but he was always on my mind. I was so curious about who Leo was, where he'd been, and why he'd come home, but the relationship building between us wasn't one of getting to know you conversations. I couldn't imagine a future rendezvous where I'd ask him about his favorite cuisine after a flogging. Questioning him about his world views wouldn't much work with a ball-gag in my mouth. So I figured to satiate my hunger for knowledge, I'd do the next best thing and pump his brother for information and hope he wouldn't find out.

Luckily, Oliver didn't find my inquiry odd and answered in between sips of his drink. "This place was our dad's, our grandfather's before that. When our parents retired and relocated, they handed it off to me. Leo was about to graduate and he was restless. He needed something to focus on after school, something to ground him after his wild stint at college. Dad and I convinced him to stay here and take partial ownership with me. Scared as I was that he'd find a way to screw it up, he took to it surprisingly well. He's got a mind for business even though he lacked a little direction in the beginning. He proved early on he has a knack for leadership."

I choked down my last bite and averted my eyes. He showed me the same thing early on. The man was a born leader.

"But that old restlessness and maybe his apt for guidance, I suppose, is what drew him away from the store for the past few years. I'm sure he told you about Marie."

My lips parted and I shook my head as a pit formed in my gut. "No."

Why did another woman's name sound so acidic in my head? Leo was nothing more to me than a coach in deviancy. That's all I needed him for. But was that all I really wanted? My dark desires could've been laced with a number of things, but why the hell was jealousy cropping up? He wasn't mine to claim.

"Leo may've been wild at one time, but our sister Marie has always been a bit of a mess."

I loathed the relief that rushed through me. Sister. Oliver didn't notice the catch to my breathing or the way my eyes shut and he continued.

"She's a single mom and she's great at picking out horrible boyfriends. Leo went to live with her when our nephew was born and help her get her back on her feet."

"And now? Why did he leave?"

"Marie's doing well for once. She needed some independence. And I think she feels guilty for taking so much of Leo's time."

I glanced at the clock and saw our lunch break was nearly over. As I stood, I gathered the sandwich wrappers and napkins from the table and tossed them in the trash. "It sounds like Leo's a good guy…why were you so worried about the way he treated me when he first arrived?" I asked, remembering Oliver's concern that Leo had been rude to me.

Oliver's mouth contorted and he wobbled his head from side to side, mulling over my question. "Leo's a great guy. He has a bit of an edge to him though. I don't know what his deal is, but I don't think he realizes how cold he can come across. He's weird." Oliver laughed. "I just didn't want a nice girl like you catching the brunt of his hostility."

I laughed a little in return, biting my lip to squash the ironic outburst. "You have nothing to worry about. Your brother is definitely blunt, but he's been nothing but nice to me."

"Slacking off in the middle of the day, brother?"

I heard Leo's voice from the front of the store along with the bell and Oliver rolled his eyes. "It's just a lunch break," he grumbled.

Turning, I held my breath as his face came into view. Straight nose and perfect teeth, he beamed a smile at me first and I felt my insides quiver. His blue eyes struck me and I let the new information about him paint my vision. The enigmatic man with the smoky voice and the black leather gloves was also a sweetheart who'd drop everything to go help his sister get on her feet and raise a child. And just like that, I was more invested and more intrigued by him. And once again, I hated that anything but lust had melded into the feelings I held for Leo.

The sweet old woman handed me a few bills to cover her assortment of gardening books with a smile and I quickly returned the change to her before bagging her purchases. "Have a good night, come back and see us," I said, passing her the bag of books. As she exited the front door, a familiar face entered. Wendy came in looking as though the store was the last place on Earth she wanted to be. She'd always been friendly to me, but the look on her face as she breezed past the register told me not to offer a greeting. I watched as she peered into the office before turning to me with a huff.

"Is Oliver here? Or Leo? I need my last paycheck."

My mouth opened and my eyes lifted to see Oliver descending the steps behind her.

"Wendy," he said, nearly breathless. "Hi. Um..."

"I'm here for my check."

He nodded fervently and hurried into the office, emerging once he had the envelope in hand. Wendy took it from him without a word and bolted for the door. Oliver rushed after her and I felt my heart seize at the bold move from the quiet man I thought I knew. Thankfully, we were nearing closing time and no customers were inside because the pseudo soap opera playing out before me was too enthralling to take my eyes away. Shamelessly, I peered at the exchange, watching their silent story outside the store front window. The arced lettering of Calloway Books canopied over their heads perfectly, framing the scene as Wendy folded her arms across her chest while Oliver spoke words I couldn't make out.

"Spying?"

Leo's deep voice made me flinch and turn to him. A gloating smile lingered on his face as he sidled up next to me and opened the cash drawer to begin counting out for the evening.

"Do you know what's going on with them?" I asked.

"They're in love with each other, can't you tell?"

I shot Leo a look but his eyes remained down, counting the last few dollar bills. When he swept his gaze to me, his eyes softened. One step and he stood behind me, lips at my ear, boldly brushing my hair over my shoulder as he turned my chair gently until I fully faced the window.

"See the way he stares at her mouth as she talks? He can't stop thinking about kissing her and he's trying to decide if acting on it will fix things or ruin it all."

I turned my head to gape at him. Oliver hadn't said a word about Wendy. In fact, he'd never mentioned a woman or any kind of relationship.

"Fix what? What do you know?"

Leo's brow creased, but a smirk formed on his lips as he tsked around a light laugh. He put a finger on my chin and put me back into place so I could continue watching.

"She keeps touching her face. He makes her feel uncomfortable—vulnerable—but she's desperate for physical contact. She wants his hands on her."

I stiffened barely and thought of how his words could've easily been about me. About us. He was right though. Wendy sighed and looked away as Oliver reached out to her with a devastated look on his face. How had I never noticed there was something between them? She pulled away and fixed her gaze on him and though it was hard to tell from the side, I thought I saw tears gleaming in her eyes.

Leo's smooth whisper rasped in my ear again, causing my breath to run shallow. "She pulls away because she's afraid of what his touch will do to her. She knows it will melt her, possess her…she knows once he touches her she won't be able to run from how she feels anymore. She won't be able to hide from it. We don't need to hear them to know what they're saying. They probably aren't saying much—but I can see it loud and clear. Can't you?"

Wendy wiped under her eyes and I turned to Leo again, my brows pulled together in the center as I examined his profile while he continued to watch them.

He turned and his eyes narrowed briefly. "What?"

I sighed audibly. "Nothing. What do you need me to do for closing?"

He shook his head and gazed at the window again. I joined him for no other reason than wanting to see his reaction. Wendy threw her hands in the air and turned, storming off and leaving Oliver with his head hung low and his shoulders on the verge of trembling.

"Whoa," I breathed.

"Go after her, you idiot," Leo murmured.

Oliver dragged his hands over his face then bounced toward the door, opening it just enough to pop his head in with an exasperated sigh. "Leo, can you close up? I gotta—"

"Yes. Go!" Leo replied. His face lit up as he shooed his brother away.

Oliver smiled and tapped his palm against the door two times. "Thanks, man," he said as he jetted off in the direction Wendy had gone.

I spun the stool I sat on and grinned at Leo. "Tell me everything. I'm dying to know what the hell just happened."

He didn't look at me. The little smile on his face faded into something almost stern but closer to stoic. He took a set of keys from his pocket and locked the cash register. "No," he said.

"No? Come on, I need the dish. Oliver's been holding out on me." My brain didn't catch up quickly enough to recognize the look in his eyes as the intoxicating mixture of lust and dominance I'd been craving. He faced me and put the keys in my hand.

"Lock the front door. Close the blinds. Meet me upstairs."

My chest flared with an electric pulse as my fingers closed around the keys. I stood stunned as he smoothly moved to the coat rack near the office and pulled something from his coat pocket. When he reached the bottom of the metal staircase, he looked at me, unmoving and wide-eyed. Penetrated by his gaze, a ripple of fear and temptation swelled inside me as I watched him pull on the pair of black gloves I'd been aching to see once more before taking his first step to the second floor.

I blew out a breath and turned for the door with weak limbs. This was it. Round two. What waited for me upstairs? The click of the deadbolt rang around the rush of my blood in my ears and I somehow found the clarity to yank the blinds down over the window, turning off the neon *Open* sign as well.

I could do this. I wanted this. I wanted him. I wanted new. I wanted that freefall feeling in my belly at least one more time.

My feet led me to the stairs and I peered up, holding on to a moment of freedom before I fell under his rule for however long he pleased. Drawing in a breath, my shoulders rose then sank down again before I took a conscious step toward my fantasies.

The door of the room where the first tendrils of our web had been spun barely cracked when he gave his first orders. "Sit at the table with your hands in your lap and your eyes down."

My right arm trembled so violently, I pumped my hand in a fist as I did as he said, urging it to stop. Leather fingertips brushed my hair over my shoulders the same way his gentle bare hands had downstairs and an involuntary shudder claimed me. My lungs ached as I held my breath to keep from panting. The anticipation sent me reeling. Maybe I couldn't do this.

"Breathe," he whispered.

Though his voice wasn't the dark rasp I knew as the one he used to command, I obeyed him as if it had been a growl. A heavy huff staggered from my nose and a gloved hand rested on the back of my neck, easing my panic. I felt him towering over the chair, finding my cheek to speak against.

"*Yellow* if you're approaching a limit and you want me to slow down. *Red* if you reach a limit and want me to stop what I'm doing. And *black* if you need to end the scene for any reason. Nod if you understand."

Slowly my head bobbed, his colorful lullaby soothing me one step further. I heard a faint sigh that sounded like it could've been a breathy laugh and exhilaration flooded me. Acutely aware of where he stood, I kept my eyes on the table feeling him straighten behind me. He tossed a pencil, a rubber band, and four black binder clips on the table. Staring at them, my eyes narrowed at first and then my imagination took off like a rocket. Shit. Where were those things going? I bit down on my bottom lip and tried to breathe. I was safe. I could stop this at any time.

"Put your hair up," he said.

Without thinking, I whipped my head to the side and gazed up at him. One corner of his mouth upturned and he simply pointed to the rogue office supplies, granting me mercy for my unauthorized glance. "Use one of those. I don't care which, just get the hair up and off your neck and shoulders."

I resisted the urge to smile and nodded. I quickly grabbed the pencil and held it between my teeth as I gathered my hair in my hands and twisted it into a bun. Securing it by sliding the pencil through my thick strands, I pulled my lips inward when I heard another less subtle laugh.

"That's better. Now listen carefully," he started. "You're going to sit there, still, while I ask you some questions. If you hesitate when answering or if you lie...or if you shiver or pull away from me, I'll start counting."

My mouth popped open but I put myself in check quickly enough that I didn't make a sound. However, Leo must've noticed my attempt. "Need to say something? Go ahead," he allowed.

I focused my eyes on the rubber band still lying on the table and twisted my lips contemplating whether I should even ask.

"Counting...what?"

"For every time you don't follow the rules, you'll get a spanking. And since you felt the need to interrupt me just now, I'll be counting by twos."

I breathed deeply and squeezed my thighs together at his gruff reply. By the end of this, I'd be wet and aching for him and I wondered if he intended to do more than spank me.

"Are you ready?"

"Yes," I whispered.

Lost in my thoughts, I flinched when Leo appeared at my side, reaching toward the buttons of my shirt. Stunning blue eyes collided with mine as his leather covered fingers popped open each button. When the fabric split open, he pushed it down my shoulders, allowing him the sight of my white bra and my bare, pale skin. The air tickled over my chest and a quick chill moved through me.

"We haven't even begun and you've already disobeyed. That's two," he sneered.

My mind raced attempting to recall the rules. Answer the questions. Don't hesitate. Don't lie. Don't shiver or pull away. Leo disappeared from sight and my hearing suddenly became keener as I listened for his footfalls to know how close he was to me.

"How old are you?"

What? I wasn't sure what I imagined he'd ask me but it certainly wasn't that. By the time my lips parted to answer, he growled.

"That's four. How old are you?"

"Twenty-seven."

"How many sexual partners have you had in those twenty-seven years?"

Fuck. I counted as quickly as I could, praying my answer wasn't a lie as I blurted it out onto the air. "Four."

Silence filled the space and I shifted barely. Feeling my shirt slipping down my arms, exposing more of me, I resisted the tremor that began rolling up my spine. But the moment a sharp zing traced across the back of my neck, I succumbed and felt goosebumps bloom along every inch of my skin as I shook the way I would if a feather dragged along my flesh.

"Six," he said coolly.

I lowered my head, shaming myself. I sat with my shirt hanging off of me, letting a man in black leather gloves do God knows what to my neck while he interrogated me. He was good at this. Better than I'd imagined he would be even after the first time. He had me in complete submission, yearning to please him. The realization filled me with sudden conflict and my mind flipped to a time three years ago when another man had wielded such power over me.

"Look at me," I heard him say from across the table.

I snapped out of my memories and into the present. He'd taken a seat opposite me while I berated myself for the cold chills I'd allowed and the submission I'd granted another. When I looked at him, he smiled the sinister grin he'd shown me a few times already. He held up a thin silver tool of sorts for me to see and twirled it between his fingers. It had a long handle, as long as a pen, with a spiked metal wheel on one end. My eyes narrowed on the tool and for a moment, I thought of my grandmother.

When I was a child, she'd tried to teach me to sew and quilt alongside her but I'd never taken to it like she hoped. The thing Leo held out to me wordlessly looked like something I'd seen her use once to…trace a pattern? I wasn't sure. I couldn't place it. And I knew damn well Leo didn't intend on turning me into a seamstress with it.

"Consider this your distraction," Leo said, pressing the sharp tines of the wheel into one fingertip, threatening to pierce the leather. He stood and moved behind my chair once more so I was blind to his movements, the sound of his breathing my only clue.

Cool metal touched my bare shoulder and I instantly stilled. No shiver, no goosebumps, no reaction. Though the sharp intake of a gasp I heard from behind me nearly made me melt. This series of quick-witted movements, each of us trying to outsmart the other, was the kind of game I'd never played. Not like this. He wanted to rattle me and I so desperately wanted to please him yet, hearing him count my eventual punishments aloud made warmth pool within me.

Confusion addled me and as I considered what I truly wanted and how this sensual interchange reminded me of unhealthier days, the spiked wheel began to roll across my skin. As he spoke his next question, he pushed down and I sank my teeth into my bottom lip to keep from stirring at the pain.

"Do you masturbate, Sloane?"

"Yes," I croaked and he lifted the tines from my skin, relief and adrenaline waving over me.

"When was the last time you touched yourself?"

My words flowed out, broken by a moan, as another prickle danced in a line from my hair down to the top of my bra strap. "This mo—*oh*—orning."

Thinking of how I'd woken up with a hand down my panties, a dream leading me to waking visions to send me over the edge, I sighed. Sleep came easier now that my body's responses were driven by release instead of stress.

Leo chuckled and rolled the wheel up my spine so quickly it felt like a knife slicing me. And I adored it. My senses were on high alert, my skin tingling, my head swimming and my stomach flipping with excitement.

"What was that?"

"This morning," I whispered.

A deep noise built in his chest and I gasped when a black glove threaded into the hair pulled up at the back of my head. His fist tightened, yanking on the strands roughly. Leo drew my head back and brushed his mouth against my temple.

"Were you thinking about me?"

The tight grip stung my scalp and the roughness of his touch and his voice triggered the beginnings of my freefall. My eyes closed and my chest heaved as a whimper left me. He was all I thought about. This morning. Last night. Every night since I first heard his voice.

"*Eight*." He tugged on my hair again. "Did. You. Think of me?"

"Mmm hmm."

The weak reply vibrated from my throat to my closed lips. A gust of warm breath expelled onto my cheekbone before he shoved my chair back away from the table. In an instant, he was in front of me with his hand reclaiming its position at the back of my neck. Leather captured my throat as Leo grasped my neck from both sides. I was completely at his mercy. With a strong twist, he could break my neck. I wasn't putting my life in his hands though. He'd done exactly what I knew he could—he saw on my face what I wanted. Though confusion still attempted to swamp me, I silently begged for escalation. I craved him moving me like his puppet. Playing with me like a doll. Made for his enjoyment.

"Open your eyes."

Pulling my heavy lids open, I came face to face with him before me, his strong hands keeping my chin tilted up. I expected a dark look. Though I was already starting to lose myself to the spin, I read his expression and swallowed hard, feeling the pressure of his palm increase—testing me. The look in his eyes was anything but dark. It was light, shining, thrilled and nearly awestruck. I watched as he scanned my face, blinking, brow furrowing then lifting as though he'd lost himself to an overwhelming feeling too.

"Did you come?" he whispered down at me.

"Twice," I choked out.

His lips crashed into mine hard and he moved his other hand to assist in strangling me. My fingers itched to reach out to him but I didn't dare. The muscles in my body lost their sense of gravity and the float began. My insides levitated as his tongue invaded my mouth. Gloved hands on me, a few sharp prickles across my skin to distract my senses and a brutal kiss moved me more than sex ever had. The interrogation was foreplay and this kiss was the main event. Though my core throbbed, aching to be filled and driven to release, I felt utter satisfaction from his mouth on mine and the penetration of his tongue only.

His hands tightened for a split second, stealing my breath as he released me from the kiss, then releasing me altogether. I panted, starved for air and freedom but devastated by the overwhelming feeling of loss without him joined with my body.

A scatter of chills rippled through me. This was so much more than I expected. I wasn't sure if I was ready for the boundless emotions that threatened to consume me. He'd gone easy on me, I knew it. If he could make me feel like this with a little warm up, what would his true potential do to me? He'd own me for sure.

"Ten."

My eyes whipped up to meet his, wondering what I'd done. He dragged a finger down my arm, drawing my eyes to the damning evidence of every fine hair standing at attention, tiny bumps turning my body into Braille for him to read.

"All things considered, you're a very good girl," he said. "But I know you can be better. You just have to learn."

I searched myself for the right word to describe the way he made me feel. His hands, his voice, his orders, his praise and his punishment left me—raw. In every sense of the word. I was unrefined, inexperienced in this lifestyle. I felt awakened by the primal urges deep in my soul. My body and mind reacted viscerally to the long-awaited and most pleasurable damage I'd ever allowed anyone to inflict on me. Was this all I'd ever needed? Was this the path to drudging up and curing my pain? By feeling it on my skin and letting it please me and someone else?

"Stand up," Leo said, snapping me back to the scene.

I rose and the motion caused my shirt to fall almost completely off, hanging on at my wrists only, the crisp fabric flowing over my backside like a train. Leo stood before me and looked in my eyes as he guided the shirt up my arms and onto my shoulders, smoothing it into place before buttoning it up. A wave of rejection crashed on me, fueled by my persistent emotional overload. He was done with me. No interest in taking what I was willing to give.

"You have a beautiful body," Leo said as he secured the button between my breasts. I swallowed hard but didn't look at him. The freefall was over and dejection loomed, ready to swarm me.

"I want to see the rest," he breathed.

His hands slid down the sides of my waist until he reached the button of my jeans. Releasing the metal button and slowly pulling down the zipper, the feeling of leather fingers and palms smoothing over my belly and hips as he pushed my jeans down shot tingles in every direction. My jeans stopped just below my knees and Leo crouched down in front of me, feeling the backs of my thighs as my limbs wobbled. Locking my eyes on a spot on the bookshelf across the room, I sighed when he pressed a kiss at the seam of my panties and spoke against my skin.

"What do you want, Sloane?"

I whimpered, holding on to my words.

"Twelve. Tell me what you want."

My own heat scorched me and only raged hotter when the tempting gloves inched my panties down to meet my jeans at the knee. Bared to him, with his face nearly nestled at my core, I struggled to breathe. He wasn't done with me and I feared that the feelings clouding my mind would mean I'd never be done with him. How long had I waited for this? My need to be wanted only outweighed by my default of wanting to be manipulated. Leo granted me both but in a way I'd never experienced. My heart grew heavy again, letting the shame and regret of my former life chain me up, denying me that floating sensation Leo offered with his breath at my sex.

"I want you to hurt me. Punish me," I whispered.

A smile broke out on his face and he moved into the seat he'd placed me in before. Then his hand gripped my wrist and tugged until I stumbled over to him, my legs tangled in my half-shed clothing. He yanked me forward, taking me over his knee like a disobedient child, my ass up ready for his assault.

I tucked my chin down and panted—waiting. Smooth, cool leather swept over the bare skin of my buttocks and when he just barely tapped the skin, I flinched.

"Fourteen," he said, a clear grin in his words. "Now you do the counting. If you don't count, I'll just keep going until you get it right. Understand?"

"Yes," I managed. It was so much more intimate this way, with my heartbeat pounding against his thigh and his arm lying heavily across my back holding me down. And then there was the fact that I didn't have even the light protection of cotton over me.

Without any more lead up, the first crack of leather against skin rang through the air. My flesh stung. He'd been holding back last time.

"One," I choked, starting the long countdown.

The raps came in quick succession with no chance for me to recover in between each one. But I gritted out my numbers, around groans and pleasure-laden sighs. The hum of my skin as he struck me had my core pulsating erratically by the time I grunted out, "Ten."

He stopped there and smoothed over both cheeks delicately, soothing the surely reddened flesh. My head dropped again and I sighed, knowing it wasn't over but too exhausted to let the anticipation rule me for a moment longer. When I fully relaxed across his lap, a blow more powerful than the rest made me cry out. Another came before I gave the count and it forced another scream from me. By the third strong slap—his promise to be unrelenting if I couldn't do as I was told, kept—my vocal chords scraped and my teeth clenched.

"Eleven!"

Harder.

"Twelve!"

Lightening shot from my clit to my belly button as arousal surpassed pain.

"Thirteen!"

My feet thrashed, not to get away from him or to make him stop, but to rub my myself against his lap, wanting nothing more than to work the growing orgasm to fulfillment. The final slap stole my breath and made me fall limp against him, the entrancing plummeting feeling taking over, but not before I whispered, "Fourteen," as everything faded to black.

SIX

CONSCIOUNESS SLOWLY CAME back to me as the sensation of warm skin smoothed over the traumatized cheeks of my ass. Leo's voice snuck out like a lullaby, his head leaned down close to mine as I lay wilted over his lap. The spinning slowly waned and I made out his words.

"You were so good," he said sweetly. "Such a good girl. It's okay. You're okay."

The tender sentiments shot another jolt of carnal need to my center and I squeezed my thighs together, the first sign to him that I'd regained my senses. His palm slowed its circles then slipped under my shirt to rub my lower back.

"How was that for spontaneous?" he whispered.

I let out a tiny snort as he reached to slide my panties over my hips. I moved, putting my feet on the ground. My hands gripped the edge of the chair beside his leg and as I attempted to push up, I felt my biceps tremble and fail me. Leo caught and guided me effortlessly, stabilizing my legs so he could help me dress. I cringed, feeling satin and denim pull over my tender ass. He made a little noise then carefully lowered me onto his lap.

"Are you all right? We're done. You can relax."

I stared at my knees, slowly coming back to earth, the clouds in my head not yet cleared. Leo's hand, free of the gloves, stroked my cheek and turned my face to his.

"Sloane? Can you speak?"

The concern in his gaze threw me, but I nodded. He smiled wryly at my silent reply to his question and my lips curved briefly.

"I'm fine," I whispered. "That was...a little intense."

His mouth and eyes hardened and he drew in a weighty breath.

"What?" I asked.

One hand rubbed at his forehead as he exhaled just as heavily. "That was nothing."

"I know that," I said.

Worry creased his brow as he examined me, easily—familiarly running his hand up and down my back. The clouds disintegrated finally and I smiled to ease the tension I saw painting him.

"Don't give up on me just yet," I said. "I can be better—handle more. I just need to learn."

His eyes sparkled and he wet his lips, changed by my thievery of his words for my own agenda. "Would you like some tea?" he asked.

Order me upstairs, tear my clothes off of me, grill me while you mar my skin with steel, punish me for my reactions to said grilling …then serve me a cup of tea? Yes, I had a lot to learn. I nodded and he tapped my arm for me to allow him up.

"Take a minute to yourself if you need one then come on downstairs. We'll have a drink then I'll get you home."

I didn't reply with more than another nod, feeling myself slip back into the spin the second his words became instructions that I so desperately wanted to follow. When he reached the door, he turned back to me with a beaming smile. "Sloane?"

"Yes?"

"Thank you."

Just like the first time, he thanked me—for what, I wasn't positive. But I knew that the acknowledgment filled me with as much satisfaction as the rest. I knew I craved his gratitude as equally as his control, approval, and brutality.

The last swallow of my tea still warm in my throat, Leo glanced at me. I relished the silence we'd been sharing. It wasn't uncomfortable and yet it wasn't truly quiet. My mind hadn't stopped chattering away since he'd walked downstairs. When would we do it again? What would it be like a third time? Was I good enough? Could he tell I enjoyed it? Did he enjoy it? Why didn't he fuck me? And the question in block letters, lit up like a neon diner sign…what was wrong with me?

"You ready? I'll grab your jacket," Leo said, rising from where his arms leaned against the checkout desk. He came up behind me and held my jacket out, coaxing me to slip it on with his assistance. His hand at the small of my back led me to the door and I stood watching him as he locked it behind us.

"I could drive you, but I liked our walk the other night. I figure, as long as the weather holds out, we should enjoy the outdoors together."

I nodded and attempted a small smile to appease him. As we walked, I felt my stomach pitch and my ears heat up. The questions still circled my mind and the chill in the air wasn't the only reason for my pained lungs.

"You think you're fucked up."

My eyes shot to him and he met my stare with a challenging brow.

"You're not," he added, looking ahead.

"How would you know?"

Leo laughed lightly and slid a hand through his dark hair. "I guess I don't know for sure. You could be all kinds of fucked up for all kinds of reasons. But what we do—what we did—that doesn't make you fucked up."

He knew I'd been thinking it. He knew I was chastising myself for every part of it. The newness I'd asked for had brought with it a sense of uncertainty. Who was I? What did this all mean? Why had I jumped in so eagerly, willingly, and without considering the consequences or the complications?

My stomach flipped. This wasn't the first time.

"It's perfectly normal to feel like you're weird or sick, but you need to understand that you aren't. Your tastes don't have to define you any more than your hairstyle does, or what kind of car you drive, or your favorite pizza topping. It's a preference. It suits you and that's all that matters."

I let his statements soak in, taking a deep breath as I began to believe them. Maybe he was right. I wasn't unhappy, just puzzled by it all.

"How long have you been doing this?" I asked.

He shot me a side-eye and grinned. He didn't have to say it, but I knew he was glad I'd found my voice again. "Since college," he replied.

As I considered what Oliver had told me earlier, my lips upturned on one end. I wondered if he knew just how wild his little brother had been while he was in school. Dominating sorority girls didn't seem like typical college guy fun.

"I have an idea," he started. "Something to help you get a little more comfortable. And it might also be a good way for me to feel out some of your limits without having to try them first."

"Okay…"

From the side, as we walked, I saw him wet his lips and begin to smirk. Whatever he was about to suggest amused him. I figured this whole thing amused him. The little bookshop girl chomping at the bit to be defiled. I swallowed down the self-reproach and reminded myself I was enjoying it.

"A friend of mine has parties occasionally. It's a safe space for people to play. He's having one in a couple days; we should go together."

"An orgy?" I balked.

"No," he chuckled. "Well—" He shook his head and smothered more laughter. "Only for people who want that. It's pretty much a free for all. Anything for anyone. But no one does anything they don't want to. For us, I was thinking we could just look…"

"You think a way to make me more comfortable is to take me to a stranger's house to watch other people fucking? I'm good, thanks."

The disparagement in my tone startled me. Leo halted and let his hand easily grip my elbow. It wasn't a strong grasp but the touch straightened my shoulders a little. It amazed me how I'd already become so in tune to him. I might've been obedient to his touch, but outside of the bookstore, my defiance—the remnants of rebellion that spurred from escaping Warren's hold—reared its ugly head. Looking at the smile on his face as he held me still with a light hand, I pursed my mouth contemptuously.

"Well, I didn't take you for a brat," he said. "But I can work with it."

Brat? I was about to speak when he stepped into me, forcing me to look up at him from only a few inches of space between us.

"My suggestion is that we go to see, in person, the variety of things we might enjoy together so that you and I can understand each other's tastes better since you don't seem big on conversation."

A sigh rushed out of me and I lowered my gaze, focusing on the waistband of his slacks. I wanted to hate the suggestion. I wanted to dismiss his idea altogether, turn my back on him and spend the next few days convincing myself that I'd had my fill of discipline—two spankings and it was out of my system for good—but I couldn't. I wanted more. I wanted Leo. I needed to see where this new endeavor would take me. The constant struggle in my mind of whether or not I was some sick fuck or just a girl with eclectic taste was exhausting, though.

His hand cupped my chin and pulled my face up to see his. Dammit, I adored that authority he maintained over me. "I want you to see that you aren't the only one who likes the things you're still afraid of liking. I can't help you with whatever's holding you back right now…but I can help you get that spinning feeling you love," he said. He moved even closer and spoke against my cheek. "I can make your life a carousel if you let me, Sloane."

The ride he offered was everything I'd been dreaming of, despite how I wanted not to believe it. The only thing I needed to get a handle on was the burden I felt weigh on me every time Warren crept in my mind, reminding me that I'd been submissive long before I'd ever shared a scene with Leo. I swallowed hard and boldly took a step backward. He didn't rule me all the time—not yet anyway. Part of me expected him to grip me harder and pull me back into place, but he let me go, his hand falling to his side as my gaze traveled up and down his body. I hugged my arms around myself, waiting for him to take a hint and say goodbye. We'd made it to my building and all I could think of was how my ass needed aloe and my mind needed sleep.

"I'll think about it, okay?" I resolved.

I watched his full lips soften and his head nod almost unnoticeably. "Of course," he replied. "Whatever you want."

A cynical scoff passed my lips abruptly and my arms cinched across my chest tighter. "Whatever *I* want? Sure."

"Yes, it's up to you. It doesn't exactly do it for me if I feel like I've pushed you into something you don't want to be a part of."

"What?" I breathed. "Isn't that the point? You make me. You command and I obey."

"No, no, no. I don't mean when I've got a Wartenberg wheel to your neck or a fist full of your hair. I'm talking about step one. When I handed you the keys and told you to lock up then come to me…that moment was no different from this one. You chose to walk up those steps. You could've just as easily walked out the front door. You choose to submit. You always have your freedom. You freely place yourself under my control for a period of time. Just a second ago, you chose to pull away from me. I didn't order you to come back because I have no right to do so…but look where you are," he said, flicking his eyes to our feet.

I'd closed the gap between us again without even noticing. His fingers linked with mine at my side as I continued staring at the tips of our nearly touching shoes. I was drawn to him in every sense of the word.

"I have no interest in stealing your submission from you, Sloane. I won't demand it or force it or even beg for it," Leo said. "I intend to earn it."

His voice cast spells on me, his touch turned my blood to fire, and one look caused me to erase all space between us. I hadn't dropped to my knees before him, but I knew it wouldn't be long before I completely surrendered, whether he earned it or not.

Staring at a nail pop in the ceiling, I let Leo's intentions swirl through my thoughts. He'd left me at my door with a simple squeeze of my hand and nothing more. With him gone, I felt all the things I wished I'd said plaguing me. I considered his suggestion of the party. Half of me envisioned some Stanley Kubrick-esque dungeon of sin and sickness full of rich people and their playthings and the other half figured it might've been as simple as a backyard barbeque with a little fun on the side. I barely knew my own wants and desires, was I really ready to see others' played out before me live and in color? Would it be inspiring? Tempting? Or would it scare me off entirely?

A breath rushed out of me as I sat up in bed and made my way to the kitchen. I reached for the corkscrew on the countertop and picked out a bottle of red. Pouring myself a glass, Leo's parting words struck me once more. I wasn't sure if I'd ever had a man attempt to earn any of my emotions or actions.

In all of the days I'd spent in Salem, thoughts of Warren had never bombarded me as strongly as they did now that Leo continued to inch his way into my life. Warren stole my submission. He demanded my energy. He forced my heart to weaken and eventually break. And he begged for forgiveness that I didn't want to give time and time again. He'd never earned a thing from me. Not trust or respect—not even my love. He stole that, too.

Three years flashed behind my eyes like an intense slideshow. I cursed myself for every single step but one stuck out in my mind as the most upsetting.

I reached for my phone and found a long forgotten number. For all the wrong I'd allowed Warren to do to me and all the wrong I'd done to myself at his silent behest, the worst of all was ending a friendship. My sister wasn't the kind of person I could even tell about Warren, let alone Leo. I loved her but she'd never been a confidant. My finger skimmed the glass screen over his name in my contacts list and with another sip of wine, I pressed on it firmly then held my breath as I listened to it ring.

"Hello?"

"Bryon?" My voice was a pitiful squeak.

I heard him sigh on the other end before he spoke. "Sloane. Hey."

"How are you?" Again, I barely recognized the meek tone I carried as fear and doubt consumed me. How long before he'd hang up on me?

"I'm fine. You got a new number, huh? Did Sugar Daddy need to switch providers so the Mrs. wouldn't catch on?"

The disdain in his voice cut me, but I knew I deserved it. I swallowed hard and bit down on my bottom lip for a second.

"We broke up."

Bryon laughed darkly. "Okay, I'll bite. Haven't heard that in a while. It doesn't sound like you've been crying so what's it been…a couple of hours?"

"About eight and a half months," I replied. "I moved. I've been living in Salem."

Silence hung on the line then I heard him draw in a breath. "Why didn't you tell me?"

"The last time we talked you made it pretty clear you didn't want to hear from me again."

"Well, why are you calling me now? Is everything all right? Are you okay?"

My heart sank hearing the man I still considered to be my best friend clamor for words to ask about my safety. Tears welled in my eyes and a smile touched my mouth.

"Yeah. Yeah, I'm fine. I just—I missed hearing your voice."

"I miss you too," he said softly. In the background, I heard the trill of whimpering baby cries and then a light curse from Bryon. "Hang on," he said.

I swiped a tear from my eye and gulped a little more liquid courage, hearing him call his husband's name.

"Sorry, I'm back," he said.

"How's Craig? And Elizabeth?"

It had been close to a year since I'd spoken to him. Our final face-to-face argument was the first crack in my foundation—the first trauma that ultimately led me to wake up and leave Warren behind. Bryon and I had been best friends for close to fifteen years and we'd been through it all. The loss of my parents, his college boyfriend Tom's suicide, break-ups and job changes, the whole gambit. He'd met Craig around the same time I met Warren and as their relationship progressed, jealousy turned me into an awful friend. I used words like weapons, criticizing how quickly they were moving and questioning Bryon's feelings, even going as far as suggesting he was looking for someone to replace Tom. I turned into the world's biggest bitch, and Bryon made no apologizes for his feelings about my relationship with Warren. Slowly, our friendship became nothing more than an ongoing feud. To me, he was masking his grief with a rebound and looking past faults for a future, and to him, I was a gold digging, naïve whore making excuses for a man who would never leave his wife.

Only one of us was right.

I spent three years denying that I had any inclination Warren was married when I first met him, but I knew. On our first date, I saw the indent on his left ring finger where a band must've sat for years. I noticed the way he checked his phone every thirty minutes like clockwork, shooting quick texts to someone clearly more important than me. From there it only became clearer. We never went to his place, he never called, only texted, and we rarely went out past our first few dates. Sure, he played me, but I entered the game willingly.

My stomach pitched and Leo's words suddenly wounded me as an aftershock. My choice—my first step—my submission allowed everything with Warren to transpire much like my decisions would be the catalyst for whatever path Leo and I travelled as well. Good or bad, I had no one to blame but myself.

"They're good. She's getting so big, Sloane. You should see her," Bryon replied dreamily, snapping me from my damning inner monologue. I hated knowing I'd never met the child that should've known me as Aunt Sloane. I broke that family bond. "What about you? You wanna tell me what happened?"

I sighed and scrubbed at my forehead. "They um…Warren and Elaina…had a baby."

"Fuck," Bryon breathed.

My voice broke and I choked out the twisted, angry sob I'd been smothering for weeks—ever since I saw the birth announcement online. That was the news that catapulted me into writer's block, insomnia, and perpetual muscle tension until Leo came around and distracted me from it. Liberated me from it.

"You'd think our fights would've been about why he hadn't left his wife yet, but our constant screaming match boiled down to the fact that he never wanted children. I'd sacrificed so much to be with him, I didn't think I could give up a shot at motherhood. One day, I brought it up and he didn't react to it the way he used to. Then he avoided the subject. Then he just became altogether distant. Eventually, I figured it out. He begged me to stay and told me he'd leave her. His reasoning, of course, wasn't because he loved me or that he wanted a life with me…it was because he didn't want to raise a child and if he left her he could be a weekend dad. I wanted to have his children and he wanted me to be the reason he abandoned one."

Remembering the night in question made my stomach turn. His words that night nearly made me vomit. I was so disgusted by him, but more disgusted with myself for caring about him—for wanting him the way I did for so long and turning a blind eye to every single one of his failings as a man. He was pathetic. I was pathetic for allowing our distorted relationship to trick me into thinking what we had was true love.

"Sloane…"

I sucked in a breath and pushed Warren away with my exhale. "It's okay. You know, I'm glad I left. I don't miss him." A broken laugh fell out of me. "And I saved so much fucking money while we were together that I only recently started working here in Salem. I just feel stupid. And embarrassed…and I'm really sorry."

I'd waited so long to say that to Bryon, I felt a weight lifted the moment I uttered it. Since the day I met Warren, I deferred to him for everything in my life, including which friends to keep. Needless to say, he didn't like me keeping company with those who didn't approve of him, which meant I lost nearly every friend I had and somehow was able to blame it on those people, not the man turning me against everyone.

"I know," Bryon said. "Thank you. I'm glad you're done with him."

"Yeah. Me too. Do you think maybe…we could start over?"

"We don't need to start over, babe. We can pick up where we left off. Have you been watching *Scandal?*" Bryon's boisterous laughter warmed my heart. The sound I'd missed deeply filled my ears and just like that, I felt my soul flickering back to life like a lightbulb that had been off for too long.

SEVEN

WE SPENT THE next two hours catching up on our favorite shows, the latest gossip from our graduating class, and every milestone his daughter had reached. I yawned and heard Bryon whisper goodnight to Craig.

"I'll let you go," I said. "Tell Craig I'm sorry I took all your baby-free time tonight."

"Oh, I'm sure he's thrilled. He's always had faith in you and he's never stopped pestering me to call you and mend fences."

A little twist in my chest made me shut my eyes. After all the hateful things I said about Craig… "So have we? Mended fences? Mended…us?"

"We at least both got the tools out tonight, babe. Maybe we could get together soon. I'd love to show off my little princess to you and I'm going to need to hear about this new guy eventually."

I froze. I hadn't mentioned Leo at all. Not even the fact that I worked for a man. "What?" I breathed.

"Come on, I can hear that shit in your voice. You leave Warren behind but wait eight months to call me? Eight months without a boy fucking with your head and you could live without me but somebody's got inside your brain now and you need me."

I couldn't tell if he sounded pissed or not. It wasn't true but it wasn't false either. Needing Bryon wasn't just about what was going on with Leo. My heart ached for a friend again—it ached for Bryon specifically.

"Bryon…it's not like that. I—"

"It's okay if it is," he said softly. "I've thought about you a lot since that last fight. Worried about you. Wondered if you were okay. I always knew he was going to break you. I just kept thinking, when they're finally finished with each other, how many pieces will she be in? You're strong and you don't need anyone to fix you; you've clearly put yourself back together. But if there's a guy, I'm glad you called because someone needs to be the one to tell you that just because you've got seams, just because you've got glue holding you together doesn't mean you're fragile. You don't have to tell me everything tonight…but, he's nothing like Warren is he?"

I sighed. "No. He's nothing like him."

"Didn't think so. Want some advice from someone who also glued himself back together?"

I shut my eyes before they could brim with tears. "Always."

"Don't hold back. Don't worry about the cracks, don't worry about that fucking *rebound* word, don't even worry about breaking again—you know where the glue is. Just don't settle for anything less than mind-blowing."

My lips parted and I wanted nothing more than to reach through the phone and cling to him.

"Jesus, Bryon."

"What?"

"I've missed you so much. I was such a bitch to you. I treated you like shit..."

He made a sad little noise. "We both did and said things we shouldn't have. But we can fix this. I'm happy you've moved on."

We made plans to meet up in the next few weeks before saying a sentimental goodbye. I took my final gulp of wine and scrolled to Leo's number next. I wasn't even sure if he knew I had it. Oliver had given me both of their cell numbers when I started working at the store in case I ever needed to reach them. My conversation with Bryon left my heart and mind feeling more open than they had in a while. Though Bryon probably imagined the relationship he was vaguely advising me about to be a romantic one rather than a twisted S&M partnership, what he said still worked. What I'd started with Leo had the possibility to be mind-blowing if I just quit holding back.

I tapped out a text message to Leo, telling myself to let go and find freedom in his promises of bondage.

Sloane: *I want to go to your party.*

A heavy breath rushed out of me as I sent it but my next inhalation stuck in my throat when I saw his name flash on the screen as an incoming call.

"Hello?" I choked.

"I don't text." His voice was the same firm and domineering tone that made me tremble, but sounded like it might've had a grin to it. "I'll pick you up Saturday at six-thirty. Wear something nice."

I opened my mouth, to say what, I wasn't sure, but he cut me off then quickly hung up.

"Sweet dreams, Sloane."

I sat with my ear to the silent phone for a few seconds, merely breathing and attempting to quiet the worry that overcame me knowing I'd just made plans with Leo to take things up a notch—maybe to mind-blowing.

After placing a final pin in my hair, I rifled through my jewelry box for a pair of earrings to wear. I found some sparkling teardrops and put them on. My hands had been trembling since I turned on the shower two hours ago. I'd taken a ridiculous amount of time to get ready and had been fretting the entire time. He'd be arriving any minute. Dressed in a simple sleeveless black dress that stopped at mid-thigh and black heels, I thought I looked nice. I only hoped I fit Leo's definition. I'd had two days to consider what to wear. Two days without seeing Leo to stew about mundane things like the color of my nails or the timing of my wax.

I jumped when I heard a knock at the door. *I can do this*. I'd made the decision to do this. Pulling in a breath, I reached for the knob and blew it out just before I pulled back the door. My lips parted and I nearly moaned at the sight of him. The man was born to wear a suit. He'd slicked his hair back a little, the style and use of hair product making it look an even darker sable. His tempting blue eyes lit up with the smile his full lips wore and I swallowed hard.

"You wore your hair up."

I absently lifted a hand to touch a lock of hair hanging near my ear, the rest strategically pinned up in loose curls. Leo toed the threshold of my doorway with one step toward me and fingered the same tendril, scanning me as he did.

"Your neck is too stunning to be hidden by all that hair," he said, letting his finger drift from my earlobe down the curve of my neck. I resisted the urge to shudder as though I was still playing by his rules, evading punishment.

"Should we go?" I asked.

His eyes danced across my face again before he nodded and stepped aside so I could lock up. We reached his car and he held the passenger side door open for me. After I buckled my seatbelt, I rested my hands in my lap and waited for Leo to start the car. I glanced over to see him staring at me with the ghost of a smile on his face.

"What?" I breathed.

"You look nervous."

I let one side of my mouth rise in a half-grin. Damn him for reading me so well. "Maybe," I replied as he pulled out of the parking lot. "I'm mostly just…curious."

"About?"

My teeth pressed into my bottom lip for a brief second and I shifted in my seat to watch him as he drove. "You. Your friends. What I'll see tonight. Everything."

Leo's brow rose but he never took his eyes off the road. "Please. Ask away," he said.

A little noise cracked at the back of my throat. I hadn't expected the freedom. Already, I was accustomed to speaking only when spoken to—a thought that made me oddly proud.

Leo laughed lightly. "Come on, I only have a few hours before this thing turns back into a pumpkin. It's okay, ask me anything."

I chuckled nervously in return and touched the loose pieces of hair around my face. "Okay. Well…how old are you?"

He grinned and tongued one pointed, white tooth before shooting me a look. The fading sun painted him beautiful amber, warming the tone of his skin to something like honey and lighting his eyes with a fire-like glow. He no doubt recognized the question he'd demanded of me.

"Thirty."

I nodded and wickedly considered asking him all the same questions he'd asked me but I resisted. I had my own line of inquires I wanted answered.

"Tell me about the party. Have you been to one before?"

Leo swiped his hand over his jaw and sighed. "Yes, I've been a few times. I met Gabe and his wife Melanie at a club a few years ago, before I moved—"

"To live with your sister?"

I instantly pressed my lips together to smother my voice from interrupting him but it was too late. A chill danced up my spine, wishing he'd punish me for speaking out of turn.

Leo glanced at me. "Oliver told you?"

Swallowing the lump building in my throat, I nodded.

"Yeah… Anyway, before that I was doing what I do now, running the store with Ollie. And like I said, I met Gabe and Melanie—the Nolans—at a club." The precision with which he spoke somehow soothed and unnerved me at once. We may not have been playing, but I could tell he didn't like interruptions. He seemed happy to answer my questions so long as he remained in control of the conversation.

"What kind of club?" I asked. I'd read three books on the topic by now and my internet search history would probably scare anyone who knew me besides Leo. I knew, but I had to ask. I had to insert myself once again. God, I was all but begging him to pull over and swat my ass.

White teeth gleamed in the headlights of the oncoming cars and he shot back, filling the space around me with his smoky voice. "What kind do you think?"

A slow smile blossomed on my lips along with a heated blush creeping up my jawline to the apples of my cheeks.

"There's usually five couples or so. The Nolans have money; one look at the house and you'll see what I mean. They usually have the dinner catered."

"Dinner?!"

He laughed. "Yes. Dinner. I hope you didn't eat already. Melanie goes all out for these things," he said. His eyes fluidly swept to mine as he smirked. "Four courses of aphrodisiacs."

I'd been too nervous to eat anything more than a handful of microwave popcorn and I'd cursed myself for not picking up another bottle of wine since all I wanted was a drink to settle down.

"Just so long as there's a bar," I muttered.

"There won't be. No drinking. Part of the reason I prefer Gabe and Melanie's house parties to the clubs is that everyone who attends knows and follows the rules. No booze, no drugs, and no means no. We have a nice meal, casual conversation, and then we all go our separate ways. They typically clear out a handful of rooms throughout the house and stage them according to specific preferences. Doors stay open though so you and I can roam around, see it all."

For the first time, I was struck by the idea that Leo's done all of this before. Of course, I knew that, we'd talked about it. I wasn't struck by the fact that he was seasoned...it was more that at one point in time he'd taken another woman—maybe multiple different women—to this house for this kind of party. What would these other couples think of me? I hated to imagine how judged I might feel walking into a room full of strangers who would instantly know I was the sub of the week.

"My friend, Ben, and his girlfriend, Jade, will be there. They're into pet play and they choose to turn dinner into a little warm up, so don't be alarmed when Jade purrs and crawls under the table to eat." Leo laughed.

After the words *couples, wife,* and *girlfriend,* it was clear that not only would I most likely be the only newbie, but also Leo and I might be the only people not in a relationship. I held back a sigh and kept my eyes on the road ahead. I knew the area we were heading toward. The edge of Salem had a mini millionaire's row, inundated with mansions and sprawling estates. When I first moved to town, I passed through it and played out a fantasy where Warren came running after me, professing his love for me. He and I bought a big house there and lived happily ever after with a yard full of kids and commercial-worthy smiles plastered on our faces. It seemed almost laughable now. I could hardly think of Warren without a sneer making its way to my lips. The thought of him touching me turned my blood to ice. The shame I felt for having loved him so long racked me at least weekly. Now, more than ever, I was happy to be on my own. But as Leo turned down the long driveway leading to the most gorgeous house I'd ever seen, I let a strange and new idea swing through my mind.

What if Leo became more than my Dom?

He parked the car, last in a line of three others, and quickly came around to my door. Leo offered me his hand and I took it, though my fingers twitched. My stomach flipped and the idea grew more powerful when he threaded his fingers with mine, giving them an affectionate squeeze as he glanced down at me.

"Ready?" he asked with a grin.

EIGHT

I HALF EXPECTED an aging butler to pull back the front door of the massive house, but Leo let us in without even a knock. The feeling of my hand nestled in his was all I could focus on. His warm skin against mine had my head buzzing as much as the anticipation of the night. Glancing over at him as he led me through the foyer toward the sound of roaring laughter, I let a deep breath expand my chest then pushed it out along with every hesitation. No holding back.

"Calloway!" a man's voice shouted as we entered the gorgeous living room.

There were plush sofas, a stunning chandelier, and one entire wall was covered with a floor-to-ceiling bookcase. Leo's hand slipped from mine as he reached out to return the solid handshake of the man who'd called his name. The man looked to be in his forties, a touch of silver at his temples adding something dashing to his otherwise dark chocolate waves of hair. He, like Leo and the other men I surveyed quickly, was dressed somewhat formally in a black suit with a deep sapphire blue shirt and a pale blue pocket square folded neatly at his breast.

Leo grinned from ear to ear as he clasped the man's hand then drew him in for a half-hug. "Gabe, it's good to see you," he said.

A beautiful mocha-skinned woman in a cherry red dress and sky high heels sauntered up behind Gabe. She slid one hand around his waist and up to stroke the lapel of his jacket as she smiled at Leo around his shoulder.

Leo wordlessly leaned in and pressed his cheek to hers. "Mel. You look great."

She replied with a modest thank you and I realized only then that I'd been carefully watching the intimate exchange between old friends. I'd been twisting my fingers and picking at my nails as I took in the way Leo smiled at them—so honestly, so graciously.

Melanie dropped her hands from her husband and moved to me in a way that made electricity shoot up into my chest. Her caramel eyes examined me as she took her steps toward me and her hips swayed with purpose. I glanced at Leo and he only shook his head and grinned at Gabe when Melanie reached me. Her hands came down on my bare shoulders softly and smoothed down my arms, stopping just above my elbows. Then we simply stared at each other. She was as tall as I was, but I remembered the stilettos and figured flat-footed I'd have a few inches on her.

Melanie traced her bottom lip with her tongue as a grin grew on her mouth. She was also most likely in her forties, though not a single silver hair lay among her natural mane of long black curls. She was beautiful and not just that—she was sexy. She exuded sex with everything she possessed.

"Sloane," she purred, lowering her chin to look at me from beneath thick lashes. "We are so happy you're here."

A jagged breath made its way in through my nose and I managed to smile and nod. "Thank you for having me," I replied in that mouse voice Leo had conjured out of me a time or two.

She turned and linked her arm through Leo's. "Come on, I'll introduce you two. Everyone, welcome Leo and Sloane," she said, pulling us both farther into the room where the rest of the guests still chatted.

Though their conversations hadn't seemed to let up, each one of them had eyed Leo and me at least once after we came inside. Everyone turned with polite faces and Melanie began.

"Leo, you of course know Ben and Jade," she said and the first couple smiled.

Leo slapped the man on the back and gave the same cheek kiss to the woman at his side. I wasn't sure if I'd ever seen such a seemingly ill-suited match. Ben looked like a linebacker, with cropped sandy hair and an all-American jaw line; he could've been a first string

NFL player for all I knew. Beside him was who I knew to be his *pet* and if Leo hadn't told me as much, I might've deduced it with a glance. The top of her head barely cleared Ben's bicep. The sleek, jet black hair, cut in a short style with bangs, framed the porcelain face she'd made up like some of the less extreme Goth girls from my high school. Sooty eyeliner, pale skin and dark lipstick gave her a startling albeit beautiful look. Around her neck she wore a collar much like a cat, complete with a little heart tag hanging from the center. Her all black attire seemed perfectly normal aside from the fur bracelets around her wrists. She smiled softly at me and then rolled her neck, nuzzling into Ben's side. I blinked twice and moved my eyes along to the next couple.

"Then we have the Miller-Temples, Ian and Jack," Melanie said, gesturing to the two oddly similar-looking men. The two stocky men both had closely trimmed full beards, though Ian wore his hair a little longer than Jack's buzz cut. They nodded at me as though we were meeting at a company picnic. I lifted my hand in a small wave and plastered on another smile, wishing Melanie wasn't standing between Leo and I as I was starting to feel overwhelmed. I wanted his sturdy frame beside me.

"And Sean and Tracy Higgins and their guest Missy," Melanie finished the introductions. While Sean and Tracy looked old enough to be Leo's parents, their guest looked like she might've been dropped off by a big yellow school bus. The perfectly suburban looking couple said hello and their sultry sidekick, with her platinum blonde hair that faded into turquoise waves long enough to completely cover her breasts, dragged her eyes up and down my body before winking at me.

The millionaires, the kitty and her keeper, the leather bears, and the triad. And of course, the bookseller and her brooding boss. I barely had time to let every name sink into my mind as well as the quick judgements and assumptions I'd made about them, when Melanie and Gabe ushered us all into yet another gorgeous room. The dining room, with its crystalline light fixtures and framed art on the walls also held a long table set for eleven.

I jumped, feeling Leo place a hand on the small of my back as I glanced at a plate with my name written on a card. I turned and caught his eyes. My mind was already so overwhelmed and the show hadn't even begun. But as I looked at Leo next to me, pulling out my chair smoothly and without hesitation, I let the worries fade and his strong presence soothe me.

A smile slowly curved his lips and he glanced down at my feet for a moment before I took my seat in the chair he held out. "You still have your heels on. Not preparing to run just yet then?"

I rolled my eyes and grinned up at him. "I'm at least going to eat first," I teased back.

He chuckled and sat next to me as everyone settled in. Just as the distinguished man in a tux I'd expected to answer the door came out with the first course, I felt Leo's hand slide over my knee, under the table but surprisingly not under my dress. I shot him a look and saw the smirk tugging at his delectable lips. I had no intention of running.

I slid my spoon through the most heavenly chocolate mousse I'd ever tasted, making sure to get the last bite of the small portion. As I licked it clean, I turned my eyes toward Leo, who watched my mouth shamelessly. My tongue swiped over my lips when my spoon was empty and Leo matched my move.

"Sloane," I heard Gabe's voice and broke my gaze away from my date. "You've been quiet this evening. Tell us a little about you."

Forcing a smile, I took a sip of water. He was right. I'd remained silent since the moment the oysters came out, save for a few agreements here and there. I was just taking it all in. Gabe and Melanie's stories of their recent Mediterranean vacation, Jack and Ian's home improvement projects, and the exciting news that Mr. and Mrs. Higgins were going to be grandparents. Aside from the muffled noises of Jade lapping up her dessert from beneath the table, the dinner had been incredibly normal. But I hadn't added anything to the conversation because every time I felt myself easing into the seemingly average dinner party, I'd picture one of them naked. I'd get so close to sinking into the night and allowing it to become normal, but then my mind would wander to the future when I knew I'd watch them all in compromising positions.

I cleared my throat. "Well, I moved here a little less than a year ago and I've been working at Leo's store part time."

"Where did you move from?" Melanie interjected.

"Blacksburg."

"You did?" Leo's voice at my side startled me and I turned to him with a furrowed brow.

"Yeah... Why?"

"I just—didn't know that," he uttered before pursing his lips and looking down into his water glass before silencing himself with a drink.

"What did you do before Leo hired you?" Gabe asked.

I was starting to feel flushed as the inquiry built. "Before I moved, I worked in marketing. But I have a minor in English so when I came to Salem I got it in my head that I should try my hand at fiction." I laughed lightly. "I'm not sure I'll keep that up though."

"Marketing? Really?"

Again, I looked over to see Leo gawking at me. My lips turned down briefly and then I nodded at him.

"Come on, Calloway, don't you know anything about the woman?" Ben asked with a chuckle from across the table.

Leo shook his head and snorted a laugh in response.

"It sounds like you're too creative to just be selling retail. You'll have to find an outlet for that imagination of yours." Melanie's voice was like silk as she spoke to me, her eyes dancing wildly. She stood from the table, glancing down at Gabe, who instantly lowered his eyes. My head ticked back when I saw the exchange, confused by the challenge of my assumption that Melanie was Gabe's submissive, not the other way around.

"Shall we get started?" she proposed. Multiple voices answered in quiet yet enthusiastic agreement.

"How about we get some fresh air for a minute?" Leo's hand slipped around my elbow as the crowd dispersed without any more discussion. My gaze drifted in the opposite direction of where he gently led me, watching everyone else file down the hallway. My stomach fluttered with anticipation as we made our way out onto a stone patio off the kitchen.

"Here," Leo said, offering me his jacket over my shoulders.

I smiled in thanks and sat beside him as he lowered into one of the outdoor chairs. I breathed in the scent of the night air and let a surprised smile take over my face when an erotic grunt sounded loudly from the house. "That didn't take long." I snickered, glancing over at Leo.

His blue eyes zeroed in on me and though his face was still, I saw something in his expression I'd come to recognize. It was the look of a hunter waiting for his prey. I knew despite the fact we hadn't talked about having a scene tonight that he was bordering on Dominant in that moment. I crossed one leg over the other, causing my dress to ride up slightly. At the sight, Leo pulled in a sharp breath before he spoke.

"You know my sister, Marie, lives in Blacksburg. We must've been living there at the same time."

"Really? Wow. I mean, I guess that's not too crazy, it's not that far away, but still…"

"Too bad we never met there; we could've started this sooner."

My eyes shot to his. Would I have even given him the time of day? Warren had a hold of my every thought and desire; I can't imagine what it would've been like to meet Leo while Warren still had his hooks in me. Maybe he would've pulled me away from him. Or maybe I would've retreated further into Warren's grasp.

"I was a different person there," I whispered to the expansive, dark backyard.

I could feel him watching me out of the corner of my eye, but I didn't look. The feeling of his gaze both unsettled and aroused me. Knowing what we'd be witnessing side by side in a few minutes was already turning me on.

"So you've been writing a book up on the second floor of the store, huh? What's it about?" he asked as though he already knew my life in Blacksburg had led us to the topic of my book.

Turning my head, I heard another sexual cry from the house but it didn't keep me from focusing on him and him alone. I searched his face and saw only his beauty. Strong, dark brows, straight Roman nose, temptingly full lips and a fierce pair of blue eyes that all but wilted me into submission. I wasn't sure how I felt about him asking me personal questions. It was easy to separate my life into two parts when Leo wasn't trying to get to know me. We weren't dating. This wasn't a relationship. What I had with him was my personal thrill. My secret awakening. Something I wasn't ready to share with the other part of my life—the part still riddled with cracks glued together from a hundred pieces.

"Answer me."

I gulped and shook my head. "No. I don't want to talk about it."

His eyebrows lifted slightly and his lips parted. I expected him to narrow his gaze and make me feel small for my disobedience. Leo looked me up and down and nodded before extending his hand.

"All right. Let's go back inside and see what we can see."

I took his hand, his fingers lacing comfortably—intimately—with mine again. My thoughts swam. He didn't scold me for my reply and I didn't know if that meant we weren't playing our roles tonight…or if the lines I'd drawn between us had already begun to blur.

NINE

"SO WHAT EXACTLY do you want out of this peep show?" I asked as we approached the hallway. Leo had dropped my hand as we made our way to the action, the pornographic sounds echoing from one end to the other.

"I'm going to watch you. Hopefully I'll be able to see what intrigues you, but I'd also like you to talk to me. Ask me questions or tell me about a limit or an interest you see. Does that sound okay?"

A deep moan ripped through the air as well an intermittent buzzing sound I couldn't place and I nodded. "Yeah."

His lips morphed into a devilish grin as we finally stood a step away from the first door. Leo swept his tilted hand out to one side, prompting the first of many reveals and I moved to look inside. My breath caught as I saw the proof that my novice assumption about Gabe and Melanie had been all wrong. Gabe hung naked a few feet off the ground from a huge four-legged metal contraption, wrapped in black rope with intricate knots across his torso. I took in the sight of his arms tied behind his back and rope leading up to the center of the obviously sturdy stand, dangling him. My eyes traveled down his body and saw his dick enclosed in a sort of metal cage, forcing him flaccid, and his ankles bound by the same black rope. His head hung and then I saw Melanie come around his side, scraping her nails along his ribs. He shivered and so did I. She'd changed into a black corset and red shorts with tall leather boots. She slapped a riding crop into her palm as she made her way in front of Gabe.

"Look at me," she barked and his head snapped up.

"What are you for?" she asked.

"My mistress's pleasure," Gabe replied.

"How do you please me?"

His eyes dragged down her body and she slapped the crop into her hand again sharply.

"I obey," he uttered.

"Correct. Good," she said. She grabbed the rope that traveled up from his wrists to the hook at the top of the metal frame and pulled, causing him to spin slowly. "Now, take your punishment."

He spun in place as she swatted him with the crop all over and my heartbeat thrummed wildly. Gabe held his outbursts in and only groaned as red marks began to appear on his skin. Melanie stopped and turned to look at me. My face flushed as she paralyzed me with her eyes. It was nearly the same look Leo gave me when in a scene. Dominance radiated off of her and her presence, along with her stunning beauty, made me swallow hard and look away.

A quiet moan claimed me when I felt Leo's hand snake around my waist from behind as his mouth met my ear. "Are you attracted to women?" he asked.

I looked at Melanie again as she trailed her red fingernails down Gabe's chest, toying with his restrained member. Pushing up on her toes, she stroked his face tenderly then struck his cheek with a hard slap that made me jump. She was undeniably sexy and just as commanding a presence as Leo, but I'd never strayed any farther than a one on the Kinsey scale. I shook my head and Leo laughed against the curve of my neck.

"The riding crop then?"

Words evaded me as I continued to stare at the couple. His punishment continued and he became more vocal as she became more aggressive. I shrugged and Leo's arm tightened around me, pulling me back flush against his chest.

"Suspension," he said firmly and I shuddered. "Mmm, yeah, that's what you want."

I attempted to turn in his arms but his strength wouldn't allow it. He held me for a moment longer, keeping my eyes directed at Mr. and Mrs. Nolan. My blood raced. The visual of their exchange mixed with the feeling of Leo's body pressed against mine made me tremble. I didn't know what I wanted more—Leo's hands under my clothes or bindings around my wrists.

"What's behind door number two?" Leo whispered as he released me and took a few steps. I followed him on vibrating limbs and soon my eyes fell on a shocking sight. With his arms chained above his head, linked through a steel ring on the wall, Jack cried out as Ian touched his nipple with the end of a long glass tube. When the glass met his skin, purple lightening shot out of the end, zapping him for a split second. Ian grinned and leaned forward to lick the nipple he'd just assaulted.

"Again?" Ian asked.

Jack's eyes slammed shut and he panted before he spoke. "Yes, Daddy. Please."

The implement tipped toward Jack's chest again and when the electric volt made contact he gritted his teeth and squirmed on the chains.

"What is that?" I breathed.

Leo's shoulder connected with mine and he leaned in to answer. "It's called a violet wand. Low current, high voltage electricity."

Ian lowered the wand and Jack continued to writhe though it wasn't touching him yet. Jack wore leather pants slung low on his hips. I felt myself clench for him as Ian tilted the end of the wand to the tender flesh above his waistband. Jack tensed then grunted out a curse when Ian shocked him five times in a row.

I tried to imagine what it would feel like but somehow I didn't think building up a charge on carpet during the dry winter months would come close. Still, just like with Gabe, watching the interwoven pleasure and pain across Jack's face during the torture made my lips swell and my skin burn.

Leo put a hand on the small of my back and we crossed to the other side of the hall to another open door. My eyes nearly bugged out of my head when I looked inside and locked gazes with Leo's friend Ben as he pounded into Jade, bent over a leather bench wearing furry black cat ears. I quickly looked at Jade instead; her face looked completely relaxed, almost serene, with her eyes closed and her lips parted. Ben had a hold of a leather leash linked to her collar, pulling her to him as he fucked her from behind. She mewed and moaned as he slammed into her, his pace quickening as his brow furrowed and his animalistic noises grew deeper.

"I'm gonna come, kitty," Ben growled.

She meowed in response and he swiftly drew the leash back tight, pulling her off the bench. He grabbed a handful of her breast and thrust hard into her a few more times before he loosened his grip on the leash and she fell forward again. She arched her back and wiggled back against him, perching her hands on the bench like delicate paws. Ben traced his hand down her spine and pulled out of her and stepped back. Then I watched as he gripped a long tuft of black fur that I hadn't noticed before, coming out of her ass like a tail. I couldn't help but let my head cock to one side to try and figure out how it was attached to her. Ben's hand slipped beneath Jade and he started fondling her as he tugged on the tail. Every time he moved it, she moaned, and it wasn't long before he worked her to her peak.

"Does kitty like it when I play with her pussy?"

She mewed again and nodded. "Yesss," Jade sighed.

One final yank on the tail as he furiously rubbed at her clit and she screamed out as an orgasm overwhelmed her. Leo chuckled when Ben glanced up at us and smirked before stroking Jade's back again as she flopped over the leather bench, spent.

I barely noticed my feet were moving when Leo leaned down to me again as we walked to the next door. "It was an anal plug," he said.

My head whipped over to him. "What?"

He grinned and wet his lips, nodding his head back at the last room. "The tail. I saw you trying to figure it out. It's a small rubber plug with a fur pelt attached to one end. Has anyone…ever explored that area with you?"

My mouth gaped then snapped shut. The amusement on his face was infectious and I felt my lips turning upward despite my embarrassment. "No," I replied, turning away and stepping toward the next open door. "Not yet," I added.

I heard a little growl creep from the back of his throat but didn't react. Instead, my eyes fell on a bed where barely legal blonde Missy lay blindfolded and gagged by a red ball with leather straps stretched across her cheeks. Crouched over the foot of the bed, Sean had his arms tangled behind Missy's knees, his face buried between her legs. Behind Sean, Tracy stood gripping his hips and pulling him to her roughly, penetrating him with a strap-on.

My mouth fell open, but by the time my brain attempted to understand the dynamics of their threesome, Leo's hand gripped mine. He whisked me into the next room over and pressed my back against the wall just inside the door and stared at me with intent.

"That's enough live entertainment. They might've tried to enlist you as a fourth if they saw that perfect open mouth of yours."

I laughed and tried to pull away but he held me a moment longer, dragging his gaze all over my face. My cheeks had been red from the start, but I knew nothing made me blush quite like Leo's intensity. I bowed one challenging brow and twisted to slip away from him. As I walked toward the other side of the room, I could feel his eyes burning into my back. A row of hooks hung on the far wall where I surveyed implements meant to punish—to stimulate and excite. My hand swept across the riding crop that hung from the first hook then my fingers brushed the flogger, the studded paddle, the whip and the cane. Under the hanging tools sat a table covered in black velvet with smaller toys laid out. The same silver spiked wheel Leo had used on me before, phallic shaped silicone, a pair of scissors and a scalpel—the last of which made my stomach clench with terror, a limit reached.

When my feet led me to the huge X in the room, a little smirk crossed my lips as I likened myself to a pirate finding her treasure. X marks the spot. The rack, called a St. Andrew's Cross per my wealth of reading materials, was made of leather and steel. It looked sturdier than the ones I'd seen photos of in books. I reached out and felt the thick padding of leather just as Leo's footsteps crept up behind me.

His hand covered mine, pressing my palm into the cushion before firmly capturing my wrist. My heart fluttered in my chest when his lips connected with the curve of my neck, leaving a tender kiss. The familiarity of it confused me, but intoxicated me all the same. The sweetness of the kiss rivaled then ultimately integrated with the severity of his hold on my wrist. His broad stance at my back turned him into a wall—a gate I'd never unlock—keeping me his caged animal for the time being.

"I'm feeling…spontaneous," he whispered and I felt the words skate across my flesh like morning fog. Enchanting, mesmerizing and oh so ominous.

I wanted to nod my head but my muscles no longer felt like they were under my control. Maybe I'd already subconsciously handed the reins to Leo. My head drifted away from him, allowing him better access to my neck, something he took full advantage of, kissing a trail from my shoulder to my ear.

"I see the way your skin puckers and I know your mind is already complying…" His tongue swept my earlobe into his mouth and he nipped it barely before letting go and dusting another kiss on my neck. "But I need you to answer this question. Are *you* feeling spontaneous, too?"

"Yes," I sighed.

With the fingers that encircled my wrist, he twisted me around to face him and pressed me into the leather padding of the cross.

"Do you remember your colors?" he asked.

"Yes."

His sinister grin sent my heart into overdrive, beating like a war drum. It nearly bruised my ribs from the inside when I saw him take the leather gloves from his jacket pocket and slip them on. When I first heard the shifting jingle of chain, I froze. Leo buckled a leather cuff attached to the cross around my wrist, keeping it down at my side then moved to do the same to my other wrist. Instinctively, I tugged against the restraints and felt the resistance of only a few inches of chain. He sank to the floor and I closed my eyes as his leather-clad hands traced up my calves and back down to my ankles. With care, he slipped my shoes off and set them to one side before forcing my legs apart, securing my ankles the same way he'd secured my wrists. It was only then, with my legs spread wide, matching the lines of the lower half of the cross, that I wondered why he hadn't hooked my hands above me. My body should've become the X, spread eagle, but instead my shackled hands were no higher than my hips.

The over analysis ceased when Leo hiked my dress up to my waist as he rose. He looked down at my exposed panties and tapped a finger to his lips.

"I hope those didn't cost too much," he mused, walking a few steps to the left and out of sight. "There's something I've always wanted to do…"

He came back into view holding a pair of scissors. My breath caught in my throat as he traced the tip of them over my thigh then slid the open blades up to snip my panties at the hip. My skin trembled, feeling cool metal brush against the sensitive area just above where my leg met my pubic bone. Then I shivered all over as my underwear fell to the floor, leaving me bared to him. He groaned, staring at the fabric for a moment before stepping to me, gripping my chin in his gloved hand.

"I like you, Sloane," he started.

My forehead flexed down and I pulled a sliver of my bottom lip into my mouth. He was always doing that, mixing something puzzling and overly familiar—guarded, even—in with the role play. As if his dominance wasn't enough to unsettle and attract me, those offhand kind words played an even better game at luring me in.

"There's so much I don't know about you. So much I'd like to learn, given the chance," he said, trickling a soft touch down my cheek.

Suddenly his hand dropped from my face and I felt the cross shift and tilt back. I yelped. My stomach clenched and my every muscle in my body flexed alternately, a futile attempt to protect myself from the falling feeling that overwhelmed me. As the cross tipped backwards evenly, I realized Leo was controlling it. Regardless of the fact that I no longer feared toppling over unexpectedly, my breath heaved as I prepared myself for the unknown. The sound of metal gears clicking thrummed in my head along with my pulse as the cross went from upright to flat as a table then upside down, in what felt like an instant.

Blood rushed to my head and gravity caused my dress to slip all the way to my chest, revealing everything from my bra down to my toes. Or rather, my toes down to my bra as it was with the new angle. My mind became a tornado of thoughts and a symphony of heartbeat and deep panting breaths as I got my bearings. Inverted on the cross, I noticed the restraints at my wrists and the surprising comfort of my arms where Leo had hooked me. He'd come around the cross and stood facing my thighs. I strained to lift my head and look up at him but only caught a clear view of his black slacks and a sliver of his chin. He glanced down at me and the sight of his face wearing a subtle smile loosened me.

My head fell back against the leather cushion, but jerked back up to see him when his leather covered fingers swatted my newly-waxed, bare pussy. I hadn't yet recovered from the intimate slap when he spread me apart, the sensation of thick leather fingers trailing along my core making me wetter than I already was.

"There's one thing I've been dying to know about you and I won't wait any longer to find out," he said, leaning over me, putting his mouth just above my slit. Hot breath enveloped my sex and clouded my senses. As he spoke, I felt the dizziness begin. "I want to know what it sounds like when you come."

His tongue darted out to lick me and I squirmed with a groan. My hands buckled against the cuffs, wanting nothing more than to grip his thighs and hold his body to mine. The loss of control, coupled with his fervent mouth devouring me, catapulted me into the spin. Upended on the cross, tied down and spread bare for his consumption, my mind splintered into colors and feelings only as my skin tingled and I lost all sense of direction.

Leo sucked on my clit and pushed his tongue inside me alternately, making me lock my knees and point my toes. The heat of his mouth as he covered me, teasing me, warmed my entire body enough to make me sweat against the cool leather at my back. He pulled away and I didn't have the strength to crane my face up to look at him. One finger, sheathed in soft leather, stroked me before pushing inside. The conflicting feeling of Leo's digit masked as a foreign object made my stomach flip with excitement and a little fear.

Just as my mind began to catch up with the swirling feeling, Leo pushed a second finger inside and claimed me with his mouth again, sucking hard enough to make me cry out. From there, he was relentless, tickling me from the inside all while dancing his tongue across every nerve of my sensitive flesh. Moans poured from my lips as I writhed, pulling against my restraints. My eyes watered and when I pinched them shut, tears trickled around my temples and into my hair. I felt the building pressure of an orgasm as wilder, unrecognizable noises echoed around me. Leo flicked his tongue against my clit, pushing me to the brink, and when I nearly burst, he let the tip of one finger press against the tight hole no one had ever gone near. I gasped and clenched, bringing forth a chuckle from him right against my sex. My head sprang up and he looked down at me.

"I don't hear any colors…" he teased, pushing in slightly then working in a circular motion.

I felt electricity pulsing in my lower half, strange new feelings consuming my mind. He grinned down to catch my wide eyes as his hands manipulated me. The fullness I felt with two fingers hooked into my pussy and the thin digit slowly sliding further into my ass stormed my whirling consciousness. And as Leo planted a kiss on my thigh followed by a quick nip of his teeth, I screamed, bearing down into the first forceful explosion of ecstasy.

TEN

"THANK YOU...LOVELY girl," I heard Leo whisper as if an echo in my mind. My throat hurt and my eyes burned as mascara and tears mixed. I'd lost time, falling into the space where everything hummed, spun, and shined a kaleidoscope of colors. As my breathing leveled and I became aware of the tangible matter of my body rather than the spiritual idea of it, I realized the cross had moved again and my back was flat. Every audible beat of my heart eased me further.

I blinked and looked up to see Leo above me. He smiled carefully and brought a tissue to my face, swiping at my forehead first, then my temples. I meant to speak but only a moan came out.

"Shh..." he whispered. "Let me get your face cleaned up, then I'll get you some water."

I sighed and nodded as he gently dabbed under my eyes. He reached down and unlocked my wrists and

I could feel his skin against mine. Another wave of relief rocked me, registering the fact he'd taken his gloves off. I flinched when his bare hand pressed something cool and damp between my legs, wiping away the evidence of my orgasm. He offered a soothing shush again. His hand landed on my knee when I attempted to lift my ankle and felt the shackles still holding me to the cross that was now more like a table.

"Hang on. Just relax. Keep breathing. You're not ready to stand," he said.

My forehead crinkled. I didn't know why he thought I couldn't stand, but staying on my back was comfortable enough and the sound of his voice made my eyes flutter closed once more. A breath filled my lungs and I trembled as I blew it out. I nearly drifted off to sleep but Leo's hand touched my shoulder and coaxed me to move. Sitting up, with his hand guiding my torso, I opened my eyes and felt the world return as the scene came back to me in a rush. Leo hadn't let up after my first orgasm. He'd grinned and dropped down in a squat in front of my flipped head and asked me if I thought I could handle more. I remember grumbling some kind of blissed out retort. With that he continued to finger and tongue fuck me, adding in the use of a large wand vibrator that he wielded relentlessly. Plus, as he made sure to explain in graphic terms, he prepared my ass to take him all in due time with the aid of his gloved fingers. I think by my third descent into intrinsic pleasure I zoned out—spinning in that most lovely way—letting him take me over the edge and back again

God knows how many times. My limbs shook and my core felt numb from Leo's bombardment.

I blinked away the blur of leftover tears and lifted one weak hand to swipe under my eye. I sighed when Leo's hand smoothed down my back. It was odd recognizing that I wasn't naked—the scene left me exposed regardless of clothing. Glancing at Leo beside me, I smiled weakly and took the bottle of water he offered, swallowing a few gulps before he gently pulled it away from my lips.

"Easy," he said. "Take it slow. How do you feel?"

His blue gaze struck me and held me more firmly than it did when he assumed the role of my authoritarian. I wet my lips, still relishing the cool water and let a light laugh spill out.

"Spent."

The corner of Leo's mouth flickered barely, a smile trying to form while concern continued to harden his features. His touch eased me as he delicately stroked my hair, still pinned up though thoroughly mussed by the thrashings of my body flipped on the St. Andrew's Cross. I searched his face and found my voice again.

"I'm okay, really. Not dizzy anymore," I added.

"The party's winding down. Think you can stand?"

I nodded, another breath bringing me over the line to normal again. Leo quickly unlocked my ankles from the cross and gave me his hand, helping me down. When my feet touched the ground I faltered, but only for a moment, and he secured his arm around my back the instant he noticed my knees buckle.

My eyes swept up his body to look in his eyes. Fire simmered beneath his stare, warming me the same as his smoldering gloveless touch. His grasp hooked at my hip and he helped to prop me upright as I found my footing before slipping into my shoes. As I straightened, finally on solid ground in more ways than one, I moved away from him. It was subtle, but I saw the quick change in him as we parted ever so slightly.

I sucked back another drink of water and followed Leo out into the hall. It smelled more like sex than before and my cheeks flushed knowing I'd contributed with my multiple orgasms. We passed the room Melanie and Gabe had occupied and Leo ducked his head inside. They were sitting together in a wingback chair in the corner of the room, Melanie resting in Gabe's lap as she stroked his hair tenderly.

"Leo," Melanie purred, "you heading home?"

Leo tapped the door frame and smiled. "Yeah. Thanks, guys. Dinner was great. Let us know about next month."

Us.

I expected my heart to clench at the quick show of his hand like that but instead I practically came again, tingles rippling through my core at the nonchalant mention of a future.

Melanie caught my eye and smiled. "We will. Hope you had fun tonight, Sloane. It was lovely meeting you."

Though she looked petite and almost childlike in Gabe's arms, her gaze remained lustful and commanding. I flashed my teeth then softened, tucking a loose strand of hair behind my ear as I returned the sentiment. Leo's hand slipped gracefully to the small of my back and he ushered me out to the car without a word.

Almost a mile down the road, I finally broke the silence. "Leo?"

"Yeah." He didn't pull his eyes from the road, but his hand reached for me over the gearshift, settling on my knee warmly.

A million things ran through my mind. I wanted his take on the scene, his thoughts on the night in general. I wanted to know if he'd meant to say "us" when asking Mel about next month's gathering. But it was becoming increasingly clear that the less I questioned this—the less I doubted and analyzed—the easier it was. A slow grin curled my lips and I tapped my tongue against the back of my teeth before I laughed.

"What was the final tally?"

He shot me a look, his intense eyes lit by the moon and the glow of streetlights off the highway. "What?"

Another breath of a laugh escaped me. "Exactly how many times did you make me come?"

Leo grinned and restricted me with a firm and sultry look. "Not nearly enough."

I smirked and faced the road again, letting thoughts of the scene swirl around us in the quiet car. We reached my apartment and inhibition stole my voice for its own advantage. "Do you want to come up?" I asked.

Leo's brow rose and he cleared his throat, adding a muttered affirmative before pulling into a parking space. There was no way we'd be engaging in anything other than conversation and I assumed he knew as much since he'd already sexually drained me. His distance as I opened my door and allowed him inside confirmed my assumption. My stomach fluttered once the door shut and we were alone in my home. Leo easily toed around, hands clasped behind his back as his eyes scanned my space thoroughly.

"Wine?" I chirped.

He smiled and nodded. Another clue that he didn't expect anything from me. Thank God. I pulled down two glasses and poured from the bottle of Riesling I had chilling in my refrigerator. I found Leo staring at my bookcase—not surprising—and offered him the glass.

"Thanks," he said before turning back to the shelf. "You have interesting taste."

I laughed and took a gulp of wine, attempting to calm the jitters he gave me. My taste in books was a bit all over the place. I had everything from brutal true crime accounts to dime store Harlequins and presidential biographies.

"What's so funny?" he asked, leading us to my couch as though he owned the space. Why had I invited him inside? His demeanor had changed from the party to here in my space but everything he said, every move he made, captivated me.

I shook my head as we sat down beside each other. Comfortably close. "Some would say the same about you," I remarked with a lingering snicker.

He didn't laugh. His eyes scanned my face the same way he'd read the spines of the books I owned. It was the same way he read me—carefully, deliberately.

"Tell me what you liked best about tonight," he said.

I looked away and drank another gulp. "I don't know."

"Are you embarrassed?"

My gaze pulled back to his face as if by some magnetic force. I was embarrassed and I hated that he knew it. Worse, I felt guilty for being embarrassed. What we did made me feel so good, I just didn't know how to process it yet.

"Maybe I am."

"What for?"

I pushed the little bit of hair that had fallen in my eyes away and sighed. "It's not so much embarrassment as it is…"

"Vulnerability."

I swallowed around a lump in my throat at his perfect speculation. His ability to look inside my mind without my permission only made me feel more vulnerable. Just like when consciousness returned to me on the flattened cross, my nakedness had nothing to do with what I wore. He didn't need scissors to free me from an article of clothing; his words were keen and sharp enough to cut through every part of my exterior, leaving me bare.

"That's what makes it so powerful. You allow me the greatest intimacy, not by granting me permission to invade your body, but your mind," Leo said.

My heartbeat slowed as I nodded. I wouldn't have known how to say it—I didn't wield words as beautifully as Leo, but he was right.

"I liked being tied," I started softly.

"What about it?" His voice was just as low and even keeled as mine.

"When I couldn't move…I was forced to feel everything in a way I never have before," I said. My face flushed just referencing the onslaught of multiple orgasms he'd doled out. Without free limbs to disperse the energy building inside me as he pumped his fingers and tongued me expertly, I had no other choice but to experience every sparkling nerve at my sex with no reprieve. When I looked up from the wine glass I'd confessed into, I saw his slackened jaw and darkened eyes. The shameless look on his face made a grin works its way onto my lips. He may've been able to disrobe me with vocabulary but my words had their own effect.

"What did you like best about tonight?" I asked boldly.

"This," he replied with a smile.

The two weeks following that night, when he'd stripped me down to my most primal state, had groomed me into someone new. Something had shifted between us and though I felt as unbalanced as I had when the cross tilted back. I lived for my moments with Leo. We broke the walls of communication over a bottle of wine on my couch and it seemed from then on his voice grew thick each time he addressed me—always my Dom. I'd never felt more aware of the senses I possessed. Turned on by the lightest touch or the most vulgar word. Getting dressed suddenly became an erotic experience, never knowing if he'd be the one to disrobe me by sundown. The sound of the bell above the door at Calloway Books signified the start of our games and the click of the lock each night was the gavel adjourning us. A truce until daybreak. His power plays during the workday varied from a simple firm grasp around my wrist and a whisper of filthy fantasies to a stolen moment upstairs where one leather covered hand gripped my throat as he slid fingers inside of me—never letting me reach my peak.

"I have a bone to pick with you," Oliver said, snapping me out of fantasy and forcing me to pull my gaze away from Leo's back where he stood across the store.

My brows cinched together. "What's wrong?"

Oliver's head ticked to one side and he huffed. "I know your secret," he said.

A wave of fear rippled through my gut. Leo wouldn't be so stupid as to tell his brother about us. So did that mean Oliver saw us at some point? Was that even possible? My face reddened and I tried to find the best way to explain myself. Leo should be the one having to explain, not me. He'd turned me into this, after all.

"You have a background in marketing?" he asked incredulously. "How could you not tell me that?"

A laugh croaked out of me as I released the breath I'd been holding onto for dear life. Relieved that was the secret he'd become privy to, I shook my head and logged another book into the computer from the new shipment.

"Nothing personal." I laughed. "It just never came up."

"Well, I could use a little help in that department if you're up for it. Since Wendy is coming back to work and with that new kid I just hired…maybe I could set you up in the office? If you kept it part time, I could probably even pay you a little more."

My hands halted above the box of new books at my side and I narrowed my eyes on him with a smirk. "Wendy's coming back?" I asked, completely disregarding the rest of his sideways offer at a promotion. My brows shot up and he rolled his eyes.

"She, um," he voice stumbled and he roughed up his chestnut hair, averting his gaze. "Yeah, I mean, since we…"

My eyes widened. "You two are dating?"

He blushed and shook his head with a smile. "Yeah. I guess."

"You guess?"

Oliver sighed and paused for a beat. "I'm crazy about her. So crazy that it scares me and I almost screwed it up and lost her for good. So yeah, we're together and I'm sure as hell not going to let her go. She liked working here and the closer she is, the better I feel," he said. "Do you want to moon over my love life some more or will you let me promote you?"

I chuckled and folded my arms over my chest. "What would you want me to do?"

"I don't know. Rebrand us? This place has been the same since my grandfather bought it. Find some publicity opportunities around town? There's that Fall Festival coming up, I'd love to get a booth. That kind of stuff isn't my thing at all. We aren't struggling necessarily, but a little boost in sales wouldn't hurt. It's time for a facelift around here and you're probably way more apt than Leo and I are at PR."

I didn't need to consider it for any longer than he took to explain. Putting my skills to use wouldn't be a problem and despite whatever I had brewing with Leo, I actually liked working at Calloway Books. In fact, these days the only thing I missed about Warren was my job at his company. I smiled at Oliver and saw relief wash over his face and warmth exude from his brown eyes.

"That's a yes?"

I nodded and he grinned. "How about I hit the pavement later this week and see what kind of advertising outlets I can find? Make some contact with other businesses we could cross promote with?"

He slung his arm around my shoulder and yanked me to his side, kissing the top of my head. "That's perfect. Sloane, I feel like you came along at just the right time," he said, pulling back and looking down at me kindly. Maybe it was the fact that he was the oldest sibling, or just his good nature, but he seemed to look at me like a little sister and a part of me wondered if he did have some vague clue about Leo and me. "I didn't know just how much the Calloways needed a girl like you around."

I felt a hearty laugh build in my chest but I stifled it into a chuckle. With the way my world had changed since finding the Calloways—one brother in particular—it was clear they'd come along at the right time for me as well.

I spent Friday morning popping into every independent retail shop along Salem's main street, offering my cheeriest of grins and my not-too-over-rehearsed pitch for the bookstore. My final stop was at Black and Brew, a coffee shop and craft beer microbrewery combo that had opened a few months back. When I walked in, the scent of coffee beans nearly made me moan in delight. I'd gotten an early start and hadn't had my normal amount of caffeine.

I stepped up to the counter and a man shot out from the swinging kitchen door with a beaming smile. Pale brown strands of hair tucked under a knit hat and a thick dark beard covered his grinning face. He stopped at the register, punching in a few quick numbers, and the muscles under his tattooed forearm flexed before he caught my eyes.

"Hey, what can I get for you?"

"A manager, please," I replied.

His face paled. "Is everything all right? I'm—I'm the manager," he said leaving the register, walking around the counter to meet me.

My hand stretched out to him without making contact and my eyes grew wide. "Everything's fine! Sorry," I said, pulling my hand back then offering it again more easily. "My name is Sloane Montgomery and I work over at Calloway Books. I was hoping I could talk to you."

The man took my hand as he chuckled. "Way to give a guy a heart attack, Sloane. I'm Ethan Corbin. The manager," he said before gesturing to a table for us to sit.

"Sorry." I laughed.

He rested his colorful arms on the table and leaned in a little, his full attention clearly given. For a second I swallowed thickly, watching as his eyes examined me while a smile lingered on his mouth.

"So, what's up?" he asked casually. I almost laughed again. He was different from every other store owner or manager I'd spoken to that morning. He was younger, calmer, and while he didn't seem unprofessional, he didn't have the same stuffy quality to him like the others did. As much as I loved Oliver, he was more the caliber of people I'd been dealing with. Neurotic, no nonsense types. Ethan seemed like he'd just hopped off of a tour bus and decided what the hell, I'll manage this coffee shop. His ease was refreshing, especially since I'd been having the same meeting over and over again.

"Do you know about the book store? Calloway Books? We're just across the street, down about a block and a half."

"Yeah, I've been in there. Cool place."

"Great! Yeah, so, we're trying to gain some new business and look for some new ways to get ourselves out there. Um, anyway, I was thinking, we serve coffee all day to our shoppers so it could be a nice opportunity for us to cross promote with you guys here."

God, I was rusty. It was my sixth on the spot meeting of the day and I'd been stumbling over my words all morning but this was really bad. Maybe I needed that caffeine sooner rather than later.

A crooked grin plastered on Ethan's mouth and he leaned back in his chair, eyeing me. Maybe caffeine wasn't the issue after all. Maybe it was the fact that none of the other people I'd met with had looked at me quite like Ethan.

"I love it," he said, crossing his arms across his chest. His gray t-shirt with the store name and logo on it stretched tight across his torso and my eyes became distracted by the designs on his skin once again. The second I wondered how far the tattoos crept under his clothes, I cleared my throat and shook the stray thought. Leo had certainly lit a match to the fuse that was my sex drive.

"How about I send you back with coffee and some discount cards to put out and in the meantime, I'll clear off one of those shelves," he said pointing to the massive display of coffee bags and logo-laden merchandise. "And you can come back in a few days with some books? We can sell a handful of titles and make sure people know to check you guys out."

I'm sure my grin was touching my ears as I nodded. "That's an awesome idea. Thank you so much," I replied.

Ethan pushed back from the table and rose to his feet, looking over his shoulder at the person who'd just stepped up to the counter. "Sure thing," he said taking a step away before holding up one finger. "Can you hang on a sec?"

I nodded and his thank you came in the form of a wink that I didn't have time to comprehend.

"Sloane?" I heard a voice say behind me.

I turned in my chair and stopped breathing when I recognized the beauty speaking to me. Melanie

Nolan walked the rest of the way over to me, dressed in black cotton pants that hugged her limbs, sneakers, and a purple zip up jacket over a tight white tank top. Her dark ringlets sat in a flouncy bun atop her head and her face was clean of makeup. She was just as shockingly gorgeous as she had been dressed in red and painted to perfection at her house party, but still the sight of her casualwear took me aback briefly. At her side stood a young woman with the same nose and mouth but her eyes were all Gabe's.

"Melanie," I croaked as I stood. "Hi."

She beamed and pulled me into a friendly hug, looking me up and down as she let me go. "It's good to see you. How are you? How's Leo?"

My voice caught in my throat. I knew why she was asking me about him, we'd all but screwed at her house, but it still made the hairs on my neck prick up.

"I'm good, thanks," I smiled. "Leo's good, as far as I know. I haven't seen him in a few days."

Her smile slanted barely and her brow jumped almost too quickly for me to notice, but I did. Melanie nodded and looked over at the young woman beside her. "Sloane this is my daughter, Angela. Angela, this is my friend, Sloane."

Angela waved and pulled her lips into a shy smile as she added a hello. I smiled back at her, figuring she was probably sixteen or so. I hated the thoughts that popped into my head. I wondered where Angela had been the night of the house party. I wondered if she knew the kinds of things her parents were involved in. I knew it didn't matter, but a tiny part of me felt judgement clouding over my thoughts of Melanie. *The mistress was a mother?* I didn't know why, but I'd just assumed a couple like Gabe and Melanie didn't have children. Melanie's hand came down on my shoulder and I relaxed under her touch, though my mind fired cannons of confusion the moment it happened.

"We should exchange numbers," Melanie said. "I'd love to go to lunch some time. I don't have many girlfriends so I end up dragging my daughter around after school." She laughed and Angela rolled her eyes. "She humors me now, but as soon as she gets her license I'll be old news."

I nodded and stuttered something like a yes as I rifled through my purse for my phone. I handed her mine as she handed me hers and we each entered our information before exchanging again. Her full lips split into another sweet smile and I suddenly felt my heart warm a little. Despite the awkwardness of our initial meeting, a new friend actually sounded pretty wonderful and Melanie was obviously a great person. I squashed the foolish judgement I'd placed on her just moments before and returned the second hug she pulled me into before saying goodbye.

"I'll be in touch," she said over her shoulder as she and Angela walked out the door.

As I turned back to the table I'd been sitting at with Ethan, I nearly jumped to see him standing right in front of me. His eyes bugged out a little and he stifled a laugh, pulling his lips in his mouth.

"Sorry, didn't mean to scare ya," he said, extending a paper cup toward me. "I made you this month's special. Caramel apple latte. On the house."

I took the drink and smiled softly. "Thank you."

"No problem," Ethan replied. In the other hand, he held a brown paper sack out to me and I took it as well. "There's a light roast, medium and a bold in there. Just let me know when you need more."

"Wonderful. Thank you so much. And I'll plan on coming back with some books soon. This is great." I grinned. My new role at Calloway Books seemed to suit me. I hadn't felt happiness fill me like this in a while and it was clear I was getting back to the old me. The me who made friends and loved to work. The me who cared about herself first.

"For sure," Ethan said. "I'm really glad you stopped in, Sloane."

His stare pressed deep into me for a split second before someone called his name and he shot me a grimace crossed with a grin as he hustled back behind the counter again.

I left Black and Brew and stopped at the tiny building that housed the historical society and an art gallery. After I filled out the forms for a booth at the annual Fall Festival, I decided to take the long way back to the store, passing through the little park I'd always looked at from afar. The leaves had started to change barely, but an Indian summer had lingered over the last few days.

I found a bench and sat down to finish my latte. The warm, sweet coffee touched my tongue and I breathed deeply, thanking Ethan silently, suppressing thoughts of the way he winked at me. Looking around at the surprisingly busy park, Ethan left my mind as quickly as he crossed it. The sight of the playground filled with happy children lit a bittersweet pang in my chest. I swatted the thoughts that chased through my mind and coated the feeling in my sternum with sugar and caffeine, closing my eyes and taking another sip of my dwindling drink.

Something brushed the hem of my dress and my eyes flew open. I smiled and reached forward to greet the little golden puppy snuffling at my shoes. Tentatively petting the downy soft fur of its head, I only looked up to who held the dog's leash when I heard his voice.

"Hi."

Leo stood grinning at me and I froze, though a smile had half-formed on my lips the moment I saw him. Leo was an impeccable dresser. At the store, he was always in either a suit jacket or a crisp button down shirt, sometimes a vest. He was trendy but he also had his own way of wearing fashions I wouldn't have picked out for him. But as I stared up at him where he held the frenzied little puppy's leash in one hand, the first thing I noticed past his stunning blue eyes was his plain black t-shirt and jeans. I'd never seen him looking so casual. My brow rose slightly as I considered the way I'd just seen Melanie at Black and Brew. Just because they wielded leather weapons didn't mean it was all tuxedoes and gowns all the time. The image I had of what Leo and his friends' world continued to crumble.

His hair looked a little damp and a tad out of place. Of course, it was sexy. He made just about everything sexy. Leo could get a spiral perm and wear nothing but head to toe acid-washed denim and I think I'd still feel a pulse of electricity between my legs at the sight of him.

"Hey," I finally breathed.

I moved my attention back to the puppy excitedly jumping up at me from the ground, its stubby legs never getting high enough to reach my lap. I scooped the sweet dog up and into my arms. It licked my cheek, evoking a giggle and I reveled in the small moment of glee. Something about affection from an animal always made me feel like a child again and it had a way of erasing any worries from my mind.

"Who is this?" I asked as the pup's squirming calmed and it nestled against my chest.

Leo shook his head and smiled. "That's Rosie and apparently she's your new best friend."

"I didn't know you had a dog," I mused.

Leo handed me the leash and sat down beside me, slinging one arm over the back of the bench as he turned his body toward me. Feeling like a child flew out the window the moment I dragged my gaze up and down the length of him once more. Though my insides still held onto gleefulness.

"She's not mine. She's Ben's. He just got her a few weeks ago and I offered to take her out on my days off," he said before leaning in a little to scratch Rosie behind one ear.

I scoffed a little laugh and quipped, "A puppy *and* a kitten? Ben's got his hands full."

Leo's eyes widened, perhaps not expecting the off the cuff joke from me—or the reference to the party—but he broke out into a laugh that squeezed my heart deliciously.

"What are you doing here? I thought you were working."

Rosie's head popped up from the two second nap she'd had on my lap and crawled over to take her place in Leo's arms instead. I watched the way his face lit up as she padded across the small length of bench between us to cuddle him. He helped her up and stroked her head whispering down at her, "Good girl."

Fire licked up my spine and warmth pooled in my belly at those words—how desperately I wanted him to say them to me. His gaze lifted and though I saw the embers of lust in his stare and recognition of his effect on me, he played it off coolly. His brows jumped, waiting for my answer as I simmered at his use of the phrase that owned me.

Clearing my throat, I looked out toward the playground again, trying to find a focal point. "I was taking a break before heading back the store. Oliver sent me out to sign us up for the Fall Festival and make some contacts for cross-promo," I replied before shooting him a teasing glare. "You know, since he just happened to find out about my previous marketing experience."

"Weird. Maybe he Googled you," he shot back.

My lips twisted, smothering a beaming smile while my thoughts raced. I'd so quickly come to adore this. Us. This banter, this familiarity outside of our sexual chemistry. I couldn't think of anyone else I shared such an easy connection with aside from Bryon. It started at the party and with our hours of discussion at my place, it only grew more unavoidable. The idea struck me like a falling meteor. From the very first moment, things with Leo had been rather effortless.

"So is this what you do on your days off? Use poor, innocent Rosie here to pick up girls at the park?"

"Is it working?" His full lips bowed and his expression softened as he shifted barely beside me, moving an inch closer.

I shook my head though my mouth betrayed me by smiling and my brain screamed the correct answer. Of course it was working.

"I'd like to have dinner with you," he said. My breath clung to my throat. "Tonight. May I?"

A series of images flickered through my brain. The first time we locked eyes over a wrecked copy of *The Scarlet Letter*, the pattern of wood grain I stared at the first time he spanked me, my shirt falling down my body as he interrogated me, his ravenous lips against my pussy, his hands slipping into leather gloves time and time again... All of that and yet none of those moments filled me with the amount of melded fear and excitement I felt when he proposed dinner.

I traced Leo's face for an instant and couldn't see a single shred of dominance. He wasn't willing me to agree and he wasn't commanding it of me. He was asking. Leveling with me…or deferring to me. Did Leo want more? The thought hadn't entered my mind. Did I know what to give or how to give it? Warren's damage remained present as faint seams, like scars on my spirit. I could give my body, I could hand over control, but could I share any more without falling apart?

Leo must've seen the wheels turning at rapid speed when he leaned a little closer. "Just dinner," he specified.

My head nodded before my emotions gave full permission and the look of relief on his face made my belly tremble. Just dinner.

ELEVEN

HE PICKED ME up three hours later at my apartment and as I climbed into his car, my heart pounded in a different way than when he'd driven me to the play party. He'd told me to keep it casual which was a relief. Since dinner itself was enough pressure, I didn't need to stress about outfit choice and which fork was which at some high end restaurant. I'd changed into jeans and a black tank top with a sheer plum-colored blouse over top of it. Leo wore the same dark wash jeans I'd seen him in earlier and a navy blue and gray flannel with the sleeves rolled up his forearms. Again, the casual clothes suited him, but surprised me at first glance.

The smile on his face as we both buckled our seatbelts attempted to melt me. It was boyish and…almost giddy. I gnawed at my bottom lip for a moment, watching the road as he pulled out of my apartment complex. Soon enough his smoky voice pulled my attention back to his face and the hard line of his freshly-shaven jaw.

"How long did you say you'd lived here?"

"Eight or nine months," I answered.

"Ah, so you've probably already been to Richie's," he started.

I shook my head. "Nope," I said. "I don't go out a lot. I don't really have any friends here so most of the restaurants I've tried have been places Oliver's bought lunch from." My brow pulled together. I chased away the little wave of sadness I felt thinking about my lack of friendships when I remembered Melanie's proposal and her number stored in my phone. I thought about telling Leo I'd run into her but resolved to keep it to myself and keep talk of the party quiet for the night.

Leo side-eyed me before he turned down Walton Avenue. "That's a shame. Yeah, Oliver hates pizza, the blasphemous fool. So I guess you're in for a treat. Best pizza you'll ever eat is right through those doors," he said, pointing as he pulled into a parking space near the entrance.

The little red brick building with its classic neon sign looked just as quaint as the rest of Salem and considering it was the last kind of place I expected Leo to take me to, it put a smile on my face. He had the unexpected down to an art. He held the door open for me and the smells of cheese and garlic made my stomach bubble with hunger. My smile lingered as I looked around the restaurant, waiting for Leo to tell the hostess we needed a table.

"I have an order for Calloway for pick up," he said.

He glanced back at me then dug in his pocket. He offered me a quarter and nodded his head toward the old jukebox in the back corner of the restaurant.

"Play me a song while we wait?" He grinned.

"We aren't staying?" I asked.

"No," he said plainly. "Nothing off the *Footloose* soundtrack though, okay? When we used to come here as kids, Marie only ever played songs from *Footloose*. She was obsessed. My dad nearly unplugged the thing once when she swiped five quarters from my mom's purse and put *Let's Hear It for the Boy* on repeat."

"Understood. *Holding Out for a Hero* it is," I teased as I took the quarter.

An absent smile crossed my lips when I approached the old style jukebox. I hated the new digital kind I'd seen in bars. I scanned the pages of albums behind glass—nothing more recent than 1995—and breathed a laugh to myself when I flipped to the *Footloose* soundtrack. I glanced back toward Leo and saw him watching me with a kind but serious look. My eyes fell on *Almost Paradise* and I considered disobeying his orders despite the fact that this night didn't feel like the kind of night that would end with a scene. Leo wasn't just keeping me on my toes, he had me levitating an inch above ground, equally fearful of floating higher or coming back down to earth. My mind was too fuzzy, racing too fast to make a choice.

"Just wait, Sophie," I heard a voice scold followed by a whine. I turned to see a young boy around twelve years old and his little sister who was maybe five waiting impatiently beside me. The little girl held a quarter between her fingers clasped to her chest as she fidgeted. A smile formed on my mouth and I crouched down in front of the two kids.

I held out my quarter to the little girl and sighed. "I'm having a terrible time choosing a song. Think you could pick one out for me?"

She snatched the coin from my hand with an opened mouth grin.

"Sophie, say thank you," her brother prompted before her little voice squeaked out, "Thanks."

"Make sure it's a good one," I said, straightening and winking at her. She nodded again and giggled as her brother hoisted her up to flip through the song pages.

When I made it back to Leo at the front of the restaurant, he held a pizza box and a short stack of paper plates in his hands and tipped his head toward the door. I opened it for him then he unlocked the car, placing the pizza box in the back seat.

"I just figured you and I could use some time alone…in a more laid back setting."

"Sure," I said with a hesitant smile as he started the car. "I trust you."

He caught my eyes and I saw that same boyishness exude from him. I didn't know where he was taking me, but it was true. I trusted him. It was difficult for me to admit as much though and the thought made my palms sweat a little. I watched as he drove us further away from the town and resolved to fill the car with something other than silence.

"So…Oliver and Wendy…"

"Finally," Leo mused, keeping his eyes on the road. "I was starting to worry he'd be a bachelor for life."

"You think they'll get serious?"

His blue eyes lit up as he shifted his gaze toward me briefly, tilting his head to one side. "Come on," he said. "They already are."

"I guess I'm blind or something. I never even picked up on it."

"No, Oliver's just… We're all different when it comes to relationships, me, Oliver and my sister. Oliver is the cautious one; he overthinks everything and it takes him forever to make a decision. But when he does, he means it. Marie is the reckless one; she acts before she thinks and she's always in over her head, usually with the wrong person."

"And you? What are you?"

His mouth popped open as though his mind had mustered a quick reply for me but he hesitated. He sighed softly then shrugged. "I'm the middle child so I guess I'm somewhere in the middle. A little careful and a little wild," he said before side-eyeing me. "You know, leap in first then think of a plan."

My cheeks tinted rose for a moment and I considered the fact that he'd just alluded to us while talking about relationships.

"What do you think of living in Salem so far?" Leo asked.

I sighed. "It's quiet. Kind of a little storybook town, you know. I like it. But everyone seems to be confused about the fact that we aren't in Massachusetts."

Leo laughed and nodded emphatically. "Fall and Halloween—the witch stuff—have always been a big deal around here. Growing up, Oliver and I were always the two smartasses reminding people that there are about twenty-six cities named Salem in the U.S. and ours has no historical significance."

I chuckled. A few miles away, up a meandering, tree-lined hill that wound like a hidden path, Leo finally slowed down. He parked the car and when I noticed where we were, I smiled. Oliver had mentioned the bluff once or twice. He told me it was the coolest place in Salem and what he called make-out point at one time. Sitting far enough away from the streetlamps of town seemed to make the night sky even clearer; all I saw were stars and all I heard were crickets.

Leo rolled down the windows and flicked on the radio before he turned the car off and motioned for me to get out with him. He grabbed the pizza and paper plates from the backseat and handed them to me while he leaned in again, emerging with a blanket in one arm and a small cooler on the other. I watched as he spread the blanket out on the grass a few feet from the car, lit by the headlights he'd left running.

"Are you serious?" I laughed.

Leo took the pizza from my hands and sat on the blanket then patted the spot beside him. "Completely."

I let go of a breath and recalled for an instant the handful of times Warren had taken me out after I learned he was married. It was always extravagant, over the top, and ridiculously expensive. Whether he was trying to hide me from the eyes of the general public by taking me to the places few could afford or if he was trying to buy my complacency, I was never sure. There was something special about Leo's choice. It wasn't boastful or showy and while it was surprisingly sweet, it didn't feel like a ploy to gain anything from me but time.

"Perfect night," he reflected, looking up at the navy blue sky speckled with stars.

I tilted my eyes skyward and sighed. It was beautiful. My ears suddenly picked out the love song station coming from the satellite radio in his car. Every detail had romance written all over it and my brain struggled to comprehend exactly what Leo was doing. Glancing down, I saw he'd pulled two beers from the cooler and popped the caps off, and was holding one out to me where I stood.

Sinking to a place on the soft blanket opposite Leo, I reached for the bottle and frowned.

"I thought you said this was just dinner…"

Leo made a face and put a slice of pizza on a paper plate and offered it to me. "We're going to eat, aren't we?"

My eyes drifted to the vast skyline in front of us where the hillside dropped down, showing every tree top for miles lit mostly by the moon. I took my first bite, finishing it before looking over at Leo as he swigged from his bottle of beer.

"This is like a date."

Leo's dark brows dipped down in the center but one corner of his mouth lifted. "Yeah…" he started. "And? So was dinner at Gabe and Mel's."

"It was?"

He scooted closer to me and concern clouded his expression. My ears pulsed with my heartbeat and the smooth sound of some cheesy love ballad I barely recognized.

"Is a date a bad thing?"

The hurt that waved over his face as he asked unsettled me. "No," I blurted. "Just…confusing. I didn't know…or I guess I didn't think that's what we were doing."

A smile parted his lips and out of nowhere, I flashed back to kissing him. "Unconventional, remember?" He laughed. "Maybe I should've been clearer. I like playing and having fun—I really like hearing you come," he said and I blushed. "But I also like you. I want to get to know you and spend time with you. Doing both of those things at the same time… that's what dating looks like for me."

"Does Oliver know you want to date me?"

Again, he smiled and I clung to the image, blinking to burn it into my mind. It wasn't exactly Jekyll and Hyde because the domineering side of him didn't frighten me, but he had these two sides that I found equally intriguing. In fact, I didn't know which I craved more in this moment. If he were to slip on the black gloves right now and tell me to shut up, I think I'd mourn this confident yet gentle man before me.

"Do you mean, does Oliver know we're dating? Because this is happening, Sloane. You're dating me," he replied with a laugh behind his words. "Sorry you missed the memo."

I couldn't help but roll my eyes, pulling my bottom lip in between my teeth.

Leo's eyes fluttered and he softened. "No, I haven't said anything to him."

"So—"

He cut me off, placing a hand on my knee. "I just want to enjoy you in any way you'll let me. And right now, I want to eat pizza, drink beer, and get to know one another. That's all I'm asking of you tonight."

He'd convinced me in a split second. His crystalline blue eyes staring deep into mine and his warm, soft touch at my knee ricocheted a complicit thought through my insides.

"Can you do that? Can you have dinner with me here under the stars and let me get to know you?"

My face tingled as a light breeze drifted over us and I breathed, "Yes."

Leo tossed the clear cellophane wrapper from the mint he'd just popped in his mouth into the pizza box and leaned back on his elbows with a huff. Our conversation had started light. We talked about books and of course, I left out any mention of my recent reads courtesy of his order of the complete fetish collection. Then we talked about Wendy and Oliver a little more.

"What about your family? Are they around here?"

"My parents passed away. My sister, Ellie, is in Blacksburg. She lives with her boyfriend, teaches fifth grade," I replied.

"I'm sorry about your parents," he said softly. "Are you and your sister close?"

"We used to be closer but she's really in to micromanaging me lately. She worries too much. She didn't agree with me moving here. She doesn't get why I left and until I started working at the bookstore, I think she was certain I was going to end up on the street or something," I said with a half-hearted laugh.

"But you weren't working when you first moved here because you were writing, right?"

The leading question made my stomach tighten. I swallowed hard and stared at one red stripe on the blanket beneath me before pushing a hand through my hair, nodding.

"Am I allowed to ask what the book is about now?"

Something about him asking my permission felt strange, but not unwelcomed. A deep breath filled me and I met his eyes squarely as I resolved to give him what he wanted.

"It's about the dissolution of a relationship that shouldn't have begun in the first place."

"Is it autobiographical?" he asked, drawing out his words cautiously.

"No. Not really," I lied.

"But there was a guy. In Blacksburg."

His tone made me feel transparent. As if I was so predictable, it was almost amusing to him. He didn't even ask. He just stated it and waited for me to confirm.

"Isn't there always a guy," I retorted, defeated.

"I'm sorry. You don't want to discuss it—"

I shook my head and exhaled. "No, it's okay. Yes, I moved here because I got out of a relationship and I started writing to work through it. I moved here…to help myself stay away. I had a bad habit of taking him back so moving away and starting over kept me from changing my mind. Backsliding."

My chest tightened as the harsh reality spilled out and I wondered what Leo would think of me. Weak, gullible, pathetic?

"Did he hurt you?" His voice snuck out as a throaty rumble and when I glanced up at him my stomach sank. I realized how much my explanation sounded like me breaking some kind of abuse cycle.

"No," I breathed. "Not like that. He hurt me in a lot of ways, but he never laid a hand on me."

Being honest with him didn't feel as bad as I imagined it would. Telling that small sliver of my history with Warren felt oddly liberating. I wanted to turn from Leo's gaze, but I couldn't break my eyes away from the stern look that'd washed over him at my last words.

As a new song poured from the radio, I broke a smile. I hooked my thumb toward the car and breathed a laugh, taking power away from Warren by pushing him from my mind and removing his presence from our date.

"This is the song I was going to play at the restaurant!"

The tension melted from Leo's expression and he glanced at the car then shot me a wide-eyed look. "*Almost Paradise?*" he barked. "What did I say about the *Footloose* soundtrack?" he teased. His hand brushed against mine as he repositioned on the blanket and I let my wrist turn, rolling into his touch. Choosing to float a little higher before planting my feet on solid ground again, I seized the moment and inched closer.

Leo erased the remaining space between us and a sigh slipped from my lips as his fingers stroked my cheek. The feeling of his bare hand on my face rippled warmth through my body. I'd never had the pleasure of his skin against mine like that. There was a time and place for those black leather gloves and his stern touch, but under the starry night sky with a love ballad on the air, I didn't want anything as a barrier between us.

He brought his face close to mine and the air between us filled with the scent of the red and white mints he'd pocketed at the restaurant. I shut my eyes when the tip of his nose brushed the apple of my cheek.

"May I kiss you, Sloane?"

My eyes blinked open and I reared back to look at him. It wasn't condescending. It wasn't a joke or a trick. Leo waited for my answer, his eyes dancing across my face. When I swallowed hard and nodded, he moved in and pressed his lips to mine, giving me the most beautiful kiss I'd ever experienced. His hand cupping my jaw and his lips moving against mine set my skin ablaze in a way completely different from the way he ignited passion in me with his commands.

As his tongue barely touched mine, parting my mouth before pressing a lighter kiss against my lips, the center of my chest lit up and radiated shockwaves out to my limbs. The song swelled in my ears and the gentle force of his kiss captivated me. Once again, my consent had led to surrender and as Leo's other hand reached up to capture my face, there was no doubt in my mind he was well aware he'd earned one more piece of me tonight. The threads lacing us together strengthened and with every second, I felt more compelled to let go of the past and let Leo show me a future.

TWELVE

TINY FINGERS WRAPPED around my thumb and I exhaled, scanning her face as she drifted off to sleep. It took Bryon clearing his throat a second time—more loudly than the first—to snap me out of my daze.

"Sorry," I whispered, not looking up but feeling his knowing grin. "She's just so sweet. And she smells so good. And her little lip keeps moving like she's talking in her dreams."

Bryon chuckled and dropped his head. "Yeah, yeah. My kid is the epitome of adorable awesomeness, I know. But you're killing me here. What happened after you two made out like you were under the bleachers?"

I hadn't seen Bryon in over a year and my heart felt fuller than it had in a long time having him in my apartment. Holding his daughter, Elizabeth, for the first time had stolen my attention from the story I'd been relaying. Everything that had happened to me in the last few weeks all seemed to fade away the moment I rocked her to sleep nestled against me. And yet, it lingered as a shadow in the back of my mind because I knew she represented what I ultimately wanted and I feared I wasn't on the right trajectory.

"We just kissed," I replied, looking back down at Elizabeth. "And then we talked a little more until it got cold and he drove me home."

Bryon's arms crossed over his chest and he glared at me, his mild smile remaining. "That's it? No whips and chains?"

I'd told him almost everything about how Leo and I began. As Bryon moved across the room, flopping down in the chair in my little living room as though he'd been there a thousand times, I smiled absently. Relief flooded me knowing we were able to pick up where we left off. I hadn't doubted for a moment whether or not I could tell him the lurid details of what had transpired with Leo, but there was still that element of liberation. I stood and gently placed the baby in her car seat where it sat on the floor near my sofa. Busying myself by refilling my glass of water, I shrugged.

"We barely even talked about that stuff. It was like we were together for the first time. He was a total gentleman. Incredibly sweet and romantic. He walked me to my door and kissed me on the cheek at the end of the night."

"So what do you think?" Bryon said.

My brow furrowed before he continued.

"Are you going to see him again?"

"Yeah, I mean, I work Monday so…"

Bryon laughed. "You know that's not what I mean. Do you like him? Do you want to be with him?"

My face fell and I met my friend's eyes meaningfully. "I'm worried."

"Why?"

"Because what if it's a mistake?"

Bryon moved to the couch and put his arm around me sweetly. "What makes you think it could be a mistake?"

A dark laugh crept out of me. "I don't know, it just feels like there's something keeping me from going all in. My track record, for one. Maybe I don't know how to pick them."

"Leo isn't married. Leo doesn't want to hide you or change you or control you," Bryon said.

I shot him a look which made him roll his eyes.

"You know what I mean. Not every guy out there is Warren 2.0. When you started the story with, *'He spanked me before he knew my last name,'* I was on board for this guy solely because I want to hear the kinky details. But I know you, Sloane, I know what you sound like when you're crushing and you've got it turned up to eleven for him. You like him. Why not let it ride and see what happens?"

"*Crushing?* Indulging in a fantasy and what happened last night are two different things. I didn't think a relationship was what I was getting myself into when he bent me over a table a few weeks ago," I retorted with a scoff.

"But isn't a relationship what you really want? Deep down?" he asked before fixing his gaze on Elizabeth where she slept, directing my eyes to her face as well. "Don't you want that? Warren kept you from the things you wanted and if you're not careful you'll keep yourself from them too."

His ability to make me see the truth as I watched a yawn take over Elizabeth's tiny, sweet face made my eyes mist with tears. I did want that. I wanted children. I wanted a future. I wanted to know love—real love—not the watered down promises and tainted emotions Warren gave me for years. I was tired of those left behind nightmares and the loneliness of walking through life without a companion. But fear was always ever-present and the insecurity Warren had conditioned in me still held more power than I'd hoped. I didn't love him any longer but the ties that bound me to him hadn't yet come undone.

Bryon squeezed his hand on my shoulder and I leaned into him as a smile chased the tears away. "I'm glad you're here," I said into his chest.

"Me too," he whispered.

Bryon and Elizabeth headed home about an hour later. I couldn't believe I'd waited so long to reach out to him again. His friendship had been the thing to pull me back to the surface after my parents died and I knew he would be a part of the final climb out of the black hole Warren had left me in to drown. Of course,

Leo was a part of that golden staircase I'd been ascending too. With the invasion of new happy thoughts, the ones Leo had managed to drum up with his unexpected mixture of passion and sweetness, old poison still found a way to leech into me. One moment I breathed easily and dug deep to forgive myself for the mud I'd caked my soul in, priding myself on the fact that I'd walked away and moved on, made friends, continued living…but shame crept in each time I thought his name. Each time I remembered his face. Heard echoes of his voice. Recalled the moments we shared.

I hadn't opened my manuscript since before the party and whenever I considered it, my stomach pitched. I didn't want to see what I'd written prior to meeting Leo, prior to my attempt to exorcise those demons in an alternative way. I put the chain over the front door and curled up on the couch with a glass of wine. The moment I reached for my phone on the coffee table, it shook in my hands and I dropped it.

"Crap," I muttered, leaning to grab it as it continued to vibrate. Leo's name made me gulp. Swiping my finger across the phone, I exhaled heavily then answered. "Hello?"

"Hi."

The thick rasp of his smoky voice caused me to clamp my lip between my teeth and sink back onto throw pillows behind me. I instantly forgot the shame and the pain.

"It's late," he breathed. "Did I wake you?"

"No."

"Good. I—I was thinking about you. Couldn't stop actually, so I figured I'd call."

My heart seized in my chest. I hadn't ever put it in those terms to myself, but I couldn't stop thinking about Leo either. Not since day one.

I sighed. "What were you thinking about?"

"*Almost Paradise*," he said. "And how next time I hear it I won't be able to think of anything other than your lips. So I guess really I was thinking about your lips."

Heat rushed over my skin and I shut my eyes, letting the memory of Leo's kiss invade my thoughts as well.

"I was also thinking how I badly I want to see you again and I was considering where we should go on our next date."

My heart swelled with every word so much so that I couldn't respond to him. I just let his words penetrate me, opening up for him as though he had me tied.

"And I was thinking about Monday and how we'll be closing at the bookstore together. Alone."

His voice dipped to a lower register with his last trailing comment and my thighs squeezed together at the implication.

"See what I mean? I can't stop thinking about you," he said.

Sex laced his words and anticipation skated across my nerves, causing the hairs on my arms to rise.

I'd been envisioning seeing him again since the moment I answered the phone.

"So, Sloane…are you thinking about me now?"

"Yes, Sir." The title slipped out without warning but the taste of it on my tongue was one I relished. Especially when I heard the little groan Leo emitted before he chuckled softly into the phone. How easily he'd shifted our conversation to be that of give and take. Of compliance and command.

"Very good. Now listen carefully. I want you to touch yourself as much as you want tonight and tomorrow. Come as many times as you like, but enjoy it, because after Monday your pleasure is mine. I'll give it and I'll take it away. And you should know, Monday won't be a picnic—not even close. It's time we delved a little deeper, don't you think?"

It was my turn to growl, moaning at the threat that thrilled me as much as sweet conversation and tender kisses. Together we were a pair of dice, both of us landing on different sides, tipping over one hard edge after the other to reveal new facets of ourselves. And yet, we were always adding up to something bigger. Why was I so afraid to let myself wade in his waters?

"Was this your plan when you called?" I asked daringly. "To make me wet and guarantee I'd dream of you?"

"That's been my plan since the second I met you, Sloane."

Another breath rolled out of me, this one uneasy and staggered. My brain began to spark, unable to compute him. I suddenly didn't know how to wrap my mind around who he was or what he wanted. And while I'd enjoyed every second of the attention he offered me, I still felt my insides begrudgingly ripple with a shadow of fear. It was the same feeling I got in my dreams where I was left behind, just moments before I realized I was alone. A mixture of safety, serenity, and utter angst as I waited for the inevitable. Had those dreams that plagued me before I ever met Leo secretly starred him? Was he in the dim driver's seat—the person leaving me behind after making me feel so secure?

"Sloane?"

"Yeah."

"What are you thinking about?"

"I don't understand this. I don't understand *you*," I breathed.

He cleared his throat and though I couldn't see him, I knew he instantly changed. "What do you mean?"

"I thought you wanted sex," I admitted. "I thought you were just looking to mark my ass until you got bored. I thought when you handed me medical records that was a very clear admission—confirmation of my assumption of who you were and what we were going to be. Sex. Kink. Fantasy. And I was fine with that. I wanted that. I needed…" My voice broke and faded into nothing but a breath. I heard Leo breathing on the other end but he waited for me to continue. "I don't understand you, Leo. I keep trying to tell myself you're not Jekyll and Hyde, but you are. You're either spanking me in the inventory room or you're taking me on a moonlit picnic, which is it? You change without warning and I don't know how to keep up. When I think you're one man, you're the other. I like you. I like both sides of you and how you make me feel. I like it all too much and I'm afraid I like it for the wrong reasons."

Finally. The admission I'd barely allowed myself to think silently left my lips and while my stomach still floated, anxiously weightless, relief began to trickle in. Leo's silence pounded in my ear as my bold speech swelled in the space around me. I glanced at the clock and the moment I heard Leo's voice in my ear, I cut him off.

"I have to get some sleep. I have a hair appointment early tomorrow," I said.

"But, Sloane—"

"I shouldn't have said anything. It's fine. Don't worry about it. Goodnight," I croaked as I hung up.

My ribs ached as I heard the words that had nearly become my catchphrase when I was with Warren. As my head reeled, I knew I wouldn't seek to pleasure myself as Leo had suggested. My thoughts raced as shame came back in full force and agony burned through my veins. Bryon was right, if I wasn't careful I'd be the one to prevent myself from having the things I wanted—and it was only now that my head pounded and tears threatened to break through the wall of emotion around me that I wondered if I was wrong. Maybe the real mistake was shutting Leo out, not letting him in.

Wendy's eyes sparkled as she gaped at me from behind the register when I pushed through the front door. My trip to the salon had come after a night of tossing and turning, attempting to make up my mind about Leo and what I would do or say come today. I kept my color the same, the one I'd changed to as soon as I got to Salem—a rich burgundy—but when it came time for my standard trim, I let a little of Leo's variability guide me.

"Cute!" Wendy cooed.

As I slipped out of my jacket, I touched my hair bashfully and forced a smile. I moved toward the computer she sat next to and clocked in without a word, but as my eyes swept to Wendy's, her grin grew.

"New man, new 'do?" she quipped.

"What?" My voice was merely a breath.

She looked past me and as I followed her guilty gaze, I found Oliver coming out of the office with the same expression. Leo hadn't waited any longer to tell his brother about us. Oliver clearly registered the apprehension on my face and he pulled his lips tight before shooting a glare at Wendy.

"Sorry," she whispered. "Didn't know it was a secret."

I brushed my hair out of my face again and shook my head. "It's okay. It's just—"

Her hand tapped my arm then flitted in the air as though she was clearing away the awkwardness. "No, it was my bad," she said. "But, for real, your haircut. I'm obsessed."

Oliver must've been the key to Wendy's cheer as I'd never heard her speak so enthusiastically. When she worked at the store back when I was just a fixture in the corners working on my book and drinking the free coffee, she'd always been nice but never this bubbly. I laughed a little and thanked her. I almost jumped out of my skin when her hand ruffled through my hair, another squeal leaving her as she turned me around by my shoulders to feel the back.

I stood facing the front door, Wendy fondling the back of my neck that now felt every waft of air that travelled over it. Cut close to the nape of my neck, the short style still hung below my chin in the front and swung at a perfect angle along my jawline. I giggled as Wendy continued to fluff my hair up.

"It's so sexy!"

Tilting my chin back up, I locked eyes on Leo on the other side of the window. His phone pressed to one ear and a black cigarette dwindled between his lips as he stared at me. As bewitched by me as I was by him. I recalled the first time I met him and the faint scent of cloves I'd picked up. Watching as he blew out a wisp of smoke, I remembered the way I'd attacked him then cut him off when we last spoke. He stomped out the butt on the ground and pushed through the front door, never dropping his blue gaze from mine.

Wendy's hands left my hair and a cold chill ran over me. Leo's penetrating stare had me glued to the floor and knowing Wendy and Oliver were watching—with newly enlightened eyes—unsettled me even further.

"Well, did you try to give him Tylenol?" Leo said into his phone.

My brow furrowed and I suddenly heard Oliver call out to Wendy to start brewing the coffee. Leo's lips firmed up and a breath rolled through him before he scrubbed at his forehead, finally tearing his eyes away from me.

"Yes, you should," he barked. "No...I'm not mad. I'm glad you called. Start with some meds and plenty of fluids, let him lay in my bed and watch *Monsters, Inc.* and call me this afternoon."

I sucked in a sharp breath and turned toward the office, afraid to hear any more. I knew it was his sister, Marie, and he was probably talking about his nephew, but hearing that sliver of his conversation made my stomach ache. It sounded like he was talking to the mother of his child. He sounded like a concerned parent and as if I wasn't confused enough already by my feelings for Leo, the idea of him having a child hurt me deeply.

I heard him approach the office door as I sat down at the computer to start working on my plans for the Calloway Books booth at the Fall Festival.

"Love you too. Bye," he said before clearing his throat in the doorway. "Sloane?"

I didn't turn around. I couldn't. I was on the brink of full-on crazy. Between our date, his orders over the phone, and the way my walls had been raising and lowering like some kind of death-trap obstacle course in a video game, Leo had created the most shocking sense of instability in me. And I knew the only reason he'd gotten to me that way was because I cared about him—everything about him; what he thought, how he felt, who he was, who he made me. Instantly. Irrevocably.

"Sloane?" Leo said again.

"Yeah," I replied without turning from the computer screen.

"Are you still closing tonight?"

"Yep. That's my shift," I snipped. "I have to finish this plan for the Fall Festival then I'm on the register from three to six. You made the schedule, you should know that."

I heard him sigh heavily behind me and grumble under his breath. "Mouthy."

Whipping around, I pinned him with a glare, hating the way the sight of him rippled excitement through my belly. "Excuse me?"

Two quick strides and Leo bent over me, caging me in with his hands gripping the arms of the desk chair. His face wore an emotion I couldn't decipher. His eyebrows cinched close together in the center and shadows cast in his blue eyes. His jaw shifted then clenched then shifted again as though he meant to speak or scream but censored himself. I didn't see anger. I didn't see rage. I didn't even see the full-fledged dominance he'd shown me before. This was different.

"I said, you're mouthy," he whispered. With his face so close to mine, I could smell the clove cigarette on his breath. Scanning me with bright eyes, Leo's tongue slipped out to wet his lips and my shoulders relaxed at the sight.

"I—"

"Be quiet," he said easily, cutting me off. I gulped and felt that familiar weightlessness in my limbs that Leo's orders cast on me. "Do you want to stay late with me tonight? If you say yes, you're saying yes to whatever I want."

"Leo…"

"It's a yes or no question. Yes or no, Sloane?"

The gruffness of his tone may as well have been a five ton brick that just fell on the partition around my heart, slamming it to the ground. Obliterating my barriers. I searched his face and as my heartbeat grew erratic, I answered without thinking.

"Yes, Sir."

THIRTEEN

MY EYES FOLLOWED Leo as he locked the front door and turned off the *Open* sign in the window the moment the clock turned six and the last customer had slipped out. He turned to where I sat behind the register and I gulped from the weight of his stare.

"You ready?"

Again, I attempted to swallow the apprehension he had a way of eliciting inside me. I nodded and stood on jellied legs. My gaze flickered to his hands and I noticed he hadn't yet suited up for our playdate. Leo turned from me and my brow furrowed as I watched him take a seat in one of the two chairs near the coffee bar.

"You agreed to whatever I want," he said smugly. "I want to talk."

Motioning toward the chair opposite him, a little smile tugged at his lips. I tongued the back of my top teeth in an effort to hide my sneer. Of course he wanted to talk. I should've seen this coming. I took the few steps to erase the distance between us and dropped into the comfy chair, crossing my legs away from him.

Leo leaned forward, resting his elbows on his knees, dropping his head for a beat before holding me captive with his blue eyes. "This isn't what I had in mind initially, but after our conversation on the phone it became very clear to me that I've misled you."

For some reason, my chest constricted and lit up with a prickle of painful electricity.

"When I first met you, I was instantly aware of your submissive predisposition—something I assume, now, you barely recognized within yourself. So I flirted and made that remark about punishment. I went home that night telling myself over and over again that I had to wait a few more days before asking you out or otherwise Oliver would kill me."

Flirted? That dark stare and whisper of a smile as he alluding to tanning my hide was Leo's definition of flirting? I didn't speak up as his words continued to flow, detonating little mind blowing bombs in me along the way.

"But the next day, you and that little laugh asking me if I'd come upstairs to punish you…I couldn't resist. Sloane, I should've asked you out first. I shouldn't have driven us halfway down a road you'd never even set foot on with my impulsiveness. But if I'd made it clear that I wanted to do more than play, be more than sex—that I wanted to get to know you, to date you, to take you places and attempt to make you smile by using more than my body I don't think you would've said yes. We wouldn't be here right now if we'd done things in order. I don't know anything about your past, why you're here, why you ran from that idiot who hurt you, but I know whatever skeletons you have in your closet…" Leo paused and sucked in a ragged breath as if preparing himself for the rest of his statement. Or maybe he was preparing me. I breathed in deeply too and our eyes met as I exhaled. "You let me race us down this road to punish yourself. You used me," he finished.

I sucked in a breath and let my eyes fall to the floor. I'd forgotten one thing. Leo read me so well; it was as though he was the creator of the cipher that translated me for the rest of the world. My silence and the way I shifted admitted without words that he was right. Guilt flooded me and the magnetism we'd had from the very start pulled my knees toward him and my eyes to his.

"I am not two different men, Sloane. I'm one man with distinct sides—differing emotions, differing actions—but I'm always me. To classify me as Dr. Jekyll and Mr. Hyde solely based on the fact that I can be both gentle and severe is…" he sighed and shook his head with widened eyes. "Honestly, it's insulting. You want to know why people talk about their respective roles when it comes to S and M? Because it needs to be crystal clear that Dominant and submissive are only titles during agreed upon times. I'm a sexual Dominant,

I'm not an asshole. And if you'd take the time to get to know me the way I want to know you, you could see who I am in totality instead of filing me away under Jekyll and Hyde because that's easier than learning who I am."

My mouth dropped open as regret churned in my stomach. My heart grew heavier with every line hardening his expression. I didn't know what to say. He'd assessed me so perfectly, so effortlessly, I couldn't refute a word he'd said. All I had was an apology resting on my tongue, unable to escape.

"So like I said," he began, his face softening a bit and easing some of the tension in my muscles. "This isn't what I thought we'd be doing tonight, but there it is."

"I—" My voice snuck out before a shudder claimed me and I rearranged in my chair, uncrossing and crossing my legs. "I needed to hear that," I said. "You're right…about everything. I'm sorry for mislabeling you—but what you said about me punishing myself—"

Suddenly, my eyes wet with tears as the rationale of scolding myself via Leo's aggression finally clicked, filling me with even more shame.

"Let me tell you something I've learned," he interrupted, leaning in once more, heating the space around me and quelling the stress I felt. "You might've initially been drawn to what I offered to free your inner demons. It's okay to feel that way. Play can be very therapeutic. But that isn't why you've continued to let me dominate you. Once you completely break through those old feelings, you'll evolve as submission shows you who you really are. Sexually submissive women are some of the strongest women I've ever known. And you are no exception."

"How does being submissive translate into strength?" I asked skeptically.

A warm hand found mine and for the first time since we'd sat down, I felt that fiery connection linking us together on a higher plane. The feeling of his skin against mine soothed me, warned me, and beckoned my heart all at the same time.

"It's like I've told you before, you're the one with the choice. The strength it takes to choose to be defenseless and to allow yourself the often incomprehensible ability to find freedom in bondage and discipline…is significant. And personally," he said with a smile, "it's the sexiest thing in the world to see."

A trickle of desire skated down my spine and settled low in my abdomen. I thought about the heavenly spinning feeling submitting to Leo had given me and indeed, it felt like freedom. It felt like tapping into a part of my soul I'd long forgotten and I wondered if my limits were pushed even further if I'd uncover my true self. My essential existence.

"If the submissive is the strong one, what does that make you?"

With startling blue flames for irises, Leo searched my face and held silent for a beat, still clutching my hand on my knee.

"Your shepherd."

I thought about Melanie as he continued to lead me toward the inevitable with his convincing philosophies. I thought about her home—transformed into a dungeon of sin once a month. I thought about her stunning good looks at the party juxtaposed with her natural, everyday beauty at the coffee shop dressed down in loungewear. And I thought about her daughter, smiling shyly, completely unaffected by what Melanie must've kept private from her. Just like Leo had said after our first planned scene, the things Leo did to me, the things he wanted to continue to do, and the levels that I wanted to explore with him in return didn't have to define me.

But could they transform me?

Leo let out a deep breath and cocked his head to one side, offering a subtle smile. "Do you have a cat?"

"What?"

"Do you have a cat? Or a pet of some sort? Something that needs to be fed? I assume you don't have a dog since I've been to your apartment, but cats have a habit of hiding."

I shook my head and furrowed my brow. "No, I don't have any animals. Why?"

"So there's no need for you to go back to your place tonight?"

Darkness settled behind his gaze and I remembered my free will. And as I shook my head and rose to my feet, I chose to fall into his darkness. I chose to wrap myself in all that he was, intent on seeing every part of him in between the two sides I'd already come to crave.

The chill in the air caused my breath to fog in front of me and I realized I was nearly panting with anticipation as Leo unlocked his door. With a hand at the small of my back, he ushered me inside and flipped on a light. From the street, the small bungalow house was as cute as the rest of Salem with its blue shutters and mums planted out front. But inside, the masculine décor screamed Leo Calloway. From the entryway, I caught a glimpse of the living room and kitchen around the corner but I didn't move. I glanced over at the office to my left behind glass double doors and saw the massive bookshelves filled and almost overflowing. The large dark wood desk with a leather chair sitting behind it sent visions of Leo deep in thought, working on God knows what, through my mind.

I took a few steps and made my way down the short hall that left me standing with the kitchen on my right and the living room spread out in front of me. Large windows on the back wall of the house showed the wooded area behind his home bathed in moonlight.

"I love your house," I breathed, taking in the gray leather, riveted sofa, metal coffee table, large flat screen TV above the white stone fireplace, and the two large abstract canvases on the wall. When my head turned to look over the kitchen, I felt him grab the collar of my jacket and the strap of my purse, slipping them off of me without a word. I made a move to glance back at him when he spoke.

"Don't move."

I sucked in a breath and kept my back to him.

"I'm done talking," he rasped. "Are you?"

Impulsiveness overwhelmed me. The need to feel his lips against mine made me turn against his wishes and reach for him greedily, pushing up on my toes for a kiss. Leo's hands, already sheathed in black gloves, snatched both of my wrists as he stepped into me, pressing my back against the wall and pinning my hands above my head.

Hot breath tickled my nose and cheeks as he moved his face close to mine, scanning me carefully. I sighed and dropped my gaze, letting go of control and praying for the spontaneity I'd craved right from the start. Only now, I wanted more. I wanted him to push me further and bend me just shy of my breaking point. I knew Leo would know where that line would be drawn and from the look in his eye, I could tell he was ready to approach it without crossing.

"I'm done talking," he repeated through clenched teeth. "*Are you?*"

"Yes, Sir," I sighed.

The groan from the back of his throat before he brought his lips to ghost over mine thickened my blood. Without making full contact, his tongue slipped into my mouth and I met him with a matched slow dancing lick. It wasn't a kiss. It wasn't anything I'd ever experienced, but the succulent sweetness of our tongues coyly lapping at each other was more erotic than the wildest of moments I'd spent with any other man. Leo's kiss had the power to rule me and this—this had the power to make me do something I never envisioned I would do…

I struggled against him and Leo let up though he still held me by the wrists and with his stare.

"What? You want to move?" he asked.

I nodded and one side of his mouth kicked up in amusement. It was as if I could hear him thinking about letting me have my way just to see what I would do. His hands loosened their grasp and slid down my raised arms. Wetting his lips, he took a step back and gave one nod.

With shaking hands, I tugged my shirt over my head and tossed it aside, then undid my pants, shucking them to the floor before stepping out of them completely. Leo surveyed my body, clothed in only a simple red lace bra and black satin panties, and brought one leather-gloved hand to his chin.

"That's what you wanted?" he breathed. "To undress for me?"

I gulped and shook my head no.

His eyes narrowed and I took a final breath. My last free breath before I gave him the thing he'd promised to earn. He'd earned it and I was ready for him to cultivate it, no longer feeling fickle or afraid of what he offered—sexually or emotionally. I was all in.

And as I slowly lowered to my knees before him, looking up into his astounded eyes just once before lowering my head, the sound of the shuddering inhale he took imprinted itself in my mind forever.

FOURTEEN

A HANDFUL OF blurred moments passed and I felt Leo's strong arms scoop me off of the floor and carry me around the corner into a bedroom. He tossed me on the bed then paralyzed me with smoldering eyes as he undressed me the rest of the way. Leo moved to a dresser drawer on the opposite side of the room while I remained immobile, naked and trembling with excitement. I let my eyes drift to see the pale gray walls of the room with nothing but a mirror on one wall and an odd looking bench and chair off in one corner. By the time I began scrutinizing the furniture, he grasped one wrist and hoisted me off the bed just enough to yank the thick comforter out from underneath me. He sat me back down on the soft sheets, but didn't look at me as he buckled each wrist in a leather cuff before securing them together with a metal chain.

He guided me forcefully onto my back. Gripping the chain between my restraints, he pulled my arms above my head, looping the chain on a hook screwed into the headboard. The idea that Leo would have permanent fixtures meant for play in his home hadn't really crossed my mind until now. As he snaked down my body, I shivered. A black strap appeared in his hand from beneath the bed and I saw the same kind of cuff attached to the end. The cool, textured leather slipped around my left ankle and I instinctively drew my right leg in in an attempt to have one last free movement before he roughly grabbed it and locked it in place.

Legs spread wide, cuffed at the edges of his bed, and arms gathered and locked above my head, I'd never been more restricted. I tugged at the cuffs around my ankles and flushed with heat when I heard Leo laugh at the sight. My eyes met his. The silence between us didn't frighten me, it exhilarated me. I waited for him to make a move but a little protesting whimper came out of me when he backed out of the room wearing a smirk.

Alone, the first splinter of fear pricked at my heart. I dragged in a ragged deep breath to calm myself. Shutting my eyes, I breathed in again and again. With every inhale, I settled down and with every exhale, my passion stirred.

I heard a scratching sound followed by a *whoosh* and the scent of sulfur filled my nostrils. My eyes fluttered open to see Leo holding a matchstick to the wick of a white candle, lighting a second one as soon as the first flame ignited. The two thick cylindrical candles sat atop the dresser and the dancing flames entranced me until I noticed Leo. Shirtless and changed out of his black slacks and into loose sweatpants, his body lit by the glow of candlelight made my mouth water.

The muscles of his chest and abs tensed as he stood still near the candles, staring at me darkly. Leo's gaze slid over every inch of my body, cast in amber glow. My bare breasts heaved with each breath. He wet his lips and I squirmed. His feet moved and I was sure he was coming for me, but again he turned to walk out of the bedroom. Once more, my vocal chords scraped in a weak protest, but then my eyes fell on his back and I gasped.

Taking up nearly his entire back was a portrait of a lion. Done solely in black, the tattoo startled me and intrigued me at once. I didn't know why but I didn't expect a tattoo on Leo at all let alone this one. The quick glimpse wasn't enough to truly dissect the image but what I saw was unexpected—yet another reason I should've given every part of Leo my attention from the start. The lion image he wore wasn't that of the roaring king of the jungle or the menacing hunter. It was docile. Simply looking back at me with mystery in its eyes.

I swallowed hard as Leo walked back into the room, this time carrying a metal bowl that he set on the nightstand beside me. He took a seat on the edge of the bed. His eyes grazed over my skin and all I could think of was his tattoo and how desperately I wanted to see it again.

"Do you remember your colors?" His voice sounded rough; it was music to my ears after the silence that had hung between us for so long.

"Yes, Sir."

A black glove reached out and I flinched as he trailed one finger in a circle around my already hardened nipple.

"Good girl," he replied and I squirmed again, desperate to squeeze my legs together. "I should punish you…"

I pulled in a sharp breath and set my eyes on him, frantically wide but without a word. Certainly without a color. He reached into the top drawer of the nightstand and pulled out a black satin eye mask. Leaning over me as I panted, he slipped the cool fabric over my eyes and let the elastic strap hug the back of my head, shrouding me in darkness.

"Punish you for back talking me, for pulling away, for stealing my opportunity to undress you by taking matters into your own hands, and for resisting me for so long—too caught up in your own concerns to think about me. Us."

With my sense of sight revoked and my limbs captured, the sound of his voice in my head was as luscious and intoxicating as wine. This moment alone made my body feel that gentle pull toward levitation and I knew whatever he had in store for me, it wouldn't take long before I spun out.

I jumped at the feeling of his gloved hand smoothing down the skin between my breasts, trailing all the way to my sex. I could feel his hand hovering above me. I tried to lift my hips off the bed to meet his touch, but I had no leverage and his presence kept me weak.

"But I want to reward you, Sloane."

I stilled and honed in on his words, focusing every ounce of my being to the tone of his voice as I felt him lean into my ear. His breath warmed the already flushed skin of my cheeks and I drew in the clean scent of him.

"Reward you for listening to me, for seeing the errors you've made, for apologizing, for dropping to your knees," he whispered and moved even closer, his warm bare chest pressing against my side. "And for cutting your hair."

A whimper passed my lips just as he smothered his mouth over mine, capturing the sound with his tongue. He pulled back, leaving me breathless. The sensation of his kiss without the ability to see or touch him catapulted me to an unearthly height. I felt his hands snake around the back of my neck, now exposed thanks to the haircut.

"This part of you," he spoke against my lips, "haunts my dreams."

He lifted my head and crushed his lips to mine again.

"It's everything you are," he said, breaking the kiss. "It's delicate but strong and while you own its every move, I will always be able to wrap my hands around it and take your breath away."

One heavy pant pushed from my lungs, coated with a moan when Leo pulled away from me. My chest rose and fell and my head whipped back and forth, blindly searching for him.

"What do you think I should do? Punish or reward you?"

I attempted to speak but nothing emerged. Cool leather plucked hard on one nipple, tugging it straight up making my lips clamp shut and vibrate with a moan.

"Come on," he said. "Be a good girl and answer me."

"Both," I choked as he let go. The answer was greedy, as the punishment was a reward after the emotional rollercoaster I'd been on with him over the past few days. I heard a rustling noise, like liquid swirling and something clinking against metal.

"Perfect answer," he said.

Goosebumps instantly scattered across my skin as something slick and chilly pressed against the nipple he'd just tweaked. Shocked, I yanked on my restraints feeling the hard little object circle around one sensitive peak. I registered the sensation as an ice cube as soon as Leo moved it to my other nipple and sucked the first one in his mouth, the heat of his tongue zapping the cold away. Gasps ripped out of me every time he alternated, swapping his mouth for a torturous ice cube, slowly circling the surely reddened buds. I bent my elbows and pulled on the hook that held me but it didn't budge, and every time I tried to pull myself up and away from his devilish actions, I felt the cuffs on my ankles mocking me.

Sucking so deeply on my nipple that a pop sounded through the air when he released it, Leo finally lifted the ice from my skin. I heard the same liquid and clanking just before a new even colder cube came to draw a line from my parted lips down my chest to my navel. I sucked in my stomach, trying to shrink away from the delicious agony of the cold but puffed a curse as Leo pressed it firmly against my skin, drawing it to the crease of my thigh. The ice moved everywhere but where I knew he meant for it to end up eventually. Heavy breaths shot from my lips to the ceiling and I reveled in the excruciating pleasure of not being able to move or see as he toyed with me.

"Do you know yet?"

"What?" I shrilled, feeling the ice slip slowly to the place where my outer sex split. The heat of my body melted the cube and cool water trickled down to mix with the wetness he'd brought forth.

"If this is the punishment or the reward?"

I could hear the grin in his voice but didn't have time to react. Leo pressed the ice cube flush with my clit and I cried out. He added a second and then a third as I gritted my teeth, feeling all three pieces of ice melting on my sex. I tried to catch my breath, but I failed and screamed as soon as Leo pushed one hard cube inside me, then pressed another handful between my legs. His firm, leather-sheathed hand cupped my sex. I felt goosebumps break out all over my legs and tears slip down my temples. Leo replaced his hand with what felt like a pillow and I whimpered. I felt the bed shift as he stood and my senses perked, anticipating a shower of ice to rain down on me. I licked my lips in between panting breaths and tried to ignore the numbness of my throbbing pussy and focus on the clues I had with sight and scent.

Footsteps.

Fire.

"Are you cold?"

"Yes, Sir," I whined, wiggling my hips in effort to melt the cube slowly shrinking inside of me.

My senses blocked out the cold the instant liquid heat splashed on my breasts. It burned for a split second then cooled and puckered on my flesh. I choked on a breath just as another trickle painted me, the burning drops splashing over one nipple. As more liquid fire spilled on to my skin, the scent of the flame pulled me toward the realization that Leo was pouring candle wax on my body. While it scorched the first second it touched me, it cooled rather quickly and the moans the sensation drew out of me were proof I enjoyed it. Droplets fell on me, coating my belly in broken stripes and finally moving low enough to make me squeal. As the velvety, hot liquid trickled close to the pillow holding ice against my sex, I screamed.

"Please!"

"Please, what?"

"Please," I huffed. "Sir." Another gasp. "I—can't."

My voice failed me and a sob slipped out just as the pillow between my legs disappeared. The melting slivers of ice fell away from me. A deep, guttural groan ripped from my lungs and I shrank inwards, flexing every muscle in my body as soon as I felt Leo's hot mouth against my pussy. His tongue pushed inside where the cube he'd slid into me had chilled my core. The temperature torture reached its peak when he unlocked his lips from me and exhaled deeply onto my flesh, attempting to steam the frozen, sensitive flesh. I felt myself melt at his attention and as the feeling came back, blood rushing to my pussy, the deep ache of an impending orgasm engulfed me. Bucking against his face, I gritted my teeth and mewled pathetically when I heard Leo laugh.

Suddenly, the weight of his body covered me and he pulled the blindfold away. I blinked to see his brooding eyes as he stared at me briefly before slinking down, unbuckling the cuffs around each of my ankles. He met my bleary eyes once again, hovering over me, letting a gloved hand fondle me between my legs. A flicker of a smile touched his lips as he shifted and I felt him push down the pants he wore. Without a moment to prepare and my mind still on overload, I cried out as he pushed his cock inside me. I shut my eyes and groaned in delight.

He sat up and gripped my hips, yanking me toward him, fucking me deeply without reprieve. With my arms still linked to the wooden headboard, I longed to touch him. But the utter loss of control and the feeling of him taking me—rewarding me—was the final push I needed to lose myself to the spin. My eyes rolled back as Leo thrust, stretching me and pushing me toward ecstasy. Then the feeling of leather fingertips slipping under my earlobe to the back of my neck made me look up at him.

The indigo stare that had struck me at our first encounter dug deep into my soul as our bodies joined as one. His hand at the back of my neck tightened into a fist, gripping the short hair as he ground into me. The symphony of sounds resounding around us only added to my dizziness. The world fell black and I sank to a dark and desperate place. A place where pleasure knew no bounds and everything was Leo Calloway. Nothing else mattered. Nothing else existed.

My body slackened as he rocked into me. I felt my arms shift and jostle then felt the warmth of Leo's skin against my wrists. I opened my eyes a sliver to see he'd hoisted me into his lap and looped my chained wrists around his neck instead of around a metal hook. With every thrust, the inevitable built inside me. My heart ricocheted beneath my breast as the spinning intensified.

Leo's leather-sheathed hands made their way around my throat. There was no pressure, my air flowed just as ragged as it had before, but the intensity of the moment—my spinning mind, my life's breath in his hands, and the driving force of his cock—pushed me over the edge. A cry tore from my lungs as my core pulsated around his thickness. Tears streamed down my face as I came—the deepest, most emotional release I'd ever achieved completely overcoming me. Just before blackness shrouded me, I locked eyes with Leo. He wiped at the tears on my face, kissed me roughly, and came with a harsh curse against my lips.

FIFTEEN

THE LITTLE SMACKING sounds of kissing lips pulled me out of my trance before I registered the feeling of those kisses peppering my face. My eyes struggled to open as Leo's calm voice shushed me sweetly, pressing delicate pecks across my cheeks. The warm flesh of his palms cupping my jaw on either side scattered a final bout of goosebumps. As I came back down to earth, I knew by the feel of his bare hands that the scene was over.

I blinked a few times until Leo's face became clear. He held me in his lap still, sitting up in bed with my arms linked around his neck and my legs encircling his waist. His thumbs wiped at the tears that had flowed down my cheeks, not in pain but in utter release. The power of his torture followed by his rough lovemaking not only spun me into the dizzying trance I desired but it pushed me to a new level of deliverance. The walls shielding the heart I'd put back together shattered from the strength of Leo's rule. By limiting my physical movements—my ability to shy away from the intensity of his passion or resist the supernova of chemistry between us—he'd freed me from the bitter heartache that had constricted my soul for so long.

"Hi," he whispered with a tender smile. "Are you okay?"

My lips curved dreamily and I nodded. His hands grasped my forearms and guided them over his head to unshackle my wrists and he tossed the cuffs to the floor beside the bed.

"Lie down," he suggested, shifting me off of his lap and reaching for the blanket shoved at the foot of the bed. My legs stretched out and smoothed over the sheets; I yelped then giggled. Leo shot me a concerned look and moved to my side.

"What's wrong?"

"Cold," I said with another laugh, reaching under the covers and producing a forgotten ice cube. His smile made my chest blaze, my heart pumping wildly. Leo took the ice from my hand and tossed it in the metal bowl on the nightstand before snuggling under the blanket with me, pulling my naked body flush to his. His soft touch evoked a breathy moan from my lips and I couldn't stop smiling as he pressed a kiss at my temple.

"Thank you," he breathed.

I snorted softly and turned to meet his eyes, our face just inches apart. "Why do you always thank me?"

Leo drew his brows together. "Because I'm thankful for you. I'm grateful every time you allow me to dominate you," he said. "You and I seem to understand each other's desires and needs so clearly. We complement each other and for that, I'm incredibly thankful I found you. I've been with women before who weren't interested in what I like, but were still great lovers… But you… When I want to push, you want to be shoved. I'm thanking you for giving me your rawest self and for trusting me to foster the side of you that you don't know what to do with."

"Tell me why you like it," I whispered.

"Why do you like it?" he shot back with a half-smile.

I tugged my bottom lip between my teeth and smothered the sinful grin his question elicited. Still reeling from the high he'd given me, I tried to categorize the reasons I enjoyed our mutual fetish. I stared at him through the darkness, feeling his breath mixing with mine.

"When my senses are limited," I began, "withdrawing into my mind where doubt and insecurity live isn't an option. The line between pain and pleasure blurs and every sting just magnifies how good you really make me feel. You're right…I become my rawest self with you because I have no other choice but to peel back the layers and experience every sensation. I get to a point where everything fades away and I'm just spinning out. For a long time, I struggled with a need to keep a firm grasp on control. But giving it to you has made me realize how futile that struggle was. Maybe control was never what I was seeking..."

His stare, shadowed by the night and the fading glow of candlelight, held me as perfectly as leather cuffs and metal chains. I watched his lips part slightly and I involuntarily wet my own.

"Then what were you seeking?"

"Liberation from the need to control."

He blinked and my mind began to ask him for his own dark confession over and over. I had to know what it was like for him. An outsider could look at him like a freak. A potential serial killer or danger to society. But I knew—even without knowing fully—that Leo's brutality was laced with something else.

"This is why we match. Why the dynamic between sadist and masochist exists...where you struggled to be in control I struggled to be heard. I used to feel weak. Insignificant. I lacked an identity. This side of me, this—habit fulfills so many of my needs. I'm heard. Obeyed. Respected. Needed. Desired. I become raw just like you. I find that place where the world fades and darkness takes over and all that's left is giving and taking. I like it most because the energy we exchange is pure. Some think sex is the highest level of physical intimacy, but what we do exceeds it. It's as much mental and emotional as it is physical. And for some, emotional release is sought after more than sexual release." Leo's hand reached out and his thumb swiped under my eye. No tears remained but it was as though he was still soothing the outburst the scene had brought out in me. "I can't tell you what it does to me to see you cry when you come."

I felt a pulse between my legs and one corner of my mouth lifted. "Rather insightful of us both," I mused. "And here I thought we were just a couple of kinky fuckers."

Leo let out a laugh and rolled on top of me. A giggle slipped past my lips as he trailed kisses from my collarbone up to my ear, pulling the tender lobe between his teeth. The pinch made me moan through another breathy laugh.

"Oh, we are," he said. He dropped beside me again and pulled me to him, stroking a lazy hand up and down my spine as we breathed in unison, a weight lifted from the space between us.

I stared at his chest and slid my hand down his sternum, watching my fingers as they moved. Though I felt like a novice still, the way he spoke made me feel like I encompassed the exact thing he was looking for. "How did you know?" I started. "That first night at the store, you said you could sense my submissive side right away. How?"

His dark brows rose and his lips downturned thoughtfully. "You had a perfect mixture of assertiveness and hesitancy with me," he said, smiling as though he remembered the occasion clearly. I knew I did. "Then, you stared at my mouth when I spoke and your breathing sped up. And when I saw the wheels turning in your head the second I told you I'd punish you, I had my confirmation."

It was true, my attraction to Leo had been instant and startling. And maybe I didn't know how to quantify it then, but I supposed I'd picked up on his dominance as well. Leo had coaxed me into the blinding and beautiful light of self-awareness and now—self-acceptance. Without his telepathy that night, I might never have welcomed this decent into indefinite bliss.

"What are you thinking?" he asked, tracing a fingertip along my cheek and down my jawline.

I breathed a laugh. "It's funny you should ask that," I mused.

"Why?"

"I was just thinking how comfortable I am with you in my head."

A smile formed on his lush lips. As he smoothed a hand over the back of my head, stopping at the nape of my neck to draw me near and kiss my brow, I melted against him.

Leo insisted we get out of bed to eat and though initially, I disagreed, hoping for another bout of games, as soon as the bowl of macaroni and cheese moved in front of me, my mouth watered.

Dressed in one of Leo's old sweatshirts, I sat swinging my legs on the stool at his kitchen counter. I stabbed at the nostalgic food and took a bite, moaning when I tasted it.

"Don't start making noises like that," Leo said, "or I'll take you right back in there."

"Promise?" I said, batting my eyelashes.

He reached out to rub my back as I continued to wolf down the midnight snack. I glanced over at him and marveled at the way he watched me with such care. Every time he looked at me, I felt the weight of his emotions. Even before I understood that he wanted more than my body, I sensed his protectiveness over me.

"Are you going to eat?" I asked between bites.

"In a while."

I nodded absently and let a moment from the day linger in my mind. "You smoke," I blurted.

Leo's head dropped, his sable hair falling over his forehead. He pushed the black strands back into place and grimaced at me. "Not usually," he said. "Only when I'm under stress."

That made sense. I'd only ever seen him smoke that morning and aside from the first night we met, I'd never smelled the clove scent on him again.

"Why were you stressed today?"

He stood to make himself a bowl of macaroni and I sucked in a breath as I locked eyes with the lion on his back for the first time in full light. Leo faced the stove and the moment he spoke, I pulled my eyes from the animal to listen without distraction.

"My nephew is sick and—my sister, she's a good mother, really she is, but it's like whenever things get difficult she forgets how to function. I guess I didn't help matters by living with her for three years and helping to raise him. It's time she stood on her own. She's perfectly capable but she's used to having things done for her."

"What about the father?"

He turned and held my gaze for a beat, bouncing his eyes over my face blankly before reclaiming the seat beside me. "He's an asshole. Not even worth mentioning."

My lips scrunched up and I stared into my quickly diminishing bowl. "I know the type," I mused.

"What are your plans for tomorrow?" Leo asked, clearing the space of thoughts of unworthy men.

I stood from the bar and lifted my dish to carry it to the sink when he captured my wrist, leading me to sit again.

"I got it," he muttered. He took my bowl around the counter and rinsed it, returning to his seat.

My teeth pinched at my bottom lip when I took the quick moment to gaze at his tattoo and consider this man before me. Everything Leo did had thought behind it. He took an expert level of care with every move he made and nothing was done without purpose.

He cleared his throat and shot me a playful glance, still waiting on my answer.

"Oh, um. I have to work," I chuckled.

"What if your boss got you off for the day instead?" Leo's eyes grew sinister and his voice dipped to the smoky register that fanned flames within me.

"I really should go in for a little while," I said with a smirk. "I need to drop some books off at that coffee shop down the street that's giving us a shelf for promotion."

Leo moved to clean his dish and place it with mine in the sink then wiped his hands on a towel. He pressed his palms into the countertop where he leaned back with ease. "You're really taking this marketing thing seriously, aren't you?"

I shrugged with a slanted smile, trying not to gawk as his stomach flexed and showcased the definition of his muscles. "Yeah," I said. "I am. I want to make you guys proud and I want to help the store grow. It's nice to kind of be back in my field."

His expression faltered and he held me firm with a gaze, my stomach twisting with anticipation. "Did you used to work with him?"

My throat worked to push down the lump that arose. I doubted Leo would ever stop bringing it up until he knew everything. The only difficult part about that was I'd only ever shared the story with one other person and Bryon watched it all unfold in real time. I hadn't relayed the sordid tale to anyone after the fact. I considered how Leo might look at me once he knew the details. My stomach flipped again and I remembered the safety Leo's gaze granted me. The comfort of his arms and the freedom of his punishment. I figured it was only fair I tell him the things I felt I needed punishing for.

"Yes," I croaked.

"Is that how you met?"

"Yes."

"Do we have to play twenty questions or are you just going to tell me?"

I breathed in deeply and glanced over my shoulder. The couch looked like a better setting for this conversation. Leo picked up on my thoughts and nodded, walking toward the open living room. I followed and sat beside him on the leather couch, curling my knees up to my chest.

"He interviewed me for the job and as I was walking out to my car afterward, he followed me and told me he was going to have his partner look over my resume and the interview notes because he wanted to recuse himself…so he could ask me out. I was young and flattered and too stupid to notice how manipulative that move was. I thought it was romantic," I said. I dragged my hands through my hair and remembered I'd cut it, distracting myself from the past for a moment before sighing. "Warren was…*is* married. I'd love to tell you that I didn't know that while I was dating him—that he'd duped me into being his mistress—but I can't."

When I looked up to see Leo watching me with a furrowed brow and a storm brewing in his darkened eyes, I felt sick. My lips twisted and I avoided his face, glancing over at the large windows overlooking the woods.

"It lasted three years. Three years as a dirty little secret, having my bills paid for me as some sort of consolation prize. I fell for him because he was charming and handsome…and powerful," I muttered.

"The wrong kind of powerful," Leo spoke up.

I met his stare and pulled my bottom lip into my mouth. "Do you think differently of me?"

"No."

"I slept with another woman's husband. For three years. I asked him to leave her. I tried to break up his marriage every chance I got."

"What are you trying to convince me of? That you made a mistake? Everyone makes mistakes. But he's the person who broke a vow. He's the one who stepped away from his wife for you. And he's the one who made you think your place was second," Leo said, reaching out to me, resting his hand on my cheek. I leaned into it instinctively, loving the tenderness his bare hands bestowed on me. "You deserve to be someone's number one. You should always be number one."

"Someone's?"

A little growl coated the breath he let go of and his thumb swept over my skin. "Mine."

The word sounded thick, cloaked in possessiveness but wrapped in adoration. I swallowed hard and nodded with his hand pressed against my cheek and our eyes locked.

"Let's go back to bed," he said, standing and offering his hand. He led me out of the living room, flipping off the lights on his way and ushered me into the bedroom, still glowing amber. Silently, he stopped me at the foot of the bed and lifted the sweatshirt over my head, casting it aside, leaving me bare. We climbed under the covers together and he resumed his hold on me, snuggling right up against me. The feeling of his flesh pressed to mine comforted me in a way I couldn't comprehend. It was safety and security and intense familiarity. Much like every other feeling that traveled between us, it felt unwavering and genuine. Nothing with Leo felt coerced. His arms snaked around my waist and he breathed against the top of my head, kissing my hair absently.

"Leo…"

"Yes?"

A tidal wave of emotion knocked me senseless in an instant. Sharing with him the truth about Warren brought the shame and disgust bubbling up inside me. I felt an immense weight on my chest. Pulling back slightly, I gazed at Leo's face and fought the anchor that threatened to pull me under.

"What is it? What's wrong?" he asked.

"I don't know how to ask you…"

I thought there was a way to cure the horrible feelings within me. It started with my confession, saying the words out loud and owning them for what they were. But the second part was harder to explain. I'd come to realize in a very short time that pain greatly enhanced my pleasure, but I also believed it did more for me than that. With every twinge of physical discomfort that caused my nerves to burn and seethe, I let go. When I sighed, relieved in between blows from

Leo's palm, I released a part of myself imprisoned by disgrace. I finally felt the pain I'd smothered below the surface. When I felt his heavy hand, the weight of my sins lifted.

"You want me to hurt you," Leo said, reading my thoughts.

Clamping my lips tight, I nodded. His eyes searched my face and I thought for a moment I saw sadness and regret wash over him. But he shifted out of sight and moved off the bed without a word. I sat up, clutching the sheet to my chest, and watched as he turned to me from the dresser. His jaw tightened and he tugged on the black gloves. I silently thanked him then sat up a little straighter when he walked to his closet door, opening it wide.

On the inside of the door hung the same kind of implements I'd seen at Melanie and Gabe's house. A paddle, a flogger, a riding crop, and a cane hung in a line from little hooks drilled into the door. Leo turned to me and my mind blanked out. His sweatpants hanging low on his hips, the skin of his chest bathed in candlelight, the striking features of his face half-lit by the diffused light from the window…his black gloved hands clenched into fists at his sides—the total vision of him entranced me.

"Pick one." The smoky tone of his voice only hypnotized me further.

I pointed to the flogger and he snatched it off its hook, stomping toward me.

"On your hands and knees, face the headboard."

I did as he commanded and drew in three deep breaths, focusing hard on the pillow underneath me. My chin tilted up and my eyes fluttered shut as I felt leather fingertips delicately drag down my naked spine. His touch did things to me I didn't know were possible. His hand slapped my ass once and I held my stance without faltering, though the sting shocked me. I could hear his breathing turn erratic and I thought I heard him gulp before that sultry rasp snuck out.

"Don't forget you asked for this," he clipped.

It felt like a blitz attack of tiny razors striking me all at once, his first blow nothing if not merciless. I tried to cry out but my voice stuck in my throat and by the time he whipped the thin leather strips against my buttocks again, I choked on my breath. Another thump, then another, and eventually I inhaled a throaty gasp followed by a sob. It was painful, but with every whip, I grew more aroused. I heard the tool lashing through the air before it cracked against my flesh and I gritted my teeth, holding in every moan that threatened to emerge. My limbs shook uncontrollably as they fought to keep my body in position. I hung my head and groaned, my mouth gaping open to moan as the burn set deep into my muscles. I could barely think and the tension settling in my back, arms, and legs wasn't what I'd been waiting for. Leo grunted as he doled out one final blow and I fell forward, choking for air, my face in a pillow.

As I regained my breath, Leo climbed on top of me. I felt the fabric of his sweatpants against the raw flesh of my ass and whimpered as he tugged them down, his hard cock pressing against my thigh. With one hand, he pushed my legs apart then lined the head of his cock up with my entrance. Both gloved hands found my wrists and pinned them above my head while his breath steamed against the back of my neck. Using his nose, he prompted my head to turn and his lips found my ear.

"Never ask me to do that again," he scolded in a whisper. "Trust that I'll give you what you need when you need it. Don't think I didn't see the pain in your eyes when you told me about him. Don't think I didn't see the way your body became rigid the second I mentioned him. But you telling me what to do, you asking for things, that's not how it works."

A shuddering breath fell from my lips. He truly had read my mind. He knew the penance I sought. The reprimanding and the pressure of his front against my back, the head of his cock between my legs, completely outweighed the welt-worthy pain on my cheeks. I softened and waited for his guidance.

"This," he groaned, pushing inside and evoking a moan from me, "is what you need."

Leo slowly retreated, pulling almost completely out before slamming back inside with force. His forehead dropped to my temple and he panted against my face as he thrust deeply, filling me to the point of delirium.

"This is for your own good," he said through clenched teeth before capturing my earlobe between his lips. "Do you understand?"

It was only then that relief consumed me completely. As he took me from behind, covering me with his weight, holding me down and sucking on my earlobe, my body lost all its tension. My face relaxed and my mind chased away all inklings of shame and self-loathing. Leo pumped into me harder, unrelenting, huffing onto my neck and kissing it as I squirmed. His hands pushed my wrists deeper into the mattress as he fucked me. I felt lightheaded, my heart mended, and began to spin as Leo grunted, biting my shoulder. My head swirled and I sank into dizzying bliss, knowing I'd only ever be blessed with release once Leo took control.

SIXTEEN

THE SPRAY OF the shower trickling over my backside made me wince, reminding me of the pain I'd endured. Though Leo insisted he rub lotion onto my buttocks once the scene ended, the marks remained and every clench shot a tiny jolt up my spine. I soaped up with Leo's bar and washcloth and rinsed my hair with cool water. Wrapped in a clean towel, I entered his bedroom and smiled, catching him slipping into his boxer briefs.

After weeks of teasing, he'd had me twice. He'd filled me with every inch of him and rocked me into a sensual storm, yet his body still seemed unattainable to me. I'd never wrapped my hands around his cock. I'd never had the pleasure of letting my fingers roam the surface of his skin freely. Someday, I hoped he would allow me the privilege of touching him as I pleased. But after what transpired between us last night, I knew he would be the one deciding where my hands went.

His hair still damp from the shower as well, Leo shot me a slanted grin as he pulled on gray slacks. "You sure we should go to work?" he asked.

I laughed and rolled my eyes, looking around the room for my bra and panties. I found my underwear and tugged them on, still holding the towel around my body, but couldn't find my bra anywhere. Leo cleared his throat and I looked up from where I'd crouched next to the bed, hoping to find it hiding under furniture. With a soft smile, he held out the lacey bra to me on one finger. I reached for it and he drew his arm back teasingly. My lips smashed together in a line, smothering the irritated smile he'd become rather good at producing.

"You want this back?" he asked smugly. "Gotta pay the toll."

Narrowing my eyes on him, I understood the moment he gestured to my towel. Butterflies invaded my belly and without a second thought, I dropped the soft terry cloth from my body and watched his blue gaze darken. He didn't move to touch me. He didn't toss me on the bed or bind my hands above my head. He strutted toward me and offered the piece of lingerie just as easily as I accepted it. His mouth fought against a smile when he turned his back to me and I bit my lip at the sight of his tattoo.

"When did you get your tattoo?"

Leo looked over his shoulder at me as he entered his closet. "About four years ago."

Part of me wanted to ask him about the significance, but I knew I didn't need to. I was beginning to understand the many sides of him and the fierce yet soft gaze of the beast told me everything I already knew. That Leo was as proud and noble as the image he wore. Strong, authoritative…and lionhearted.

I found my jeans from the day before folded on the dresser and knew it must've been Leo's doing. I pulled them on, cringed, then sighed, wondering how I'd get away with wearing the same thing two days in a row without eliciting a few snickers from Oliver and Wendy. I ducked out of the room to find my purse with my coat where Leo had hung it and went back to his dresser, facing the mirror above it. I popped one pale blue pill into my mouth from the oval compact and swallowed it dry then dug for my lipstick. It wasn't much but it would have to suffice. Leo reappeared and I watched him walk up behind me through the mirror. He set a shirt on top of the dresser and took hold of my hips, turning me gently.

Leo leaned into my space, pressing his hands against the dresser. "My sister left a few things here once. It might be a little big on you but it's better than swimming in one of my shirts," he said.

I glanced over at it and smiled softly. Before my eyes swept over to him, I caught a glimpse of the gloves lying near the shirt. They looked so innocent without his hands filling them. Leo followed my eyes to the gloves and then we looked at each other. I didn't dare ask him to wear them, not after last night. I sucked in a small breath when he slowly reached out for them, putting them on. With my sore ass butted up against the wooden dresser, I breathed heavily in anticipation. To my amazement, Leo picked up the tube of lipstick I'd pulled from my purse. He removed the cap and twisted it up to see the shade. His brow rose and one hand gripped my chin while the other painted my lips for me. The intensity with which he watched the creamy lipstick coat my mouth sent a shudder rolling through my body. My mouth hung open after he'd finished and smirked devilishly, looking over his work. Slowly, he sank to his knees with the lipstick still in hand and unbuttoned my jeans, tugging them down just a little.

I shivered again when he looked up. Though kneeled before me, I still recognized his authority and offered myself to him to do as he wished. I watched as he Leo brought the burgundy lipstick to the skin just above my panties, drawing a single word. My breath ragged and my core tingling, I lit up the second he stood. He turned me around to look at myself in the mirror and though it was backwards, I read his handwriting along my flesh and gloried at the branding. *Mine.* His. His number one. The four-letter word thrilled me and I couldn't keep the sexy grin off my rouged lips. We locked eyes in the mirror and he simply handed me the shirt he'd brought out.

"Get dressed," he commanded. "I'll warm the car up."

With that, he removed the gloves and returned them to their resting place and left me quivering in his bedroom, stunned by the unexpected scene.

Stealing glances at Leo across the store all day made for a permanent blush on my cheeks that Wendy was snarky enough to point out. By mid-afternoon, I'd gathered up a box of books to take over to Ethan at the coffee shop. A handful of bestselling titles mixed with a few books on local history, some kids books and a couple thick art collections were tightly packed into the old paper box I'd found in the office.

Oliver came around the corner with a bottle of furniture polish and a rag. "What's all that?" he asked, gesturing toward the box.

"These are the books I'm taking over to Black and Brew. The manager told me he'd clear shelf space and keep track of sales for us. I think it's a really nice fit, working with them. What goes together better than coffee and books?"

A slanted smile morphed his face and he nodded absently. "I can't tell you how much I appreciate your help. Is everything all pulled together for the festival?"

"Yep! I have all the books I think we should take with us already pulled. I have table decorations, flyers for the Black Friday sale, and coupons for the first twenty-five people at the table."

"You are phenomenal," Oliver exclaimed.

"Just doing my job," I said. "Do you know where I can find Leo?"

His grin turned knowing and I blushed again. "I think he's upstairs."

I thanked Oliver and made my way up the metal staircase to the room Leo where had first inaugurated me as his sub. The door creaked open and I saw Leo standing at the table that held a few memories. He picked up a book from the strewn about mess and squinted at the title before lifting his eyes to meet mine. Expecting a sultry brood, I melted at the boyish expression he wore, beaming a genuine full grin at me.

"Hi," he crooned.

"Hey." The trembling breath behind my voice was one I'd no longer be embarrassed by. Leo's effect on me was evident in every moment we shared and I wouldn't try to hide it any longer. "I'm going to head down to the coffee shop. You want to walk with me?"

As if it were possible, his lips split wider and his eyes set alight. "Always," he said, dropping the book back on the table.

I led the way downstairs and the moment we were out the front door, Leo carrying the box of books easily under one arm, he slipped his hand in mine. Brisk air rushed over my cheeks and I felt autumn finally breeze through Salem.

"Are you okay?" Leo asked quietly.

I turned and caught his eyes from the side, his handsome profile distracting my mind for a moment. "Yeah," I said. "Why?"

"Last night. It was a lot to take in. If it was that serious for me, I can only imagine how you feel."

My bottom lip tucked into my mouth as he squeezed his hand around mine. I'd never considered the fact that a scene might be intense for Leo. I realized I'd never considered how it affected him at all. We approached Black and Brew just as my thoughts formed properly and when I opened my mouth to ask what he meant, I heard Leo's cell phone buzzing in his coat pocket. He let go of my hand to dig for it then huffed.

"Hang on, sorry. It's Marie."

"Sure, yeah. You've got to take it," I said fumbling to take the book box from him as he grimaced. "I'll meet you inside."

His face contorted and he nodded before answering. I left him on the sidewalk outside the shop and pushed through the door using my back. I found the shelf Ethan had promised to clear and set the box on the floor near it. Ethan came into view just as Leo entered through the front door.

"Hey, Sloane! You changed your hair. I like it," Ethan said with a cheery grin.

I smiled at him and felt a hand touch my lower back when my greeting rolled out. I nearly faltered, catching the scent of Leo hovering behind me. "Yeah, hey," I said. "Is it okay if we start shelving these books?" I hooked my thumb over my shoulder at the display.

"Totally," Ethan said. His eyes drifted over my shoulder and offered a weak smile to Leo. "Hey, man. You work at Calloway Books too?"

I heard a scornful noise build in his throat and shot him a glare as he reached for Ethan's hand contemptuously. "I'm the owner," he pressed.

His tone reminded me of the red signature he'd scrawled on me earlier and I suddenly felt aware of how the makeup made my jeans stick to my skin.

"Cool," Ethan said, letting go of Leo's firm hand. His lips pulled up in a tight smile and he glanced at me. "I'll be behind the counter if you guys need anything."

I forced a little smile and turned to Leo the second Ethan walked away. "What was that?" I asked, attempting to keep the irritation out of my voice.

Leo smirked and started unloading the books. "What was what?"

I rolled my eyes and helped him arrange the display using the bookstands I'd brought. "Is everything all right with your sister?"

"Yeah, she wanted to give me an update. His fever is gone and he's coughing less."

I placed the last book on a stand, facing outward, and smiled at him. "That's good," I said. "It's really sweet how much you help her. I bet your nephew just adores you."

The absent smile that claimed his mouth was heartwarming as he clearly thought of his nephew. "Barry's great. You'd like him."

"His name is Barry?" I asked, my mouth falling open. "Oh, that's so cute!"

Leo chuckled and picked up the empty box. He took my hand and began walking me out the door. I stuttered some kind of protest and looked over my shoulder to find Ethan. I wanted to thank him again, but Leo's grasp on my hand kept my feet moving and when I didn't see him behind the counter I pushed the thought away, letting Leo lead me.

Heading back in the direction of the bookstore, Leo kept his fingers laced with mine. He cleared his throat and my skin prickled with goosebumps, waiting for his voice to ring out on the air as though I could sense it coming.

"Would you want to meet him?"

"What? Who?"

He shot me a sidelong glance and his face fell serious. "Barry. And Marie. They're coming for the Fall Festival. My parents are, too. I was thinking...I could introduce you to everyone."

"You want me to meet your parents?" I asked breathlessly.

Instead of answering me, as we reached the front of the bookstore, he squeezed my hand tightly and pressed a kiss to my temple before opening the door for me. The ache in my chest swelled and subsided in the same moment watching a nearly undetectable tender smile twitch on his lips.

Leo drove me home after work and I felt déjà vu as he pulled into my apartment complex. My mouth took charge, inviting him in without my full permission. He smirked as though he knew the effect he had on me and followed me into the kitchen.

"You hungry?" I asked.

"Sure. You cook?"

I laughed. "I'm decent. I'll see if I can come up with something to compete with your mac and cheese."

He took the opportunity to nose around my living room while I watched from the little cut out window above my sink. Washing my hands, I followed him around the room with my eyes, pulling in a breath when he stopped in front of the photograph sitting on my windowsill. I watched his brows dip together in the center as he reached out to pick up the frame, frowning. It was the last family photo in which my family was still intact. He turned and caught me staring at him and I quickly averted my eyes, moving to preheat the oven. I grabbed the ingredients I needed from the refrigerator and my cabinets and starting prepping a lasagna with my eyes down.

As water boiled and the ground beef sizzled, browning in the pan on the stove, I heard him clear his throat behind me. I turned and saw him leaning against the kitchen doorway.

"Was it insensitive of me," he started. "To ask you to meet my parents considering..."

"Considering I have none for you to meet?" I finished his thought with a snap that surprised us both. "Sorry," I muttered. I wiped my hands on a towel and folded my arms across my chest, leaning back on the counter to stare at him. "No. It wasn't insensitive. I know you didn't mean anything by it. Family is a tough one for me. And it's not just that, it's—I'm still feeling a little off balance here. What we are. What we're doing. This...whatever you want to call it—"

"Relationship."

I sighed and continued. "This *relationship* is still really new. I like it, I like you, I like...us. But...."

He strode toward me, concern painting his face, and picked up the wooden spoon sitting on the trivet and began stirring the browning meat for me. I busied my hands by mixing the other ingredients, hoping silence wouldn't plague us the rest of the night. I glanced at him as my insides coiled tightly. He never stopped pushing the meat around the pan. He kept his eyes down and sighed.

"I get the feeling you think you're the only one off balance. Sloane, I don't know what the hell I'm doing. I've waited for my opportunity to have a person like you in my life—someone I can be myself with inside and outside the bedroom. And yet, I'm lost. I could've easily asked you out—made it clear that I wanted something different in the beginning. But instead, I played the game I know how to play. The one I'm good at. I could've given you my phone number but I gave you my medical records. I wanted to know things about you but instead of asking, I held an interrogation scene. I invited you to Gabe's house mostly so I could have a meal beside you. I sometimes feel like I'm just a timid young man alongside you—pretending to be in control, pretending to be more. I'm drawn to you in way that makes me feel as though I'm the one on my knees. I think I was made to be your Dom, Sloane. But I want to be more. I just don't know what it takes. I'll be anyone you need me to be. Just show me how."

I reached out and stopped his hand from stirring the food. He looked at me, then dropped the wooden spoon and faced me fully as I kept his hand in mine, surprised by his sudden honesty. It was possibly the most normal moment we'd ever shared. That moment between a couple when they admit they're scared and being scared can only mean one thing. They care. Deeply.

"You don't need to be anyone but who you are. You're not pretending. Just be," I breathed, reaching out to touch his face. "Just be with me and I'll be with you."

Leo leaned into my touch and shut his eyes. I didn't realize how much comfort I'd get from seeing him like that. Soft and vulnerable. A moment passed and Leo let a soft smile touch his lips before turning to press a kiss on my palm.

"What else do you need help with here?"

I swallowed and dropped my hand from his face, turning toward the stove. He was so good at taking the perfect opportunity to delve deeper into us and changing the subject as though he only had enough energy to express one thought at a time.

I asked him to grab the pasta sauce while I drained the noodles. Each time I asked for assistance, he was there, tending to my request. He opened a bottle of wine while I carefully spread the layers of ingredients in a glass dish. I slid the lasagna into the oven and set the timer just as Leo offered me a glass of Cabernet, ticking his head to one side, gesturing for the sofa.

We sat together as we had after the party and I remembered what I'd felt that night. I could've laughed thinking about the way we'd both been so blind to each other's intentions.

Leo's free hand reached out, his delicate fingers trailing down the back of my neck. He let out a throaty sigh. "I really love your hair like that," he said.

I grinned. "I can tell."

"I haven't told you enough how beautiful you are."

My chest burned with the kind of lovely ache I'd always wanted to feel. His voice had a way of enthralling me and coupled with his gentle touch—the one I rarely expected—I was lost to him. There was time for him to call me beautiful. Time for him to touch me and kiss me and leave marks on my body for days. Time for us to have the conversations we needed to have—slow and steady. One at a time. I hadn't planned on Leo and I doubted he'd planned on me but suddenly, as I stared into his eyes over the rim of my wine glass, watching the way he carefully examined my every inch, I knew I couldn't walk away.

"Do you ever talk about them?"

His question pulled me from the starry-eyed soliloquy waltzing through my head and my brow furrowed.

"Who?"

"Your parents."

I inhaled through my nose and took a quick sip of wine. It wasn't a topic I usually sought out, but I didn't dread telling Leo about my family the way I did with others.

"Not often, but of course I talk about them. What would you like to know?"

His face fell—crumpled into a darkened state. His silence brought a sigh from me and I reached out to take his hand. Suddenly, everything felt easier with Leo. As if his honesty after the savagery of our play had somehow balanced him in my eyes. It balanced us.

"I was fifteen." Leo squeezed my hand. "They were going out for my mom's birthday. Dad got her a limo and they were headed to pick up some of their friends. Semi driver fell asleep at the wheel." I swallowed and shrugged when tears sprang to my eyes unexpectedly.

"I'm so sorry."

I forced a pained smile and Leo took my glass of wine, setting it on the coffee table alongside his. He pulled me close to him, clutching my face between his hands so our eyes locked.

"You've been strong for a long time, haven't you?"

My chin trembled. He wasn't really asking me the question. He knew the answer, just like he knew every part of me. I still didn't understand how, but I didn't care. I allowed him inside, where he searched my soul and traced the seams where I'd once been broken. Once again, a storm of uncertainty rolled into my heart. He was memorizing my pieces, figuring out exactly how I was put together but I still had so little understanding of how he was arranged inside.

"How do you do that, Leo?" I asked.

His eyes narrowed. "Do what?"

"I can see you making sense of me in your head. How do you do it?"

His thumb brushed over the apple of my cheek and he stared at my lips. "You let me."

Sadness coated his response and before I could beg an explanation from him, he guided me back on the sofa, propping me against the arm, leaving my hips lifted by throw pillows. His hand traveled down my body slowly and popped the button of my jeans open.

I gasped. His eyes remained on mine as he dragged the zipper down and pulled the fabric apart. I swallowed hard and remembered the word he'd written just above my sex.

"What are you doing?"

He stared at the word on my belly.

"I wrote this because I want to call you mine," he whispered before looking up at me. "But all the insight into you in the world—your thoughts, emotions, your past, even the little things like how you drink your coffee and the way you scrape your bottom lip when you're feeling anxious …everything you've ever let me read about you through your eyes, through your touch, and through the wordless exchanges that say the most, none of that knowledge says you belong to me. You know that, right? I don't think I own you. You don't belong to me."

When he'd inscribed my skin with the word, I hadn't felt a loss of independence. I thought it was sexy. Erotic. It was foreplay to a later game in which I'd hand myself over to him. But it was clear that Leo felt some sort of regret. The same way he'd alluded to feeling our other scene seriously, I could see in his eyes he was struggling with what he'd done before we left for work.

Butterflies filled my stomach. I glanced down at the smudged lipstick across my abdomen and remembered how it had made me feel that morning. I remembered how Leo had always made me feel. Even when I felt confused by him, I wanted him. I trusted him. No one had ever made me feel as good as Leo. Even with his authority lorded over me and the way he infiltrated my mind, I felt strong and capable. Beautiful and wanted. Warren no longer laced himself intricately in my desires for punishment and my life finally felt like a new chapter, completely clear of him.

I held him with my gaze as firmly as he usually held me. "What if I choose to belong to you?"

SEVENTEEN

ONE HAND TRACED over my knee and slowly slipped between my thighs. Even through the fabric of my panties, his touch demanded a response. I turned to meet his eyes where he sat beside me in the red leather booth. Leo licked his lips and the darkened stare he wore was enough to trip the switch of my orgasm. He'd trained me to crave his looks alone.

"We're in public," I breathed in weak protest as he started to rub me through silk.

He grinned. "I know. Isn't it fun? Why do you think I told you to wear a dress? Now, be a good girl and keep quiet."

I let out a pant and my eyes darted around Richie's Pizza Place. I met one smiling pair near the door and pushed Leo's hand away. "They're here," I said, gulping as I straightened my skirt when I stood.

Bryon and Craig made their way over to us and I heard Leo chuckle at my back.

"Hi, sweetie," Bryon said, hugging me. I stumbled through a greeting and he eyed me. I didn't pay his look any attention and reached for Craig, pulling him to me.

"Craig, it's so good to see you!"

He squeezed me then held onto my arms as he looked me over. "Love your hair like that," he said.

I grinned and tongued the back of my teeth before stepping aside to offer introductions. "Bryon, Craig, this is Leo."

Leo stepped forward and my face paled as he shook each of their hands firmly with the same hand he'd just used to torment me under the table we were about to share a meal over. The four of us sat down and Leo's hand returned to my thigh, under my dress, and dangerously close to my panties. When I caught his eyes, he merely winked.

"Thanks for driving all this way, you two."

Craig smiled. "Thanks for inviting us! We needed an adult night out. I would've driven to Ohio."

Leo chuckled. "You two have a daughter, right? How old?"

Craig whipped out his phone, eyes sparkling, and held out a picture of Elizabeth to Leo across the table. "She's ten months. Elizabeth Sloane."

My heart sank and my mouth dropped as I looked at Bryon. "What? You never told me that."

He smiled and shrugged. Leo's hand rose from under the table to smooth sweetly over my hair as I melted; the darling child was also my namesake.

"Oh, she's adorable," Leo said, staring at the photo on Craig's screen. "My belated congratulations."

"Thank you, Leo. She is pretty spectacular," Craig said, mooning over his own photo for a beat before putting his phone away.

Bryon met my eyes again and a knowing look passed between us. I continued to tread lightly with Leo, but it was easy to see he was the opposite of Warren—a fact only my best friend would be able to validate for me. And he had with a simple smile. The four of us filled the space with small talk before we ordered and the conversation flowed effortlessly as we took our first bites.

"Okay, I owe you five bucks," Bryon said with a laugh just moments after the food arrived. "That's the best pizza of my life."

Leo chuckled and took another slice from the tray in the middle of the table. "I wasn't kidding."

"I love that they have a real jukebox here," Craig commented, nodding toward the machine near our booth. "Not one of those crappy digital ones with the advertisements flashing all over the screen. This place is classic."

"Right!? Isn't it cool?" I chimed in, shooting Leo a wink for his perfect choice of date locale.

"Why don't you go play something?" Bryon said, pulling change from his pocket. Leo did the same and between the two of them, they had five quarters. Craig's mouth upturned as he looked at me expectantly.

Leo nudged me and his firm stare coupled with his soft mouth held my attention before I moved to stand. "Remember my rule?"

A tempting shiver claimed me. He had so many rules and yet I remembered every single one. Batting my eyelashes, I stood. "Yes," I said then leaned in close to whisper, "But where's the fun in rules?"

I followed Craig to the jukebox and he was happy to help me tease Leo. We combined our quarters and played five of the most popular songs from the *Footloose* soundtrack. When we made our way back to the table, snickering, I felt a wave of contentment consume me. I couldn't recall a time I'd felt more free and at ease with friends. Cozying into the booth beside Leo again, I tentatively touched his hand where it rested on the red leather seat and held my breath when he locked eyes on me.

"Thanks for doing this," I said quietly as Craig scooted into the other side with Bryon. Leo's brows knit together then he tugged my hand into his lap, placing it on his thigh possessively.

"Of course."

A few minutes later, the first few notes of the title track from the soundtrack blared and Craig burst out laughing the moment Leo's gentle gaze morphed into a scowl. I plastered a grin on and watched him crack, sliding his tongue over his teeth behind closed lips as a smile threatened his stoned expression. Bryon chuckled and shook his head as Craig explained our mischief.

"Cute," Leo said, letting the smirk slant his mouth. But the look simmering behind his blue eyes told me I'd pay for my bratty ways and the thought had me on the verge of squirming for the rest of dinner.

After dinner, Bryon and Craig had requested to see where Leo and I worked and they followed us to the store. It was after hours but Leo unlocked the front door and flipped on the lights, offering a tour to a very interested Craig. I heard him telling the story of when his grandfather had first bought the store, but my attention flicked to Bryon when he put a soft hand against the small of my back. I turned and smiled at him.

"This was fun," he said.

"It really was," I replied. "Why haven't we ever…" I started to ask the question just as the answer flashed in my mind. Bryon's tight, solemn smile told me he'd thought the same thing. We'd never had the chance to have a fun double date before because of all my bullshit with Warren.

"I like him," Bryon said.

My bottom lip tucked into my mouth and my eyes trained on the floor. "Me too."

He lifted my chin with a gentle hand and narrowed his gaze. "It's not a bad thing, Sloane. You can like him. You can...more than like him," he pressed.

I forced a smile and only nodded as Craig and Leo approached, Craig with an arm full of children's books. Bryon rolled his eyes when he saw the haul his husband had. "She won't be able to read for a few years."

Craig made a face. "Not with that attitude. We're buying them. We should be reading to her more."

I saw Leo holding in a chuckle then he waived his hand. "Consider them a gift. From me and Sloane for Elizabeth."

The twinge that struck my heart was half sweetness and half discomfort. It was the kind of clashing sensation Leo was so well versed in giving me. Craig and Bryon protested but Leo insisted. He bagged up the books and as we said our goodbyes, Bryon squeezed me tightly, whispering in my ear, "Don't hold back, remember?"

"Good night, guys," Leo said. "Drive safe."

One last look at my friends as they headed out the door and a deep breath filled my lungs. The evening had been a new experience for Leo and me, and just like everything else, the comprehension of it brought forth conflicting thoughts. As it turned out, we were sort of good at the couple thing. But something was still holding me back. Something unnamable lingered in my heart and I didn't know how I'd remove it.

A hot kiss planted on the curve of my neck and I shut my eyes, all of my concerns disintegrating when Leo's tongue dragged a line up to my ear.

His steamy breath tickled my lobe as he spoke. "You whined. Pushed my hand away. And you spent my quarters on Kenny Loggins."

A sigh rushed out of my lungs. "I'm sorry, Sir," I said with a grin on my slackened lips.

"You were a bad girl. And I want to do bad things to bad girls."

I moaned as his leather sheathed hands settled on my bare forearms. "Get your ass upstairs. Now," he growled before swatting my butt through my dress. I jumped and giggled, hustling up the stairs, knowing he was quick on my heels. I spun around, the fabric of my dress twirling as I locked eyes on him stalking toward me, cornering me in the room that had started it all. His smoldering eyes dragged up and down my body and in a few swift moments, I dropped my dress to the floor. I couldn't keep the smile off my mouth as Leo lunged for me, grabbing me by the throat and easing me onto the wood floor. Feeling the cool wood against my back, I sighed and waited for his command. I gasped as he unbuckled and whipped his belt from its loops. My body slackened at his rough touch as he caught the belt behind one knee and around my elbow, linking my two right limbs together. He fixed the belt in place and gripped the long end for leverage, pulling my legs apart.

"Hold your panties to the side," he said. "Show me how wet being bad makes you."

I did as I was told, breathless and still grinning dreamily. Leo groaned at the sight of my slick, reddened flesh and I wondered if he could see me pulsing with anticipation. He undid his jeans and shoved them down along with his boxer briefs only far enough to free his cock. Holding onto the belt with one hand and finding my hip with the other, he flipped me onto my stomach and returned his strong grip on the belt. With a sturdy tug, he spread me apart and made sure I knew I was half bound and completely under his rule. His body covered mine from behind and his free hand shoved my panties off to one side again as he drove his cock into me. A deep moan fell from my lips and my head dropped to the floor as he thrust powerfully.

"Are you bad, Sloane?" he huffed against my shoulder.

"Yes, Sir."

"Tell me how bad you are."

The leather belt cinching my leg to my arm tightened every time he pushed inside me. I sighed and loosened further, relishing the intensification of his thrusts—the force behind his fucking. "I'm a bad girl, Sir. I've been thinking about this all day," I moaned.

"What, you've been thinking about being my little fuck doll?"

The vulgar name rippled delicious chills up my spine and I clamped down on my lip. "Mmm hmm."

"Say it," he growled.

"I'm your naughty little fuck doll, Sir."

Leo puffed a faint sigh against my cheek and I could feel him smiling. His thrusts quickened. He never lost grip on the belt that held me as he fucked me harder. A quick, hard slap against my ass brought forth a broken a moan. Deep grunts syncopated with every buck and as I felt myself begin to quiver, Leo's gloved hand grasped my face sternly, turning my head. Our lustful gazes collided, his forehead wrought with tension and his teeth gritted.

"Say you're mine," he breathed. The tone wasn't that of the lion pounding me into the floor. It was the voice of the man who'd held my hand walking through a darkened parking lot hours before. My heartbeat faltered and my eyelids fluttered; the beginnings of the spinning affliction upon me as he drove deeper inside.

"I'm yours," I whispered.

Still gripping my face, he claimed my mouth with a rough kiss as he came and sparks crackled in my veins. He slowed, but didn't stop, letting go of my face to stroke my clit. It only took a moment of his deliberate caresses and I shattered under his hands, shaking and eventually wilting against the floor. As ecstasy and sweat flashed over my skin, I felt his lips at my ear.

"Mine," he panted. "Thank you."

EIGHTEEN

MY CHEEKS BURNED and my palms sweat as my new psychiatrist's retort echoed in my mind. Dr. Keith's expression looked more challenging than questioning as she held her pencil to the pad of paper on her lap.

Did I think my relationship with Leo was healthy?

From the very start, it'd been unconventional. Leo even labeled it as such, but that didn't mean it was unhealthy. We'd vaguely talked about my feelings of shame surrounding Warren. I'd never felt pressured by Leo to engage in any play we'd explored. I didn't feel controlled outside of our sex life and I didn't regret a single thing we'd done. And yet, there was something still brewing below the surface. My feelings for Leo were almost too intense—too wrapped up in the sway he had over my body and the window he had into my mind. One look from him left me quivering. His smoky voice held me spellbound and delirious. And his touch—rough or gentle, bound or freed—possessed me like nothing else in this world.

"I'm not sure," I croaked.

"Why not?"

I gulped. "I don't know. I don't know if it's him or me but…it's like as much as I want it to just be as good as it seems, there's a shadow between us. Something holding me back."

"Holding you back from what?"

The sound of my blood trudging through my veins swarmed my head as I breathed deeply. "From falling completely in love with him." I whispered the word I'd never said aloud in reference to Leo.

"Do you think it's lingering feelings for your ex?"

My brow furrowed and I glanced out the window on to my right, watching a massive tree blow wildly in the wind. "No."

"Lack of control?"

I scoffed and shook my head. "No."

Unstable and moved in every direction, yet rooted deep in the soil with little to no chance of crashing to the ground, I was that tree and Leo was the wind. He led as we danced and just when I thought I'd break from the bend, he'd steady me. Just as I'd imagined, his power had transformed me. Shedding my leaves, he left me no weaker, only bare.

"Do you trust Leo?"

I unglued my eyes from the captivating tree and fixed them back on Dr. Keith. "Yes. I trust him."

"Sloane, I'm hearing apprehension, but I can't figure out what it's linked to. It sounds like the intimacy between you two is strong. Extreme, albeit unorthodox. The fact that you opened up to him the way you have is impressive in terms of communication among partners. Sloane…are you sure you haven't already fallen in love with him and the shadow you're talking about isn't your anxiety holding you back from admitting that?"

Tension racked my face, my jaw, and in between my shoulder blades. The same pain I used to feel when waking up from my stressful nightmares seemed to ripple through me, reclaiming its position the instant she made the suggestion. I cinched my bottom lip between my teeth and glared at Dr. Keith. Her face fell and she jotted something on her paper before offering me a pained smile.

"I'm sorry, Sloane. Our time is up. If you talk to my secretary on your way out she can schedule your next appointment," she said. "I think it's important you come back so we can continue this."

I blinked away tears and nodded, pursing my lips as she stood to usher me out of her office. As soon as her door closed, I bypassed the secretary and headed straight for the elevator. Pressing my back against the wall as it lowered me to the ground floor, I felt my chest heave. I filled my lungs with air, held it while I shut my eyes, then exhaled. With the release, I felt the tension in my body melt.

I needed to see him.

Our last night together had been unlike any other night we'd shared after our scene at the store. Leo took me home and held me in his arms in my bed as the lullaby of his heartbeat rocked me to sleep. Nothing more. The potency of our energy exchange left me drained and yet filled with a passion I'd never known possible. I was still coming down. The following morning, I woke to find a note from him and a pot of coffee already brewed and waiting for me. He had to go into the store and it was my day off. Waking up alone felt strange. Waking up to the scent of him on my pillows felt heartbreakingly precious. It was then that I knew I was in trouble. That I did belong to him.

I'd called Bryon, hopeful he would be able to analyze me enough to help me. God love him, he told me I needed a shrink. At first, I laughed, but by the time we'd hung up, I was frantically scrolling through internet listings of psychiatrists in the area. Dr. Keith was able to get in me the following day early in the morning—before my shift at the store.

Stunned by the revelation and still angst-ridden about what it all meant for the future, I exited the elevator in a fog and drove to the bookstore, sure that seeing Leo's face would put it all into perspective.

I parked my car, glancing at my eyes in the rearview mirror. What had I been so afraid of all this time? Leo pushed me to new heights. He imposed a new sense of self in me. I'd stopped painting myself with a scarlet A and began remembering what it was like to love myself. I'd tossed that manuscript full of dark memories and sickening guilt out, turning the page on the past. It was a prologue at best.

Another breath flowed in and out of me, lessening the last bit of stress in my lungs, and I headed inside. The bell rang above the door and I searched the space for Leo. My brow furrowed when I noticed no one sitting at the front desk and the door to the closed office. The store looked abandoned and I was about to call out, when I heard a giggle.

The sound came from the children's section where two bean bag chairs and a small table and stools had always sat for kids to lounge in. I took one step then paused. Leo descended the stairs and when he saw me, he grinned. His teeth stamped his bottom lip quickly then he drew a finger to his lips.

"Ready or not, here I come," he hollered.

Another tiny laugh snuck out from the children's section and I watched as Leo tiptoed his way over, glancing back at me every few steps with a wide smile. I swallowed thickly and took in yet another facet of him. Leo snatched up the red bean bag chair and a squeal rang out as he dropped to the floor, laughing like I'd never heard before. I could only see the top of Leo's hair, the rest of him hidden behind the small table.

"Gotcha!"

"Wonkle Leeee-ooo," the tiny voice whined through a fit of giggles.

My heart seized in my chest when Leo lifted his eyes, catching mine as his face barely peeked out from above the kids' seating area. His beaming smile and mussed hair captivated me in a brand new way. Leo drew in a deep breath that seemed to brace him as he looked back down.

"Hey, buddy, wanna meet my friend?"

Just like always, Leo had seen consent in my eyes. I didn't want to hold back any longer. I didn't want to be afraid of moving forward with him. I wanted to shine light on the shadow and allow myself to fall. Leo rose and when he looked at me, his brow lifted barely—an attempt at asking me if it was okay. I smiled and nodded as he came around the kids' table. Glancing down to the boy whose hand Leo was holding, I resisted the urge to sigh. Cherubic cheeks and a mop of chocolatey curls on his head, Barry was as cute as I'd imagined.

"Barry, this is Sloane," Leo said.

I instantly crouched down to his level and smiled. "Hi, Barry. It's really nice to meet you."

Doe eyes matching the color of his hair widened and met mine as a shy, crooked grin formed on his lips. "Hi."

He barely resembled Leo but parts of him looked so familiar to me, it made my heart ache. The shadow all but vanished when the thought of a child that looked a little like Leo and a little like me chased through my mind. Slowly, I stood, facing the man with whom I'd just envisioned having a baby.

The softness in Leo's gaze struck me and I melted under his touch as he reached out, cupping my shoulder and drawing me near. He pressed a kiss to my cheek and I shut my eyes in an effort to feel it deeper in my heart.

"I hope this is okay," he said against my ear.

I hummed a response and knew he understood my concerns had faded. There was nothing to fear with Leo. Holding back from something this good, someone this amazing, was idiotic. Every step on the next rung of the ladder had been a faltering one for me. I tripped every time Leo changed the script on me. But this time I needed to let go and know that I wouldn't plummet to some terrifying place, I'd fall into the most wonderful spin of my life.

"Bear? We gotta go, buddy." A woman's voice caught all of our attention and we collectively turned to where it had come from. In the doorway of the office stood a petite young woman with long dark hair and Leo's same stunning blue eyes. Though fatigue seemed set in them, she was beautiful. She walked toward us and I mustered a weak smile. "Hi," she said tentatively.

"Mommy, that's Miss Sloane," Barry said in his little mouse voice.

I peeked down at him and grinned, earning a bashful look.

"Oh," his mother said, drawing the word out, forming her lips in circle as her eyes lit up. "You're Sloane." She glanced at her brother then extended a hand to me. "I'm Marie. Leo and Oliver have told me a lot about you. It's great to finally meet you."

I pulled in a sharp breath and took her hand. I knew the ferocity with which my sister and I both cared for each other and I could only imagine what Marie was thinking as she looked at me. What all had Leo told her? He'd always been three steps ahead of me after all.

Marie's eyes flicked to Leo's, a silent exchange about something of which I wasn't privy.

"Did you get ahold of him?"

She pursed her lips and shook her head. "It's fine."

Leo huffed and dug for his wallet, pulling out a twenty and handing it over to her. Marie stared at it for a second. I was sure my presence didn't help the awkward negotiation.

"He's going to need lunch, Marie," Leo grumbled. "And Mom and Dad won't be here until late tonight."

Marie's jaw stiffened and she glanced down at her son then back at her brother before snatching the bill from his fingers. I saw Leo's brows lift slightly, directed at her, and she let go of a sigh.

"Thank you."

"You're welcome."

Leo dropped down into a crouch beside Barry and the tension on his forehead vanished as a smile covered his face. "I'll see you tomorrow at the park for the festival," he said, ruffling a hand through Barry's brown curls. "I heard there's going to be a petting zoo and carnival games. And lots of cotton candy."

Barry put on a crooked smile and peeked up at me again. "Will Miss Sloane be there?"

Leo tossed his head back with a laugh then looked down his nose at his nephew. "You little flirt," he said. "Ask her yourself, Romeo."

I laughed and nodded when Barry stared up at me. "I'll be there," I assured him.

Leo shook his head, chuckling at the way Barry eyed me. I glanced at Marie and saw her zoned out, staring at a spot on the floor in front of her. Leo cleared his throat and her head snapped up.

"Okay, bud, time to go," she said. She reached for her purse behind the register as Leo grabbed Barry's jacket from the coat rack and helped him put it on, zipping it all the way up to his chin. Leo held out his hand and Barry slapped it once before holding his hand out for Leo to slap.

"Peace out, bean sprout," Leo said.

"Bye, broccoli head," Barry retorted.

Laughter bubbled past my lips and I lifted my hand to cover my mouth. Leo shook his head and waved as Marie took Barry's hand and led him out to the car. As the door shut and sound of the bell dissipated within the store, we both stood staring out the window at them.

"Do you want children?" he asked.

"What?"

"I mean...eventually."

"I, um—" My brain and mouth fought each other, cancelling out one another as I struggled to reply.

It was all I'd ever wanted, but I'd denied any fantasy of that future so many times I had to remind myself of the truth. "Yeah. Someday."

Leo turned to me. "I never considered it until I moved in with them. Those few years helping her made me realize I'd like to be a father. Someday."

I swallowed hard and kept my eyes on the sweet curve of his lips. "You're great with him."

He smiled wistfully as he looked out the window once more, watching Marie pull out of the parking space in front of the store.

"I missed waking up beside you."

The change in Leo's tone sent a shiver down my spine and set a dreamy grin on my lips. We turned simultaneously and I watched his brows dip down, knitting together in the center as he took two steps toward me.

"Are you okay?"

I love you.

I didn't say it, but my mouth fell open and my eyes widened as though I had. Leo smiled and ducked his head closer to me. Staring up at his eyes and the sooty rim around them from his thick lashes, I felt heat rush through my body. My heart seemed to pause while he scanned my face, trying to read me, and my skin puckered with goosebumps when his hands found my waist.

"Cat got your tongue?" he asked, cocking one brow. Since the second I met him, I noticed the way sex permeated off of Leo. It radiated out of every fiber of him, setting the world around him a little brighter. Even when he was sweet, something smoldered behind it. His brand of sweetness was that of cherry; some bites were going to be tart, but every bite was luscious. With his hands on my hips, his soft but purposeful grip on my body, and *I love you* still swimming around behind my eyes, I wanted nothing more than to surrender to him. A chain reaction occurred in my mind as everything drifted into place. Every wall crumbled, every barricade circumvented. Leo's pleasurable torture tactics and invasive intuition had caused me to flourish—my life, my spirit, and my heart.

My hand slowly rose to stroke his face and he seemed surprised. Grazing my eyes over every inch of his face, I committed the moment to memory. The moment I let myself leap then fall. My fingers drifted down his jaw and settled on his chest where I stared for a moment.

Leo's hand appeared in front of my face and he snapped his fingers, the sound popping through the store. I instantly looked up at him and dropped my hand to my side.

"Say something," he said. "You're scaring me."

I realized then I'd been silent for too long. Off alone in my mind where I recounted every one of his actions that had eventually earned not only my submission, but also my adoration. I gulped and straightened my shoulders, keeping my eyes locked with his.

"Thank you," I whispered.

The fingers that had snapped in front of me spread and slowly skated over my jaw. He held my chin with two fingers and his thumb while he examined my face. I couldn't say the words that had sparked in my brain. I couldn't tell him about the emotions currently drowning me. But I could thank him the way he thanked me every time he donned those black gloves. He thanked me for letting him own my body for a moment. I had to thank him for possessing my heart.

Silence flowing between us, something repentant tinted Leo's expression before he brought his lips to mine. His soft mouth covered my bottom lip and a rhythmic dance began. Two hands cupped my cheeks, keeping our lips fixed on one another. Closing my eyes, I drank in the taste of his tongue in my mouth and let love blaze inside of me.

NINETEEN

LEO'S HAND GLIDED over my shoulder blades, rubbing soap suds along my skin as the shower rained down on us both. I turned and his hands never lifted from my body, only finding a new place to settle on: my breasts. I sighed feeling his thumbs roll over my nipples. His palms slipped effortlessly due to the slick bubbles covering both of our bodies.

His gentle touch skated upward, cupping my neck, guiding me to tilt my head back under the water to douse my hair. When I straightened, I boldly reached out to him, grazing my palms against his firm chest. Though mild in comparison to all the parts of him I wanted to trace my hands over, the sensation of touching him sent lightning through my veins. Electricity coursed through me, colliding into a supernova at my core. Leo ducked his head and kissed the wet flesh of my throat, eliciting a moan. Chuckling against my skin, he let his hands begin to roam again.

"This is how I want every shower to be from now on," he breathed. "Getting clean with a dirty girl."

My eyes snapped open when I felt his fingers drift between my legs. So warm and soft, it threw me for a moment and Leo must've noticed the shift because he stopped short, never touching my pussy.

"What's wrong?"

"Nothing. I just—you've never touched me there."

I looked at the wicked grin formed on his lips and gulped, wishing I hadn't reacted so his fingers could be inside me.

"You have a terrible memory," he said with a laugh.

"Not with your bare hands."

His eyes snapped to mine and I shrank inward under his surprised gaze. "You're right," he said. "I guess this is where we blur a line. I wear the gloves so you know without a doubt when I'm being your Dom and when I'm not…you understand that, right?"

I nodded. "Yes, but—"

His brow lifted and he waited for me to continue. His hands, however, kept moving over my body, rounding over my hips and sweeping gently up my back where warm water trickled down my skin. "You're always my Dom, Leo," I whispered. "And I don't need to see the gloves to know the difference. I feel you change. I feel myself change. Gloves or no gloves, I'm always ready…and if I'm not, I know what to say."

Leo's expression had fallen as I spoke and when I saw him gulp, I began to pant. Silently, he traced a hand over my ass, around my hip, and down the front of my thigh. Instinctually, I widened my stance, allowing him access. He held me paralyzed with his electric blue stare as his warm and gentle fingers slipped along the slit between my legs. I huffed out a breath then sucked in another gust of air. The soapy water trickling down my body mixed with the wetness created by his touch, his voice, his every move.

As he pushed one finger inside, he stepped forward, causing me to inch back and lean against the wall of the shower. He didn't wait for me to settle into the new pose before adding a second digit. The pressure shot tingles through my limbs and my eyes fluttered shut.

"No," he whispered, putting his forehead to mine. "Look at me."

I pulled my heavy eyelids open and stared into his eyes as he pumped his fingers in and out of me. My breath puffed against his lips and he tilted his chin forward to kiss me. His lips danced over mine but he pulled away, denying me the forceful connection I craved. Greedily, I reached out and dragged my fingers through his wet hair, coaxing him to my lips again. Leo complied, kissing me roughly but pulling his fingers out of me as he did. I whimpered against his tongue as he devoured my mouth.

"My way or your way?"

The twinkle in his eye and the ghost of a smile on his reddened lips weakened me. His way. Always his way. His way had changed me. It had revealed a new woman hidden beneath the surface. Leo's way was a path into the light masked by the darkness of our shared desire. His way delivered me.

Carefully, I pulled my fingers from his hair, enjoying the intimate touch one last moment before lowering my arms to my sides.

"Yours, Sir."

The second he flashed his teeth, my arms were over my head, pressed into the cold tile by a strong grasp. He held both wrists in one hand as the other pushed those two fingers into me, fulfilling the ache that had pulsed there a moment ago. His mouth claimed my neck and collarbone, trailing his tongue along my skin before biting down on my shoulder. Moans poured out of me as I catapulted toward an orgasm while his hand fucked me. My body began to shake, my core began to clench, and his hand left me once more. I nearly screamed.

Wide-eyed, trembling and on the edge of a cliff, I groaned while Leo licked his lips and stared at me blankly.

"Later."

"What?" I panted.

He loosened his grasp on my hands, sliding his touch over my shoulder and down one arm as they fell.

"You'll come later. Until then, you can think about it the whole day. Every time you look at me."

I huffed and dragged my hands over my face, clearing my eyes of water to get a better look at his evil grin. He'd doled out this kind of torture before. Once at the store after a quick tryst in the inventory room, he'd brought me to the brink then denied me release just for his own fun. The chuckle he let out as he shut off the faucet and opened the curtain was equally infuriating and adorable. He handed me a towel wearing a smug smile, then winked. I clutched the fluffy towel to my front, burying my face in it, still reeling from the sensation I could only describe as blue balls. Stepping out of the shower, I swatted his shoulder and his mouth dropped. Leo lunged and I squealed as he chased me out into the bedroom. Barely covered and still peppered with water droplets, I cracked a laugh when he caught me, gripping my hips roughly, tossing me on his unmade bed. He pounced on top of me, caging me in with his arms pressed into the mattress. My eyes grazed the chiseled muscles of his chest and I sighed when our gazes collided again.

A chill overtook me as he dragged one fingertip across my lips. "You make it difficult," he said.

My brow flexed in the center and a tender smile bloomed on his full lips as he continued to stare at me. "It's hard for me not to give you everything you want. But I know behind those little frustrated noises and that pouty mouth is a thank you."

I gasped when his thumb began stroking me. "That's what I thought," he growled. "Wetter than before. Dirty girl."

Tempting strokes at my clit had me approaching the boiling point in a matter of seconds, my breath stolen by his painfully slow caresses. "Tell me I'm wrong. That the denial—my control over your pleasure—doesn't make you want to come just as much as my fingers do."

My lips parted, sucking in a ragged breath. He wasn't wrong. The gruff tone of his voice alone had the potential to push me over the edge. His eyes danced across my face wrought with agonizing pleasure. The hooded stare he wore darkened slightly as he pulled his hand away from my sex and brought it to my lips. I gulped as he pulled my bottom lip down with his middle finger before sliding it along my tongue as far back as it would go. The taste of my arousal, salty and foreign, rippled through my mind as I watched him watching me. He stroked my velvety tongue with his finger, drawing it in and out of my mouth as I closed my lips around it more eagerly with every stroke. His stare grew lustful and wildness consumed me, convincing me to suck deeply on his finger as he pushed it in my mouth.

A pulse at my thigh startled me and he bit his lip when I started swirling my tongue around his finger. His hard cock pressed against me as Leo lowered his weight on me. Weakening. He pulled the finger from my mouth, letting it pluck my bottom lip on its way down, snaking in between us. I followed his hand with my eyes and saw him wrap it around his dick. I licked my lips and I didn't know if it was my attempt at a silent request or agreement, but either way, Leo noticed and quickly stood at the side of the bed. One hand gripped the back of my neck and drew me toward him. I pressed my knees into the mattress and spread them wide as I bent to reach him. Leo sighed as I took one moment to point my eyes up before closing my lips around his cock.

At first, I treated his length in the exact way I'd treated his middle finger, sucking deeply, swirling my tongue and pulling my lips tight with every retreat. But Leo didn't let my control last long. His hand fisted in my damp hair and began to guide me, slow at first and then more wildly by the second. He glanced down at me as I looked up, lips closed tightly around his thick cock. Maybe he saw the smile in my eyes. Maybe he could tell my arousal had increased even more than before just by his powerful hand finding the back of my head, but he wasted no more time in getting off. I shut my eyes and loosened, allowing Leo to fuck my face as he pleased. He grunted and I reflexively swallowed the warmth spurting into my mouth as his tempo slowed and his grip relaxed.

I sat back on my heels, hands placed gingerly on my thighs, looking up at him where he stood panting. When his eyes opened and he saw me, submissive position, whisper of a smile on my lips, soft and sultry look in my eye and not a drop of cum left in my mouth, his brow furrowed and his eyes narrowed.

"Oh, what the hell. Good girls get rewarded," he growled.

Leo swiftly pushed me back on the bed and a giggle slipped out of me. He yanked my knees out from under me, hoisting them over his shoulders. His face nestled between my legs and the second his heated tongue grazed my throbbing core, I cried out and my hands found his head. He laced his fingers with mine and held them firmly on my thighs while he sucked and flicked my clit with his tongue until I came.

A few moments later, my breathing returned to normal, Leo's head on my bare stomach while his hands rubbed circles on my sides. My fingers drifted into his hair, twisting the strands, letting the comfort of satisfied silence fill the air around us. He shifted, placing his palm on my belly, propping his chin on it to look at me.

"Thank you," he said.

I smiled. "You're very welcome, Sir."

A little noise croaked in the back of his throat and he climbed my body, settling beside me, rolling me on to my side to clutch me against him. He traced the curve of my cheek and I sighed.

"You thanked me yesterday," he said. "What was that for?"

I swallowed thickly. "For seeing me the way I was meant to be seen. And for making me see myself that way too."

His jaw stiffened as he caressed my cheek once more. "You are very welcome, my love."

His utterance of that word, that soft and subtle title, made my heart seize in my chest. I wanted to say it but my lips didn't open. How could I love someone I hadn't known more than a few weeks? In the same moment I wondered that, I asked myself how I could've thought I loved someone for three years but never really did. Love was unpredictable. Spontaneous.

"I love you, Leo," I breathed.

Our eyes met and every trace of authority cleared from his expression. "I—"

"Don't feel obligated—"

He took my face in his palms, blue eyes wide and sparkling. He pulled my lips to his in the gentlest kiss we'd ever shared. Tears wet my eyes, suddenly overcome by the culmination of moments that had led me here and the silence from him now pounding in my ears. I gulped and tried to shake the desolation threatening to crash on me. It was okay. He didn't have to love me. It was just a word. Leo pulled back from the kiss and stared at me, opening his mouth to speak just as his phone rang on the nightstand. He sighed and reached for it, letting go of me completely.

"Hey," he answered. "Yeah, we're getting in the car now. We won't be late. Jesus, Oliver."

He hung up and glanced at me for a beat, something indecipherable in his eyes. A huff fell from his lips and a smile morphed there as he darted toward the closet. "Boss man is freaking out about the Fall Festival. We'd better get dressed, okay?"

I forced a smile and nodded, hating how much I wanted to hear him say he loved me.

As soon as we found Oliver at the park setting up our table for the festival, he put us to work. Between staging books, making sure we had enough change, and spreading a giant pile of candy for people to take, I didn't have time to think about Leo's lack of response to my confession. The park looked amazing. The leaves had changed to beautiful reds and golds and though it was starting to get chilly, the sun shone brightly as people began trickling in for the festival.

"There they are!" a voice called out.

"Wonkle Leo! Wonkle Ollie!"

I recognized Barry's tiny voice and his adorable mispronunciation. I turned to see him charging toward his uncles, his chocolate mop of curls bouncing as he ran. Leo crouched down and scooped him up just as he nearly barreled into him. I beamed, watching Leo settle Barry onto his hip, offering him a high five before setting him on his feet again. Barry darted over to Oliver, who squeezed him in a bear hug and swung him around rowdily.

The voice I'd heard before Barry's holler must've belonged to the white-haired woman walking towards us holding hands with a man who very clearly resembled Oliver only with silver hair. She waved and Leo's face shined with the most genuine smile I'd ever seen on his face. He moved toward them, closing the distance. The woman wrapped her arms around Leo and he hugged her back, gently placing a hand on the back of her head before kissing her cheek. I watched shamelessly as he hugged the man, clapping a hand on his shoulder afterwards. The three of them approached the table, talking in words I couldn't make out from where a stood a few feet away. Leo caught my eye as I attempted to busy my hands, straightening the already pristine table thanks to Oliver's particularity.

"Mom, Dad, this is Sloane," Leo said.

I spun and felt a hot, red blotch bloom on my neck. Willing a smile on my lips, I said hello in a voice I barely recognized.

"Sloane, these are my parents, Kathy and Michael."

I glanced at Leo, taking in the sweet and utterly serene look on his face before looking back at his parents who offered smiles and kind greetings to me.

"Where's Marie?" Leo asked his mother as Barry zoomed past my leg making fighter jet noises.

Kathy made a face and Michael folded his arms before answering, "She didn't feel up to it today. She's at Oliver's."

"Of course," Leo snapped. "She's got four babysitters here, why would she come?"

"Leo!" his mother scolded.

I felt my chest constrict watching the intimate exchange among family, feeling more out of place than ever. Barry zoomed around one more time then stopped to dig through the Halloween candy Oliver had strewn on the table.

"Mom, don't act like you're not thinking it, too. When is she going to grow up?" Leo's voice hit a volume that pulled Barry's attention over and I watched his little face crumble into a grimace.

I shot Leo a glare I knew I had no right to offer and crouched down beside Barry. "Hey, remember me?"

His cherubic cheeks rose as a shy smile pulled at his lips. "Yeah," he replied in a hush. "You're Miss Sloane."

"That's right. You wanna go find some cotton candy with me?" His eyes grew into saucers as he nodded. I stood and he took the hand I offered him. Oliver eyed me with a lifted brow. "We're going to walk around for a minute while Leo and Grandma and Grandpa keep talking," I pressed. "You okay at the booth by yourself for a second?"

"Yep." Oliver smiled and I could only imagine what he was thinking of my bold move. I gave a glance to Leo over my shoulder as Barry and I walked away. He met my eyes and a pained smile crossed his face as he nodded at me.

"So, are you in school?"

Barry glanced up at me and a flash of familiarity struck me. Sure, he looked a little like Leo and a bit like Oliver in other ways but there was something else.

"Preschool," he said matter-of-factly. "I get to go to Kindergarten next year. And ride the bus!"

I laughed. "Very cool. Ooh look, there's the lady we need to see," I said, pointing to the little trailer that sold cotton candy, funnel cakes, and caramel apples.

Barry picked up the pace and dragged me along as I chuckled. We queued up in the short line and I looked down at him again.

"Two questions. One, are you willing to share some of this cotton candy with me?"

"Sure!" The smile on his face was infectious and it made me snicker.

"Thank you," I said with a smile. "Now, question two—this one is super important—pink or blue?"

I expected a gut reaction answer of blue from the four-year-old boy, but instead his little lips twisted on his face and his pale eyebrows tensed. "Hmm. Blue turns your mouth blue, pink doesn't," he started his line of reasoning.

"True." I held back a laugh.

"They taste the same…"

The people in front of us moved with their order in hand and we stepped up to the window. I gave Barry a questioning look and he shrugged. "Blue."

"One bag of blue cotton candy please," I said around a laugh.

Heading back to the bookstore's booth, Barry held onto the bag, pulling pieces of sugary fibers off and handing one to me every time he took one for himself. I breathed in the autumn air and caught a quick whiff of coffee just as a familiar face came into view. Ethan Corbin from Black and Brew stood grinning at me from behind a table just a few feet ahead. I saw a sign in front of him that read *Hot Chocolate* and nudged Barry. He wasn't my kid, I could sugar him up.

"You like cocoa?"

"With marshmallows?!"

"I'll take that as a yes." I laughed as we stepped up to Ethan's table.

"Sloane, hey."

I tucked my hair behind one ear, suddenly made anxious by his stare. Ethan hadn't exactly been subtle with me, at least it felt that way. Maybe I was wrong about him, but the smile he flashed at me along with the way he leaned over the table as I neared didn't feel like he was just being friendly.

"Hi, Ethan. Could we have two hot chocolates?"

The wink he offered was the last clue I needed. I forced a smile as he quickly poured two paper cups full, snapping lids on top before handing them to me.

"Who's this?" he asked, smiling at Barry.

"This is Barry. Barry this is my friend, Ethan. Barry is Leo's nephew."

Ethan waved at Barry, who couldn't be bothered to respond as he stuffed his blue lips with more cotton candy. I stood awkwardly for a moment and started to say a quick goodbye when he spoke again.

"And Leo, the guy from the bookstore," he started. "He's like your…"

"Boyfriend."

My heart leapt in my chest hearing deep Leo's voice over my shoulder. Ethan clearly hadn't noticed him approach behind us and his face fell. I turned and my eyes landed on his stoic face, blue eyes blazing with something I didn't recognize. *Boyfriend.* My head swirled with confusion and the admission of my feelings from earlier echoed in my mind.

Leo smiled down at Barry then slipped his arm around my waist, bending to kiss my cheek. A blush tinted me all over and I glanced at Ethan, who simply nodded.

"Right. Well, you guys have a good one," Ethan said.

"Bye, Ethan," I replied.

The second I turned and relaxed under Leo's arm draped over my shoulder, I breathed in the scent of his clothes and smelled his clove cigarettes. That had to be about more than the looks Ethan gave me. Maybe it was the stress of Marie and the conversation he'd had with his parents. Maybe he was mad at me for saying what I'd said. My eyes tilted up at him as he led Barry and me over to a bench near our booth.

"Is everything okay?" I whispered.

He didn't look at me as we kept walking, me clutched to his side and Barry's hand firmly in his. "Yeah," he said. "I just don't like the way that guy looks at you."

We reached the bench and I chuckled under my breath. Leo's response of an intense glare gave me pause and I examined the strange look on his face. He'd always been intense but his eyes had never made me feel so small. For the first time, I didn't see dominance behind that intensity. I didn't see lingering lust and a hunger for play. It felt different. My stomach rolled but I tried to swallow the ominous feeling as he gestured toward the bench. Barry climbed up in between us with no assistance needed, though we both offered a hand. I gave him the little cup of hot chocolate that'd had time to cool and watched him take a sip.

Leo's hand smoothed over Barry's hair and it hit me—the reason he looked so oddly familiar to me. Barry looked like a memory. Sitting beside him with Leo, I remembered a long forgotten vision of a child I might have one day. A lost hope. I'd spent so long wishing for a future that looked like this moment. Only now, something strange and secretive sat behind Leo's gaze, my feelings remained unrequited, and the child wasn't mine—just like before.

TWENTY

A HAND TUGGED on my pant leg as I handed out the last of the flyers I'd printed. I glanced to my side and saw Barry looking up at me quizzically. The double dose of sugar had hit him hard, prompting his grandparents to take him over to the mini petting zoo for the last hour. The festival was winding down and they'd come back to the booth.

"Miss Sloane," he chirped.

"Yeah, buddy?"

"Barry, we're working," Leo snapped before his nephew had the chance to answer me. I whipped my head to the side and caught sight of Leo, head down, straightening the remaining books on the table. His mood had been off since the morning. He'd barely spoken to me since we began manning the table after I took Barry for his snack.

"What is your problem?" I whispered to Leo.

Blue eyes flicked up from the table to slice right through me. I felt sick. "Nothing," he said. "He needs to quit pestering you. And you don't need to be so concerned with entertaining him."

I flinched, retreating from him at the harsh sound of his voice.

"Miss Sloane," Barry whined.

"Barry, knock it off!"

"Leo," I hissed.

"She got a big spider on her back!"

I froze and turned to Barry at my hip with wide eyes. "What?"

His curls flounced as he nodded at me, urging that he was telling the truth. I instantly yelped, grabbing the bottom of my sweater, shaking it as I cringed. My skin crawled imagining what Barry's idea of big was. As I continued to shiver, praying I'd lose the spider, I suddenly felt a hand skate over my shoulder.

"I see it, hang on," Leo said.

My imagination had turned it into an entire swarm of tarantulas and knowing Leo could see whatever monstrous spider was creeping up my clothes, made me squirm even more. Desperate to get it off of me, I wiggled and flapped at my shirt some more. Then Leo gripped my elbow and rasped in my ear the voice that always made me obey.

"Hold. Still."

I calmed under his touch and shut my eyes. Pulling in a breath, stifling another squeal, I felt him pluck something from my sweater before he smoothed his hand all over my back for reassurance.

"It's gone," he whispered. "You're safe."

I turned on my heels to look at him and saw the care in his eyes. His hand came down on my shoulder and slid to my elbow as his mouth tightened into a pained smile.

"Thanks," I muttered.

Leo nodded and his smile grew more relaxed. I could see the stress marring his face and knew the arrival of his sister must've brought up some lingering issue he'd yet to share with me. Oliver began packing up the table as the sun set in the distance and I figured Leo and I would have time to talk once we left.

"Sloane?"

I turned and came face to face with Leo's mother, Kathy. She offered a sweet smile and glanced past me a Leo before she spoke.

"Would you like to join the family tomorrow afternoon for dinner? We didn't get to talk much today and I'd love to hear more about you, dear. Seeing as my sons—and my grandson," she laughed, "are so fond of you."

Including Leo? I thought. At this point, I wasn't too sure. My throat worked to gulp down the quick bit of fear that bubbled up in me. I looked over my shoulder at Leo wearing a subtle glow. For a split second, I wondered if my mother were still alive if her hair would be as white as Kathy's.

"Of course, Mrs. Calloway. Thank you."

Leo's house was dark; we walked in in silence. My head had been a mess the entire day. The only time I didn't feel nervous, out of place, or on edge due to Leo's attitude had been when I was alone with Barry. Leo had remained quiet on the drive back to his place after we dropped everything off at the store where Wendy was closing up for the night. My mind raced with all the things I felt I needed to say to him. All the questions I wanted to ask burned painfully behind my eyes.

Leo walked to the kitchen and poured us each a glass of water, handing me one without a word. I watched as he gulped the liquid down then put his glass in the sink. He turned to walk to his bedroom, stripping his shirt over his head as he made his way there. When he glanced back at me, I sipped the cold water but his stare chilled me more.

"Come in here when you're done," he said.

I chugged the water and followed him, preparing my voice to speak. I couldn't surrender to him without first clearing the air.

"Leo, this morning when I said—"

"Stop," he interrupted. He moved slowly around the room, lighting candles and switching on the bedside lamps before turning off the overhead light, leaving it dusky.

"But—"

He faced me, shirtless, jaw tight and darkness clouding his stare. "Stop," he repeated. "Get undressed."

Acid raged in my gut and I choked down the saliva the sight of his body had brought forth. "Leo…"

He raised a careful hand and rubbed his forehead—not yet wearing his gloves—and I saw agony painting him. "Please," he begged in a hush. "Please do this for me."

The pleading whisper mixed with the despondency I saw in his gaze convinced me. Just as I'd needed his heavy hand to wipe away memories of Warren and punish me in the way I'd never be able to punish myself, I knew Leo needed this. Whatever storm had been brewing in his veins that day was ready to be unleashed and while the anguish consuming him bordered on frightening, I knew that ultimately I could always end it. I took a deep breath and he watched with a heavy lidded stare as I tugged my sweater then my tank top over my head, dropping them to the floor. My stomach pitched when a thought chased through my mind.

The regret I felt over telling him I loved him would fade when his rough touch sent me spinning. I needed this too.

It was as though we'd always find ourselves here. Bound by this twisted kind of loving that hurt and healed all at once. Leo's ability to make me feel was unique to him alone. Of course I wanted to talk more. I wanted to creep inside Leo's mind the way he always crept in mine but I didn't have the same power he did. My intuition wasn't nearly as strong when it came to him. I only ever felt sure of one thing with Leo—that surrender was freedom.

I unbuttoned my pants and pushed them to the floor along with my panties, stepping out of them as I unhooked my bra. When all had fallen to the ground and I was bared to him, he closed his eyes and breathed in deeply. He grabbed his gloves off the dresser, shoved his hands into them and moved me by the shoulders to the center of the room, near the foot of the bed.

He ducked into the closet as I stood naked and waiting and with my own deep breath, a strange feeling washed over me. Clarity. Calm. No matter what had transpired between us earlier, the worry I still held onto from my hasty confession, or the mystery plaguing Leo, I still felt most at peace under his rule. His touch would be my undoing and I hoped for his sake I could bring the same to him.

He came into view with multiple items in his hands. He tossed a few things on the bed and I didn't dare peek. He lowered in front of me and pushed my feet apart, placing a long metal bar between them. He secured cuffs around my ankles that attached to the bar, making it impossible for me to spread my legs farther apart or close them. From the bed, Leo grabbed the cuffs with the chain between them that he'd used to hook me to the headboard before. He unlatched the chain from one cuff and looped it through a metal ring at the center of the bar between my feet then reattached it. His hand grabbed one of mine and tugged. I had to bend at the waist for my wrists to reach the cuffs and when I did, Leo captured my hands in the leather, tightening them perfectly. Bent low in the compromising position, Leo and I were face to face where he knelt on the floor.

His eyes lifted to mine and he wet his lips. "Yellow to slow, red to stop, black to end. Got it?"

"Yes."

His brow furrowed and I felt leather fingertips pinch and roll one of my nipples, causing me to cry out. "Yes?"

"Yes, Sir," I choked.

Leo rose and I hated how obstructed my view was. Not only did he move to stand behind me, but with my wrists shackled just a few inches higher than my ankles, I couldn't crane my head to see higher than waist level. A quick smack on my bare ass jolted me out of my thoughts and made me realize how easily I could fall over if I wasn't careful of keeping my balance in the position. I sucked in a breath as Leo grasped handfuls of my ass, squeezing me so hard I squeaked with my exhale. A few more quick slaps of the flesh and I actually smiled. By the time his gloved hand trailed up my curved spine, I moaned.

"Are those happy noises I hear?"

I caught my lip between my teeth and sighed after one more spank. "Yes, Sir."

"Hmm. Interesting."

His hands left my body and I heard him gather something from the bed. Just like when I'd been blindfolded, I had to deduce what was happening around me by my sense of sound. I heard a squirt, like gel from a bottle, and then something wet. I jumped and nearly fell forward as Leo's hands spread my ass once more, this time even rougher.

"Take a deep breath," he commanded.

I obeyed, but held the breath I'd pulled into my lungs the moment I felt something cool, hard, and wet pressing against my asshole. My entire body tensed and even as the abrupt pain melted into something like pleasure as the small, teardrop shape settled inside of me, I didn't breathe. Leo let go of the cheek he'd pulled on roughly and tapped the exterior of the toy. A groan burst forth from me as well as the breath I'd been clinging to as a shockwave of foreign sensation rippled through me. I felt it rush up my spine and pulse through my sex. While I focused on the new kind of lovely torture, Leo's feet came into view. He crouched down to my level and took my chin in his grasp, examining me.

"Do you want to fuck Ethan?"

"What?" I gaped, a surprised and incredulous laugh coating the retort.

His finger pinched my chin harder and he tilted my face up at an uncomfortable angle. "Wipe that smile off your face. Do you want to fuck him?"

"No, Sir," I murmured.

"Have you thought about it?"

"No, Sir."

"Who do you think about fucking?"

I swallowed and watched his flaming blue irises dance across my face as I whispered, "You."

He softened barely and rose once more, resuming his position at my backside. "Do you think about fucking Warren?"

Paralyzed by the question, I didn't even make a noise when he spanked me for not answering him. My eyes locked on the floor and I illogically considered Leo's mood being linked to Warren. But how?

"Tell me how he hurt you."

A swift blow from something flat and leather and much harder than Leo's hand struck my ass, the impact sending another shockwave of sweet discomfort rolling through me. I recalled a paddle hanging among Leo's tools and figured that must've been his instrument of choice for the evening.

Another crack against my ass burned the flesh and I cried out.

"Tell me, Sloane. Tell me what he did!"

"He lied to me," I said through clenched teeth.

Another thump and another shout.

"And?"

"He used me!"

He stuck me again and my head began its reliable decent into a spinning trip where pain and pleasure met. Where shame and forgiveness melded together. And where my contradicting, spiraling thoughts dragged me beneath the surface of reality.

"What did he make you feel?"

"Alone," I purred, the trance cast on me.

The paddle whacked my already stinging flesh and I groaned, having fallen in love with the sensation. "Tell me more. How did you feel with him?"

High from the strange bliss Leo awarded me, my lips moved independent of my clouded mind but the truth made its way out. "Like a whore."

I heard Leo panting as he struck me again. Then the paddle clattered to the floor and his hand resumed the punishment, spanking me relentlessly. "He used you and lied and made you feel like a lonely little whore, Sloane. What the hell were you thinking?"

Heat flooded my body and my pussy throbbed, the emptiness during the revealing exchange unbearable. "I—" I tried to speak. I tried to think of an answer, but I'd been searching for that one on my own for so long I wasn't sure I'd ever know.

I whimpered the moment I felt his cock press against me. His hands latched onto my hips and pulled me back, impaling me on his length. Stretched in both openings, bound by leather, metal and words, I let go and fell into complete surrender as he fucked me. My lips closed, humming the sounds of gratification with every angry thrust Leo gave. Pumping into me, I heard him growl as his grip on my waist strengthened. While my mind blurred, dizzying by the second, I still felt the tender skin of my ass bumping against him. For every pulse of fiery ecstasy his cock gave, the marks of his aggressive inquiry lit with pain.

"Oh God," I moaned.

Leo's arms wrapped all the way around my waist and he hunched over me, breathing hotly against my back. His hands found my breasts, tugging on my nipples with brute force. The spin had too great a hold on me to allow a try cry to fall from my lips, but I whined—half begging for mercy and half begging for more.

"Tell me why you left. Tell me what he did that made you leave. What was worse than lies and disrespect? What was worse than making you his whore?"

The corkscrew of my consciousness faltered and I tumbled into a state of lucidity as my answer screeched inside the confines of my head. Leo fucked me harder, panting and groaning wildly at my back before coming with a harsh curse. The spinning had slowed and I was in my body, ready to tell Leo the truth about the end of my relationship with Warren when he pulled out and slapped my ass again.

"Answer me," he huffed. Another spank and I shut my eyes, flinching as the skin ached with tenderness.

"He had a child," I barked as he slapped me yet again. The assault stopped and I heard Leo's breathing hitch. I sighed and hung my head as my legs trembled. "He had a baby with his wife," I breathed. "That. That was worse."

"Black," Leo said.

My head rose as far as it could. "What?"

Leo dropped beside me and unlocked my wrists and ankles with quick, gloveless fingers. He tossed the spreading bar and cuffs aside and as I barely moved to straighten, his hand pressed firmly on my back to keep me bent. I felt him ease the plug out of me and did my best to breathe through it, sighing relief when it popped out completely.

"Did you say black? I'm confused. What did I do wrong?" I relaxed and fixed my body upright, feeling the harsh sting of my punishment and the tingles still pulsating in my sex.

"Nothing."

I moved to see Leo, but he brushed past me. My panicked mind took in the sight of the lion etched on his back as he stomped into the adjoining bathroom. And my heart constricted in my chest as he slammed the door shut without another word.

TWENTY-ONE

STUNNED IN PLACE, I felt my hands trembling at my sides as I stared at the bathroom door. I took a few solid deep breaths and grabbed my tank top off the floor, yanking it over my head. I found my panties and slipped into them then marched to the bathroom door with every kind of emotion flowing through me.

My knuckles rapped hard on the white wood. "Leo?"

No reply. I knocked again, harder. "Leo, what the hell is going on?"

I heard the sink turn on and the sound of splashing water as I knocked again relentlessly. "You're freaking me out. I—please." My voice cracked and I felt a wave of rejection douse me. The books I'd read in the beginning of our arrangement—before Leo showed me he cared, before he was mine, before I loved him—made it clear that aftercare was sometimes the most important part of a scene. Even when I thought Leo was just my fun fantasy, he'd wipe away my tears, hold me and shush my sighs as I came down from the tornado he knew how to stir inside of me. To be held afterward did more for me than I'd ever realized until now. That first time, he'd kissed my cheekbone tenderly, dried the few tears on my face and sweetly asked if I was all right. It was simple and juxtaposed the scene so greatly I almost wondered now if I started falling for him then. Leo had shown me more care and attention than anyone else had ever before. Standing alone and cold in his bedroom with this barrier between us made my stomach wrench.

I banged on the door and gripped the handle, gasping when it opened without any force. Pushing the door open, I saw Leo standing at the sink with his palms pressed into the vanity, staring at himself in the mirror with no expression.

"Leo?"

"Do I sicken you the way I sicken myself?"

The grave tone of his raspy voice sent a shudder through me. I rushed toward him, breaking his gaze from the mirror and inserting myself in his eye line.

"What? Leo, no."

His eyes settled on me but he looked a thousand miles away. Gone was the Dominant man who held me captive with looks alone. Leo's gaze was lifeless and despondent. I reached up and touched his face, but he flinched away from me, grimacing.

"You do *not* sicken me," I said. "What's going on?"

His Adam's apple bobbed and his eyes zoned out once more, staring at my shoulder as he spoke. "That got out of hand. I'm sorry."

I took his face in my hands and made him look me squarely in the eyes. "It's okay," I pleaded. "I'm okay."

His lips parted and he averted my gaze yet again. I watched his mouth open and shut as though his words were trying to form. When he finally looked at me again, he sighed.

"I'm not."

My forehead tensed and I swept my thumbs over his cheekbones, at a complete loss of how to care for the man who'd never acted as though he needed caring for. He swallowed thickly again and clutched my fingers, holding them to his face as he stared down at me. Leo drew in a deep breath, blinking a few times, bringing a little light back to his eyes. His grasp on my hands loosened as he exhaled and his shoulders dropped.

"I'm sorry," he said again with a breath. "That's never happened to me before."

"What?"

"A drop."

My brow furrowed and Leo lowered my hands in his to settle in between us. "You know how you spin? That really nice weightless feeling—whatever heavenly plane you drift to when you're completely taken by the moment?"

I nodded, still scrutinizing him as his voice returned to normal.

"Imagine the opposite. Spinning out of control and into a bleak place. Somewhere dark and burdensome."

"That's what happened to you?"

"I didn't feel like I could stop. I shouldn't have said those things to you. I don't know why I took it there. I shouldn't have—"

"Hey. You did stop. You stopped yourself. You and me…" I trailed off with a weak smile. "We don't always know how to talk. That, out there, is how we communicate. It's how you first spoke to me and it's how I first responded to you. We should probably work on speaking."

He puffed a sad laugh through his nose and placed a hand under my ear, smoothing his thumb over my jaw. The tender look in his eye warmed me as he scanned my face.

"There's a lot I need to learn. I'm afraid I don't know how to treat you anymore…I've never loved a sub before."

Air stuck in my lungs. "What?"

One side of his mouth curled up. "I love you."

"But—" My voice squeaked out and my lips pursed in a pout as confusion flooded me.

Leo's tongue touched his bottom lip and his grin grew. I finally recognized the man in front of me as his hands dropped to my waist and pulled me to him. "I said, I love you. No buts."

"Earlier, when I said it you…you acted like you were mad at me all day. Like I'd disappointed you."

His face fell. "I'm sorry about that."

Eyeing him carefully, I let it sink in. Leo loved me. It radiated through my chest and it shot of fireworks in my brain.

His darkened stare, not ominous, simply brooding, held me. "I did not expect you, Sloane. Not at all."

I hadn't expected him either. A weak smile moved his lips and he pulled me into a hug. My face pressed against his chest as he repeated his love for me, his mouth against the top of my head. I sighed and linked my arms around his back, attempting to let go of the pestering thoughts from earlier in the day. His mood, his stare, his reaction to Ethan and Barry and the questions he demanded of me while I was restrained. As he dropped a kiss in my hair, his chest broadening with a deep breath, I felt something looming. The shadow between us. With our acknowledgments of love freed to one another, I tried to push the idea of a problem away.

I looked up at Leo and tried to read him the way he read me. Why had he lost control? Why had he gone to the dark place? Why had he asked those things of me? And why hadn't he said a word about my final answer—the one that made him use the safe word? His brows knit together briefly and as I clung to him tighter, I realized how blindfolded he'd always made me feel and how much that scared me.

The moment we walked into Oliver's house, Wendy grabbed my arm and helped hang up my jacket. She pulled me aside and her eyes grew wide.

"God, I'm glad you're here," she said.

I stared at her, unable to think with how quickly she'd whisked me off to one side as Oliver and Leo greeted each other.

Wendy rolled her eyes. "Don't tell me I'm the only nervous one. Dinner with the parents? Kind of a big deal. Ollie told me I'm being crazy. But I'm glad you and I are in the same boat."

"Right," I said. "I mean, I met them yesterday. They seem nice. We'll be fine."

"There's wine," she said looking down her nose at me. "Want some?"

I laughed and nodded. "Sure."

She headed off toward the kitchen as Leo's hand settled on my shoulder. I glanced up at his small smile. My unsettled nerves had nothing to do with sharing a meal with Leo's entire family. I had bigger concerns than impressing his parents. I'd spent almost the whole night staring at the ceiling of Leo's bedroom, running through every second of our relationship. Trying to pinpoint the moments when Leo acted differently toward me in effort to figure him out proved difficult. In the beginning, I loved the mystery of him. It was part of the thrill and intrigue. His silent seduction. But now, every whiff of clove cigarettes and brooding stare was a tally mark in the secretive column. Pensiveness was no longer sexy, it was unnerving. Our silent communications that I'd categorized in my mind as some kind of telepathic connection stood out as moments of misperception and ambiguity. For hours, while Leo slept soundly beside me, I'd wondered if I really knew him or if I'd simply repeated my old mistakes and convinced myself of who he was.

Looking up at him, I sighed. I prayed I knew him. I prayed I fell for someone real and not a version of him I'd manifested in my mind alone.

"Are you okay?" I asked.

His eyes flashed with surprise for an instant before he nodded. "I'm just still a little tired," he replied.

It had taken him a few hours to return completely to himself after what he'd explained as his drop. He held me in his arms and told me he loved me over and over. Each time he said it I felt contentment followed quickly by doubt. What if he was repeating it to convince himself? He'd apologize and I'd tell him he didn't need to. But he never spoke of Warren again. He never asked me about my responses during the scene and I never pressed him to tell me why he'd questioned me. His exhaustion was evident, worn out by the energy of his emotions and the labor of his sadism; he finally fell asleep against my body.

We made our way into the living room and Leo's father rose from a recliner. "Hey, kids," he said, embracing Leo quickly and smiling at me. "Sloane, I'm glad you came. Good to see you again."

My lips split and a genuine smile claimed me. I hadn't been around people parents' age in so long, I hadn't realized how comforting it was. "Thanks for having me," I said.

From around the corner, Barry padded in with a stuffed elephant under one arm, rubbing his eyes with the other hand. He yawned and the mussed curls on his head looked especially out of place. Behind him, Marie followed.

"He hasn't taken an afternoon nap like that in a long time. You guys must've worn him out today," she said to Michael.

He chuckled. "Yeah, Grandma's worried she's going to have grandchild withdrawals once we head back south. She may've gone a little overboard today running him all around town."

Barry glanced up, drowsy-eyed, and saw me. His sleepy expression never changed but his feet led him straight toward me where he simply held his arms up, silently asking me to hold him. My chin jutted out and I bent without hesitation, scooping him up as he clung to me.

"Well hey, buddy."

I locked eyes with Marie and she smiled though disbelief painted her. "Wow. He's pretty taken with you," she said.

My arms held him tightly as he melted against me. "I guess so," I mused with a faint laugh. I found Leo with my gaze and felt my stomach clench as his eyes narrowed and his jaw tightened. Unreadable and yet unsettling, his expression held firm as he turned to his brother.

"I'm going to see if Mom needs help," he said.

He glanced at me one more time and left the room. Wendy arrived at my side with a glass of wine. Her mouth fell open and she sighed at the sight of little Barry latched around my neck.

"What a sweetie!" she whispered. I smiled and moved to sit on the sofa, settling Barry beside me. He snuggled to my side and I let my arm drape over him.

"You waking up?"

"Yeah," he exhaled.

Marie took a seat on his other side, stroking a hand over his hair. "Do you have any nieces or nephews?" she asked.

I forced a smile and shook my head. "No, not yet."

"Well my son seems happy to give you a taste of what it's like," she said with a laugh.

"I'm honored," I mused, looking down at Barry as he pulled in a deep breath, straightening as he continued to wake.

"Dinner's ready."

My eyes swept to Leo standing in the entryway of the living room; his expression had changed but hadn't eased. His blue gaze flicked to Barry nestled at my side, then to Marie and back to me. A deep breath widened his chest and I felt the room darken for us. I wanted to rush to him and beg him to speak to me. But his father rose and clapped a hand on Leo's shoulder.

"Ollie said he's got beers in the basement fridge. Go grab us a couple, will ya?"

His eyes tore away from my face and a chill slithered up my spine. "Yeah, Dad."

Everyone stood and headed for the kitchen. As we crowded inside, Kathy reached for me and planted a kiss on my cheek that warmed me unexpectedly. Leo had so much more to offer than just himself. This family—the idea of it at least—full of loving embraces, kind words and the potential for new friendships had already slowly infiltrated my heart.

"I'm glad you're here, honey," Kathy said, topping off the glass of wine I'd yet to sip. I laughed and shook away the heaviness Leo's stare laid on me. I let the warmth of the Calloway family envelope me and wash away whatever troubles brewed between us.

"Me too," I said with a smile. "Dinner smells wonderful."

Barry darted through the kitchen, apparently reaching his second wind in record speed. His head bobbed past the island and a little hand reached up to the chocolate cake resting on a platter.

"Barrett Fitzgerald Calloway!"

Marie's scolding stopped my feet from moving. I blinked and swallowed as a cloud rolled into my mind. My brow furrowed and I gulped red wine while thunder rippled through my every thought. Oliver's soft touch at my arm pulled me into the space again.

"Here, grab a plate," he said offering me a white paper plate. "We're fancy if you can't tell." He laughed and I gripped the plate carefully, still staring into a void as my mind brewed a squall.

"Barry's name...is Barrett?" I managed to utter.

The room hummed with customary conversation as everyone began filling their plates from the spread Mrs. Calloway had presented over the countertops and the island. Oliver picked up a napkin and handed me one as he answered.

"Yeah," he said, lowering his voice to a hush. "His good for nothing father was adamant Marie give him his family's middle name but didn't want her giving him his last name. So she just gave it to him as a first name instead."

Those deep brown eyes.

The cherubic cheeks and soft curls.

The spitting image of a child I'd made up in my mind as my own.

Because I'd seen photos of him as a child.

Barry looked like a memory to me; the kind of sweet boy I'd wanted during my time with Warren Fitzgerald Barrett.

I set my wine and my paper plate on the countertop. "Excuse me for a second," I muttered. Ducking out into the foyer, I hurried toward the door when I heard Leo's voice in the kitchen.

"Who wants a beer?"

My hand gripped the knob and I shifted the door open and slipped out onto the porch. My chest ached as I struggled for even breaths. I glanced around in a daze at the houses on Oliver's street and wondered how long it would take me to walk home. I didn't care. I didn't care that my jacket was inside because the cool air waving over my boiling skin gave me the slightest bit of relief. Dread began to swallow me whole. My eyes burned as tears welled up and my lip stung as I bit down hard on it.

The sound of the door opening made me turn from where I stood at the bottom of the porch steps. I barely remembered walking down them.

"Hey, what's up? You okay?"

Leo's voice sat in my ears and nauseated me. I took two steps up and the porch lamp lit my face for him. I watched as he registered the tears in my eyes and the anguish that I wore.

"What's wrong?" he whispered.

I shut my eyes. "I'm trying to figure out how long you've known."

The events of the previous night came rushing back and sickness surged within me. As he held onto his response, silence filling the chilled air between us, I did the math on Barry's age. I'd probably met Warren around the time Marie had him. I wasn't just the mistress, I was the replacement mistress. The spare.

"When did I first say his name? When did you realize?"

My chin trembled as I noticed the subtle relief on Leo's face. At least he wouldn't have to hide it from me any longer.

"Answer me!"

"I first suspected it…when you mentioned working in marketing in Blacksburg, but you said his name that night at my house. When you told me he was married."

My face crumpled and my hands balled into fists at my side. "Does your sister know?"

"No."

"Were you ever going to tell me?"

Leo's wild eyes danced over my features and for once, his wordlessness truly spoke volumes. I wasn't guessing or grasping—I wasn't inserting my own words into void between us. I knew. He wouldn't have told me.

"Did you just think I'd figure it out one day and we'd deal with it then?" My voice cracked as damning evidence of the pain engulfing me.

He reached up and rubbed harshly at his forehead, shutting his eyes in a wince. "I didn't know how to tell you."

My arms flew up and I stomped toward him. "Of course not, because you don't know how to talk to me! I thought it was me. I almost blamed myself for this disconnect I was starting to feel. I thought, what did I do wrong to make him shut down and shut me out? But here I am taking the responsibility—shaming and picking myself apart because of another lying man who found a way to own me."

"Sloane, please…" He reached out for me and I jerked away, wide-eyed and breathless. He reached out again and gripped my arm. I pulled from his grasp and forced my palm against his cheek without thinking. The sound of the slap rebounded around the porch and Leo turned his face with the weight. His head moved and I reared back again, slapping him once more. And then a third time, before a sob claimed me.

"Did it make you feel better? To punish another one of his whores? Did you feel like you were getting back at him for screwing your sister over? Or were you hoping to humiliate me and teach me a lesson about how stupid I was for being with him seeing as how I wasn't even his number two?"

Leo licked his lips and touched the cheek I'd assaulted as he gulped. When our eyes locked, I saw the redness at the rim of this lashes and the gloss covering his blue irises.

"I didn't know…" Leo sighed and tugged his bottom lip in his mouth. "What are the chances of that, Sloane? How could I have known? It's not right and it's not fair, but I didn't know. And I'm so sorry. I never expected to fall in love with you."

It all pieced together in my mind. Every second we'd shared.

"You could've done it all so differently, Leo. But now…with this…this huge thing. It just feels like every moment was calculated. And I don't know how I can look at you again after you watched me love that little boy knowing who his father was to me."

Leo dragged his hands over his face, speechless. I pulled my phone out of my pocket and with a few rushed taps, a car was on its way to pick me up.

"You should go back inside," I mumbled.

"Sloane, please don't do this."

My eyes met his and I hated the fading embers of passion burning in me at the sight of him despite what he'd done. I swallowed thickly and hugged my arms around myself.

"Maybe I had it coming. I always liked the way you hurt me."

TWENTY-TWO

A RUSH OF chills flashed through me and my flesh swelled with quick heat as my fingers swept over black leather gloves. The feeling against my skin catapulted me into memories of Leo and my heart seized in my chest. I shut my eyes and gripped the gloves as I breathed.

Every day. I thought of him every single day. It felt pointless to try and forget him when everything reminded me of him. For the last two months, everything had sparked a memory. The smell of cloves, eighties love songs on the radio, every book I opened, every glass of wine I drank, every walk I took, and the sensation of leather under my fingertips.

The day after I walked away from him on his brother's porch, I packed a bag and went to my sister's house for a week. I never imagined I'd find myself running back there after running away nearly a year before. I explained everything to her for the first time and though I waited for a shaming look and snide comments about needing to get my life together, I got the opposite. Ellie welcomed me into her home without judgment. Travelling back and forth, spending my savings again, I tried to keep myself busy by constantly moving. I'd come to Salem and hole up in my apartment watching movies and drinking until I fell asleep and then I'd head to Blacksburg and spend time being a normal human alongside my sister and Bryon.

Only he never left my thoughts. Leo loomed in the back of my mind like an unpaid debt—churning my stomach acid all while feeling too colossal to take on.

He called my phone at least once a day. That didn't help to rid him from my daily life. His name popping up on the screen continued to both thrill me and devastate me. In the beginning, he left messages. He begged me to answer, tried to explain, apologized, he even demanded I call him back once, thinking maybe he still had the power over me. Truthfully, that message in particular nearly broke me. The rough, smoky tone of voice that held me captive once almost pushed me over the edge. My hand had hovered over the phone, itching to dial his number back and hear his voice in real time. But I didn't do it. I poured myself a drink and willed him away. Eventually, he stopped leaving messages though his calls still came in like clockwork.

Whenever I was in Salem, I made sure to stay in my apartment. I even brought my groceries back from

Blacksburg so I wouldn't chance running into him. I didn't even want to see Oliver or Wendy. I wanted it to be how it was before I met him. I wanted to go into the bookstore I loved and drink my coffee and be invisible. But I couldn't. Leo had seen me and his stare made me whole. His touch made me real. His voice made me function.

Breathe, I reminded myself. Sucking in a breath, I chased Leo from my mind like I did every day and pulled myself back to the present. Anger set in as it always did when I saw the parallels between my first few months away from Warren and now, these first two months separated from Leo. Warren had made me feel stupid, but Leo made me feel conned.

"Those are nice."

Bryon's voice sounded at my back and I turned to him with a weak smile. He touched my shoulder and eyed me with caution.

"You okay?"

I nodded and looked back at the gloves I'd been handling. Suddenly the holiday music playing in the store swelled in my mind and I registered the noise of bustling shoppers. I hated Christmas. After my parents died, it acted as a reminder that no gift would ever be what I truly wanted. When I was with Warren, it was a magnifying glass on the true dynamic of our relationship as he showered me with lavish gifts but didn't spend any time with me for almost the entire month of December. Though I rarely allowed myself to envision a future with Leo during our short time together, I had once considered sharing a holiday with him; it was the first time I'd looked forward to that time of year.

Bryon picked up the ladies' black leather gloves and flipped over the price tag. "Hey, they're on sale. You want them? I have no idea what to get you."

I stared at the gloves with narrowed eyes and a dark laugh snuck out. Bryon gaped at me. I hadn't laughed in weeks. What would it be like to put those gloves on? I wasn't drawn to them because my hands couldn't stand the chilly air outside. Something else pulled me toward the slim fitting, soft leather gloves. I wondered what it might feel like to keep those in my coat pocket, ready to wear whenever I felt the need. I imagined the thrill that might lace through me the moment I slipped my hands inside them. Would I feel powerful? Would I feel in control?

"Earth to Sloane," Bryon sang.

My eyes snapped to his and I gave an apologetic smile. It wasn't uncommon for me to drift off into my own little world these days. Bryon was used to it but I hated feeling like I was a walking zombie. "Sorry. Yeah, I—I like them."

He snatched the gloves up and grinned. "Good. Don't watch me pay for them and act surprised in front of Craig."

I matched his grin and saluted him as he hurried off to get in the long line for the register. Turning back toward the display of gloves, I stroked the finger of a pair identical to the one's Bryon was currently buying for me. Wild visions raced through my brain and suddenly my shoulders straightened and my breath flowed differently. I jumped at the feeling of my phone vibrating in my pocket and pulled it out only to see Leo's name. Gritting my teeth, I hit the decline button and stared at the blank screen a beat longer.

Scraping my bottom lip, I glanced back at the gloves, then at the screen once more. I'd told Leo I thought I secretly wanted liberation from my desperate need to have control, but what if I was wrong? It didn't take a shrink to trace back my control issues to the sudden loss of my parents. Add in my choice of Warren—the safe bet, the man I'd never truly have to be with—and I was a damn stereotype. Maybe I didn't have to be though.

Scrolling through my contacts list, I found the person I knew I could talk to about the unexpected contemplations plaguing me. I tapped out a quick message and with one last glance at the gloves, I hit send.

Sloane: *Could we have lunch soon? I want to ask you some questions.*

I headed toward the line and met up with Bryon. He smiled and put his arm around me. After Christmas, I'd be back in Salem and with the new ideas rolling around in my mind I wondered if I'd end up staying there. I could turn my life around. I all I had to do was own it. I didn't need a man to guide me or show me who I was. I needed to grab my identity with a strong fist and never let go.

My phone vibrated at my hip in my coat pocket and I grabbed it, reading the response as a genuine smile curved my lips.

Melanie: *Of course! Coffee at Black & Brew in the New Year?*

Bryon stepped up to the register and handed the cashier his armful of items, the last of which were the gloves he planned to buy for me. He shot me a look as the woman rang him up and raised one brow.

"Leather, huh? I figured you were more the cashmere type, but leather will look good on you."

Biting my lip as a smirk overwhelmed me at his reaction, I tapped a response before gently slipping it back in my pocket. They weren't even mine yet and already the gloves had evoked a subtle change.

Sloane: *Perfect. Looking forward to it.*

TWENTY-THREE

Leo

EVERY TIME THE bell rings above the door, I look to see if it's her. It never is. She won't pick up my calls and I haven't seen her since that night. Well...I saw her once. Two weeks after she left dinner with my family, I drove to her apartment. I was too much of a coward to knock on her door, but I sat in my car and stared up at her window. I scolded myself not only for my cowardice but also for my disturbing behavior. I'd never likened myself a voyeur, but Sloane turned me into one.

Sloane turned me into a lot of things I'd never imagined I could be.

I watched her pass by the window and the quick glimpse of the curve of her face caused my heart to stammer beneath my sternum. Her hair, the color of red wine, cupped her cheek and led me to the sight of her lips. I called her and watched as she ignored me, cutting me deeper than I expected.

Explaining what happened that night at Oliver's house to my family was difficult to say the least. No one grilled me about it quite like Barry though. Watching confusion storm his sweet face as I told him Sloane had to leave and that she wouldn't be coming back pierced my heart.

It'd been over two months and I tried desperately to return to a daily routine and gain some sense of normalcy without her. The door to Ben's apartment cracked just as I closed Rosie in her crate. She'd tripled in size since the day Sloane met her—because that was how I gauged everything…in relation to Sloane.

Ben's face appeared wearing a crooked smile as he glanced at me then down at his dog. "Hey, man," he said. "I didn't know you were coming by."

I cleared my throat and shrugged. "Well, I was off today so I just figured…"

Ben eyed me as he approached with two bags of groceries in his hands and I remembered how much of a giant he was. Towering over me, his face wore a grimace. "Leo, it's Sunday."

A deep sigh overwhelmed me and my hand rose to my brow as I shut my eyes. I heard the sound of Ben setting the plastic bags on the counter top nearby then felt his palm land on my shoulder. "It's okay, man. You wanna sit?"

I nodded and followed him into the small living room to sit down. He hurried to the kitchen, rustling with the plastic bags again, putting away his groceries. When he returned, he held a green bottle of beer out to me, which I accepted. Ben sat beside me and didn't say a word. For a moment, we drank in silence, but eventually my thoughts needed expelling.

"Have you ever…had a drop?"

His eyes grew wide and one hand skimmed the top of his crew cut. "No. Thankfully, not."

"Sloane and me…our last…I dropped. And the next day she left me." I sighed. "I don't know if I'm depressed because I fucked up and lost her or if I'm still sunk. Or both."

"Jesus."

"The scene wasn't that intense, but I was exceptionally cruel with my words that night. I went dark. I'd been keeping a secret from her for days and my guilt turned me into someone I didn't recognize. I failed her."

Ben drew in a heavy breath. "I don't even know what you're supposed to do after a drop. I mean, Jade's had one or two and we just lay off for a couple days…reconnect on a different level until she balances out. But—"

"I can't do that because I lost her, Ben! She's gone. She won't talk to me. I haven't even seen her face in weeks and it's killing me. What? So if I never reconnect with Sloane I never recover from this?" I shook my head and stood from the couch. "Well, I fucking deserve it, don't I?"

Ben followed me as I headed toward the door. "Don't leave, man."

Glaring at him, my jaw stiffened. "I should be alone. To think."

"No. You shouldn't."

"I'll be fine," I said, ignoring the protesting noise he made as I slipped out of his apartment.

I thought about going home, but she haunted me there just as much as she did anywhere else. Each night I stood at the foot of my bed and remembered the way it felt when I heard her tell me what I already knew—that Warren had a child with someone other than her. Only we knew of different children and I had no idea that was the reason she'd left him. As soon as the twisted vines of his betrayal lined up in my mind, I realized there was no way the revelation of Barry's parentage wouldn't break her.

I turned into the bookstore and figured if thoughts of Sloane continued plaguing me I could at least work while she continued to whisk through my mind. I climbed out of my car and clutched my coat closed at my neck as a whipping wind of snowflakes blew down Main Street. My gaze flicked across the road and my heart plummeted at the sight of deep burgundy hair. Feet cemented to the snowy pavement, I watched her begin to turn at the door of the coffee shop as though she was waiting for someone. My eyes burned as I torturously drank in the blurred vision of her beautiful face framed by her hair and a white scarf tucked around her neck. I wouldn't be so lucky as to see the part of her body I adored the most. I squinted and saw the door open and her face light up all at once. Balling my hands into fists, I couldn't look away as Ethan grinned at Sloane. I'd met him twice and both times, I'd wanted to knock the beard off his face for the way he looked at her. *Mine*, my brain growled even now. Waving her inside, Ethan held the door open for her. She smiled at him and ducked under his arm and into the shop and as I watched his stare drift over her body when she passed him, rage swarmed my senses.

    I swallowed an acidic lump in my throat and attempted to breathe, but the truth held my lungs hostage. I couldn't allow this distance between us to continue, not because she was mine—but because I was hers. Pulling my lighter and a black cigarette from my coat pocket, I slipped the flavorful bad habit between my lips and lit it. Inhaling, I let it sink in—what it felt like to belong to someone else.

What to do while you wait for book two, *Leather Bound* (coming 2016)

Write your review.

Sign up for the mailing list for exclusive news, content, and prizes.

Check out Kate Roth's other romance novels
The Low Notes
Reckless Radiance

The Confession Records Collection
Natural Harmony
Sway

The Desire Resort Series
Last Resort
Best Laid Plans
Many Times, Many Ways
Peachy Keen

Gift, lend, recommend… If you loved *Bindings*, tell your friends! Sharing on social media and via word of mouth is the best gift you can give an author!

Follow Kate on Facebook (Kate Roth: Author), Instagram and Twitter (@KateRothWrites)

ACKNOWLEDGEMENTS

Thank YOU! Thank you for reading this book. Thank you for even picking it up and taking a chance. Thank you to those of you who have read me before and came back for more. Thank you to anyone who has read my words and felt them in your heart the way I meant them to be felt.

Thank you to my amazing editor, Erin Roth. I'm forever thankful to have found you.

Thank you as always to Britni Hill, the number one girl in my corner since day one of this journey.

Thank you to Josh Zimmerman. Friendship like yours is a rare and spectacular gift and I do not take it lightly. Thank you for all of your support over the years and especially on this book in particular.

Thank you to Lauren at All Good Things Editing, I appreciate your final glance!

Thank you to my beta readers Adrianne James, Leigha Taylor, JA Hensley and Mo Sytsma. Your time, energy and opinions were invaluable on this project.

Thank you, Adam, for your constant support.

ABOUT THE AUTHOR

Published since 2012, Kate Roth is addicted to all things romance. Her passion for love stories, both traditional and unconventional, has led her to write in various sub-genres of romance including New Adult, Paranormal and Erotica. Kate is inspired by everything from music to the real-life romance tales she's heard through her years as a professional hair stylist.

Kate Roth's goal is to give her audience steamy connections, sassy dialogue, and strong heroines & heroes.

Kate is a small business owner in Indiana who spends her time away from the keyboard with her insta-love husband, Adam and their faithful pound puppy, Sampson.

You can find more about Kate and her work on her website **www.katerothwrites.com**

Made in the USA
Middletown, DE
06 February 2016